THE ENIGMA OF NJAMA

Anthony D. Wilbon

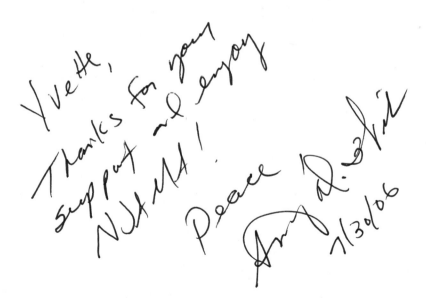

WingSpan Press

The Enigma of Njama
Copyright © 2005 Anthony D. Wilbon

Printed in the United States of America.

Published by WingSpan Press, Livermore, CA
www.wingspanpress.com

Ordering information available at
www.overlookedbooks.com

The WingSpan® name, logo and colophon are
the trademarks of WingSpan Publishing.

ISBN 1-59594-017-0

First Edition 2005

Library of Congress Control Number: 2005926545

Acknowledgements

All long journeys have countless opportunities and challenges and mine is no exception. As with most authors, the development of this novel was done in artistic isolation. But as one emerges from their creative cocoon, feedback from others is so important to ensure that you are crafting something that is worthy and of interest to others. Thanks to all of you who encouraged me to get this project published, without seeing a single word in print. Your expressions of faith in my talent are more valuable that I may have shown.

A special thank you to my wife who was the first to read this story and provide encouraging feedback about its potential. I would also like to thank David Collins for providing editorial comments that enhanced the story's structure tremendously.

THE ENIGMA OF NJAMA

Anthony D. Wilbon

1

"Purpose. What is my purpose in this life?" Dr. Montgomery Quinn whispered to himself.

He opened his eyes and emerged from his meditative state just in time to see Jovan Givens cruise around the semicircular drive at the end of Hains Point park. He pulled up to the curb and slowly rolled his scarlet Corvette to a stop. Montgomery admired it from a distance as the sun made the paint glisten like a large ruby stone.

The chrome rims shimmered from the polished finish. Jovan loved that car as much for the color as for the speed. He lived for the second looks he got driving through the city. The personalized license plate that read *CMYVETT* helped get your attention if you somehow failed to see the blaring color or hear the roaring engine.

Jovan slowly exited the car and began walking toward Montgomery, eyes cast downward and hands in the pockets of his blue khakis. His frame bulged through the wrinkled turquoise body shirt as he walked, leaning forward like someone facing gale force winds. His dark, bald head reflected the sun as much as his car rims.

Montgomery had unwrapped his long frame from the Lotus position and already begun walking towards him. Wiping the beads of perspiration from his caramel colored skin, he put on his glasses and noticed Jovan's defeatist posture. They grabbed hands and embraced in a firm hug.

"Had a rough weekend, huh?" said Montgomery.

"Brother, you just don't know," said Jovan, looking directly into Montgomery's eyes. "I've got her this time Monty."

Here we go again, thought Montgomery. Jovan's wife, Nia, had him acting more like a wimp than he'd ever seen. The two had been having problems for months and this was all he ever talked about.

Nia Givens was a computer scientist at the National Security Agency. From the start, their relationship was at the upper end of the sexual explosion scale, and often led to a pretty volatile mix of love and hate. The fact that Jovan never finished college and she had a Ph.D., created a great deal of insecurity about his worth in the relationship.

The pressure between the two rivaled that of an engine radiator after racing one hundred miles per hour. Everyone knew it would explode once the cap was removed. Unknowingly, Jovan was slowly untwisting it with his jealousy. He had an overwhelming distrust and suspicion of Nia having an affair. Montgomery often found himself the recipient of Jovan's constant whining.

"Jovan, come on man. I told you to stop being a punk before you get an ulcer."

Montgomery laughed and punched Jovan in the arm setting up in a boxing pose. They always played liked this. But obviously Jovan wasn't in the mood. He stood there with a blank look on his face.

"Listen Monty, I'm serious this time. I've got evidence to prove it."

"Unless you caught some dude in your house with his pants around his ankles, I can't imagine any evidence that could justify losing yourself in this misery. And since you're standing here and not in jail for murder, I assume that's not the evidence you're talking about."

Montgomery knew that his sarcasm blared. Jovan turned and started to walk toward the water, hiding the wells of tears forming in his eyes. Looking out at a yacht coasting toward the distant waterfront restaurants, Montgomery joined him hesitantly. Since he'd rarely seen Jovan this low before, he thought he would just listen.

The rising April sun broke through the clouds, promising a welcome reprieve from the spring rains. Montgomery knew his running time was getting shorter. The Washington, D.C. humidity made jogging unwise. Not only did the heat make it unbearable, but also the air quality sucked away the little oxygen he did have after a mile or so. As they reached the concrete boardwalk along the river, Jovan composed himself and slowly began to open up.

"She told me she was going to hang out with her girls yesterday afternoon," he said. "I said cool, but I knew something was up. I don't know why, but I needed to know what she was doing, to ease my mind. Too many stories of late meetings at work that weren't adding up. I went online a couple of weeks ago to this website where they sell surveillance stuff, you know like the private eyes use. Ordered this portable device you can put on cars to track people's movement, called um...'

Montgomery quickly chimed in, "A global positioning system?"

"Yeah, that's it, GPS," Jovan replied. He looked briefly into Montgomery's eyes and smiled, then turned back towards the water. "Some serious Minority Report type shit ain't it?"

Not really, Montgomery thought. They both had seen the Tom Cruise movie several times and loved the futuristic action thriller. Jovan exaggerated often, especially when it came to things he misunderstood. His experience with technology was limited to the Internet, car audio systems, and home wiring. He surprised Montgomery that he had even thought of the GPS himself. But desperate men are pretty imaginative and resourceful.

"I've had it for a couple of weeks but I didn't want to use it. I was scared somebody might discover it over at NSA if I put it in her car. Nia said the security over there is tighter than a hooker's skirt since this Iraq war started. With my luck, they might find it when she rolled onto the complex and think she was part of the al Qaeda or something."

"They're pretty common now, I doubt they would think anything of it," said Montgomery.

"Maybe. Anyway, so I wait until she gets in the shower yesterday afternoon and put it in the trunk of the car. I'm thinking, so this is it. If she's telling the truth, I'll drop it and stop making a fool of myself. If she's lying, I can move on, but she would be the fool because I caught her ass. Either way, I'm good. I just need to know which way to go. I stayed in the house all day after she left, watching ESPN. She left at four o'clock in the afternoon and didn't get home until two this morning!" The anxiety in Jovan's voice heightened.

Montgomery grabbed his arm and guided him to a bench. Once they sat, Jovan began ringing his hands and bouncing one leg up and down rapidly like a jackhammer.

"So what did you find out from the GPS?" asked Montgomery, trying to cut through the fluff and get to the main part of this twisted tale. Jovan told great stories, but they tended to drag on too long.

"I acted like I was asleep when she came in," he continued, ignoring Montgomery's question. "I could hear her rummaging around in her office downstairs for a while. When she finally eased in the bed she was snoring within ten minutes. I waited until about four-thirty, got up and went downstairs. I had to put a pillow over the loud-ass alarm to turn it off so I could open the garage door. When I looked at the GPS, it showed that she had been way out in Maryland. Somewhere in Calvert County, near the Bay. I got the exact location and everything. Now you know we fish out there all the time and there is no place for someone like her to hang out. Hell, ain't even no black folks out there period."

"Jimmy Blake and his wife live out there," said Montgomery.

"Like I said, ain't no black folks out there." Both of them laughed relieving the tension, momentarily.

The noise from a jet departing from Reagan National Airport just across the river interrupted their conversation.

After a moment of silence, Jovan said, "Monty, I'm headed to this place to see where she went. I need you to go with me in case I have to bust somebody in the head."

Montgomery shook his head. "Come on Jo. You're kind of jumping to conclusions man. I know it sounds suspicious, but I think you're blowing this thing out of proportion. Go home and talk to Nia. I've told you before that all of this sneaking around was leading nowhere. Even if you're right, which I have a hard time believing, are you willing to go to jail because you jumped on a dude over some woman?"

"She's not just some woman."

Indeed, Nia wasn't just any woman.

2

The sun peeking through the vertical blinds in the master bedroom awakened Nia Givens. She sensed she was alone and squinted over at the digital clock on the nightstand.

Seven thirty four? He's up pretty early, she thought.

Last night she didn't want to wake Jovan when she came home. It was late and she knew it would only lead to friction. But she so looked forward to a passionate session of early morning sex. No one had ever made her feel more like a woman than Jovan. She'd spent the past two months trying to convince him how much he meant, but he seemed to withdraw into this empty hole of despair. Jealousy was probably his only fault. And lack of patience definitely was hers.

She saw the recent fights as a waste of time and wished Jovan would just get over this silly childishness. It had become so unpleasant and unattractive. She'd been busy lately, but another man was far from her mind. Other things more important vied for her attention. Things like making sure they had a stable financial future.

But Nia couldn't discuss that with him now. The appropriate time would come soon and she could tell him everything. For now, she desperately just wanted to convince Jovan that she could be trusted so they could get back to the fervent lovemaking she missed so much.

Pulling her petite frame out of the king sized bed, Nia buried her peach painted toenails into the plush carpet. She reached for the red silk robe lying across the cherry chest at the foot of the bed and slipped her slender arms into it. Strolling to the bedroom door, she listened for any activity downstairs. Silence.

"Jovan?" Nia yelled. No response.

She shrugged her shoulders and found her way to the stairs, wiping her eyes as she descended. A large mirror hung in the foyer at the bottom of the stairs. She caught a glimpse of herself and stopped to take a look. Her straw colored skin showed the paleness of frequent overuse of makeup. Her red eyes sank in the dark circles forming underneath. She removed the blue scrungy from her shoulder length brown hair that she usually wore in a bob style. Fluffing the strands, the blond highlights went in every direction.

Man, do I need to get my hair done today.

This was the first day she had off in months and she planned to take full advantage of it. Not only was there a hair appointment, but also a greatly anticipated visit to the day salon, courtesy of a valentine's gift from Jovan. Closing her eyes, she imagined the relaxing massage taking all of the knots from her stress-filled shoulders.

Nia walked around the corner and into her small office, still a little groggy. On a table next to the door sat a coffee pot. She turned it on and walked around the walnut desk, sinking into her black leather desk chair. She opened the laptop, and as the machine booted up, reached behind her into the corner and pulled up the light blue carpet underneath the baseboard. Beneath the carpet was a small silver key. She took the key and unlocked the bottom right drawer.

What the hell!

Nia snatched the drawer fully open and ran her hand in the empty space. Her mind raced as she tried to recall whether she might have misplaced the missing small black box. She sat back in her chair now fully awake. Even though it was late and she was dead tired, she recalled putting the box in the drawer before heading to bed. Standing up, she tried to retrace her steps. *I came in the house through the garage. Put down my coat on the barstool. Turned on the alarm. Came to the office ....*

It had to be there. She sat down in the desk chair and looked closely into the drawer one more time. *Am I losing my mind?*, she thought, cursing under her breath.

Finally, Nia quickly grabbed the mouse and went to the computer management tools on the laptop. She opened the customized trace log created to monitor events on the computer. After working at NSA, tracing activities on her computer had become a habit to make sure unauthorized users didn't access data without her knowledge. She scanned the results from the program and noticed the last three identical entries at the top from yesterday.

Access attempt - Aborted. She clicked on the item at the top of the list.

Time: 1:07am
Program Access Aborted
Filename: Crucible

That bastard! I can't believe he tried to access files on my computer!

Leaning back into her chair, Nia tried to catch her breath. All of a sudden the room began spinning like the teacup ride at Six Flags. "I need to get that box back," she whispered.

Reaching for the portable telephone and calming herself, she dialed Jovan's cell phone number. This was the last straw, he's about to catch hell now. *So much for my massage,* she reflected as the phone rang.

3

J ovan, I have a class to teach at ten o'clock. Why don't you-"

Suddenly, Kool and the Gang's *Celebration* began playing.

"What's that?" asked Montgomery.

Jovan smiled, reached into his pocket and pulled out his cell phone. "You don't know anything about this, bro," said Jovan.

Montgomery had told him about the website that allowed them to create cell phone ringtones from their own digital recordings. They loved 70s R&B music and constantly competed to see who had the coolest rings. Jovan looked at the number, held up his index finger, and walked toward the rail of the boardwalk. With his broad back to Montgomery, he answered the phone to talk.

The waves of the Potomac River slapped against the concrete wall providing some welcomed serenity. Montgomery stroked his manicured mustache and watched Jovan whisper into his cell. He contemplated how to talk himself out of this situation. He didn't believe that Nia was being disloyal and thought Jovan was taking this too far. He just wanted to finish his work out and move on with his normal Monday routine.

Montgomery reflected on the joy of having a relationship without this type of drama. With the money problems, he and his wife Gabrielle had issues. But after listening to Jovan's griping, he really wondered whether his complaints held

11

any validity. Their relationship was a lesson in blissful love compared to Jovan and Nia's train wreck.

Jovan hung up the phone and returned to the bench. "That was Nia."

"So ... "

"Monty, you don't need to get involved with this. I understand you have your own life. I'm going to take care of this." Jovan seemed rushed and flustered by the phone call.

"Jo, please don't do anything stupid."

"I have to go. But let me finish telling you what happened," he said, sitting back down on the bench. "So since I was at home all day I did a little snooping. I went on her computer and looked around. She had a couple of files that had passwords on them. I tried to guess a couple of time but couldn't get in. And she has this one drawer on her desk she keeps locked. I figured out how to jimmy it. Last night nothing was in it. This morning, I checked again and – BAM! This was in there."

From his pocket, Jovan snapped up a small black box that looked like a jewelry sachet for a small bracelet. Montgomery looked at the box, and then looked at Jovan waiting for an explanation. He just glared with a smirk on his face.

Okay, I guess inquiring minds want to know, thought Montgomery.

"So what is it?" Montgomery asked.

Jovan opened the box and revealed a flash memory drive inside. The small device, sometimes called a thumb drive, provides more storage capacity for larger software programs.

"I pulled up the program on here and saw some strange symbol. I kinda heard Nia rustlin' around upstairs so, I had to close everything down in the middle of the program." He put the lid back on the box.

"By the way, she somehow figured out I got the thing and she wants it back. She was pretty hot that I broke into her desk." A sly smile crept across Jovan face, reminding Montgomery of the Grinch that stole Christmas.

"So you admitted to this foolishness?" asked Montgomery, trying desperately to keep his calm.

"Hell no," Jovan chuckled. "You know what I say, 'deny everything, even if they saw you doing it.' I told her I didn't know what she was talking about. So now I need you to hold this for me and tell me what's on the thing before I put it back in the house."

Jovan pushed the thumb drive toward Montgomery.

Keeping his hands clutched in his lap, Montgomery said, "Jovan, you're loosing it man. Take the damn thing back to Nia, and try to work this out. I really don't want to get involved with this nonsense."

Jovan's eyes seemed to pierce Montgomery and a vein popped up on the top of his forehead. He bit his bottom lip, jolted to his feet and stormed pass Montgomery. He stopped after a couple of steps and peered into his eyes.

"Monty, I need you to be with me on this one. I'm telling you there is more to this than you may want to believe." After a moment, he calmed himself a little and looked away slowly. "I'm going to find out what the hell is going on here one way or another."

Several seconds later, he turned, "I'm not asking you to get involved. I'm just asking you, as my boy, to help me out."

He held up the device and reached into his other pocket for the portable GPS. Montgomery took them reluctantly and put them in the pocket of his work out suit.

"I really appreciate this man. You're the only person I can trust with this. And believe me, I'm not crazy." He held his arms out to Montgomery. He stood up and they embraced.

"I'll call you later, okay?" Jovan turned and began to walk toward his car with the empty black box in his hand, leaving Montgomery staring out at the boats on the marina. He walked to the end of the Point, rested his forearms on the metal rail and looked out at another Boeing 757 taking off to the south. Taking a deep breath he noticed an odious aroma of dead fish.

He could hear the roar of the Corvette engine behind him. The horn blew, startling him. He turned around, dismayed by how he got himself involved with this mess.

"By the way Monty, promise me that you won't tell anyone

about any of this, especially Nia." Jovan yelled from the window.

"It's between us man," responded Montgomery.

Jovan smiled and hit the accelerator, raising smoke from his oversized tires in a sustained screech around the bend in front of The Awakening sculpture. Montgomery turned again and watched as a bird landed on the rail directly across from him. He stared out passed the bird at the slow moving waves.

Somehow, his meditative state had escaped him like a possessed demon fleeing from an exorcism. *This is certainly not a good way to start a week,* he thought.

4

This damn phone better ring soon, Nia thought. She sat with her arms crossed, staring at the wireless phone in her bony fingers. Jovan said he would call back and it had been twenty minutes. When she talked to him earlier, she could tell he was outside, which was not unusual. As an electrician, he often worked at construction sites during the spring.

The whispering concerned her, as if he was trying to hide something. Or someone. Even stranger was the sound of airplanes in the distance.

Nia had a thousand thoughts all at once. She stood up and looked out of the window into the wooded backyard. The view of the weeping willow tree and the blooming Japanese maples calmed her momentarily. Two squirrels chased each other around one of the trees until one scampered up and the other decided to call off the chase. She watched this game of tag and recalled the joys she and Jovan had over the years.

The two met at the Dream nightclub about five years ago during a professional networking function sponsored by the Urban League. Jovan had accompanied Montgomery, realizing that the events typically overflowed with gorgeous women. As they entered the club, Jovan noticed Nia first and they spent the entire night talking at the bar.

From the first meeting, his touch sent an electrical charge through her body that filled her with warmth. They use to talk for hours about topics that no other man dared to broach

15

with her. Nothing deep or complicated, just talk about life and love and mutual passions. They shared the same dreams about finding a way to live comfortably, yet enjoying all the fruits of their hard work.

She didn't care that he wasn't a lawyer or doctor or college professor. There weren't many eligible men to choose from in Washington, D.C., so adding requirements like degrees made the selection process even more difficult. This was especially true if you hoped to find a Black man.

Nia learned hard lessons from years of setting the companionship bar too high and constantly coming up empty, and lonely. She was getting older and tired of waiting for the numbers of professional men to catch up with the women. The competition was intense and she was ready to play in another arena. She was relieved to find an intelligent man, a great conversationalist, and someone who knew how to treat a woman. His career never seemed to matter. She fell deeply in love with Jovan the man, not the credentials.

Many of her girlfriends warned her against marrying Jovan because he never completed college. Nia ignored them all and considered herself the smart one for lowering her expectations and finding a jewel. Her friends still continued their search for that mysterious doctor. She luckily found her one true love because she willingly dropped the pretenses.

Now things had changed. The one thing she chose to overlook became a burden to their relationship. No matter how much she tried, she couldn't get Jovan past his insecurities about their differences in academic credentials. Recently, he had become less and less trusting of her. Jealousy bred lack of confidence in himself, and it became unappealing.

She hadn't been completely honest with Jovan about a lot of things. Her secrets certainly contributed to their problems because he attributed her secrecy with an affair. He never understood that she sincerely believed that no man could ever compete with him. She only aspired to have a better life for them. She focused on their future, not the past. Nia could sacrifice her reputation for perceived dishonesty now, if the results proved worthy later. She needed to get him to understand this, but she couldn't tell him why. At least not now.

The stillness in the office surrounded her as she turned and stared at the colorful abstract painting on her earth toned office wall. The pleasant scent from the bowl of crushed rose petals on the desk drifting into the air. Her mind descended into blankness as the rage began to overwhelm her senses.

Sipping coffee from the cup that read *The best things come in small packages*, the bitterness made her snap out of her fog. She forgot the sugar.

Nia picked up the phone and pushed redial. Jovan picked up on the second ring.

"What happened to calling me back in ten minutes? Where the hell are you?" she said.

"I've got something to do," he said. Nia could hear the annoyance in his voice, which annoyed her.

"Jovan, I don't know what your problem is," she said. "But I know you broke into my desk so stop denying it. I need that thumb drive back."

"You hiding something on there you don't want me to see?" asked Jovan.

"So now you admit that you did it. Unbelievable! Will you grow up! You're about to fuck up everything."

"I didn't admit anything. And what am I about to fuck up, Doctor." Jovan often called her that when he was pissed. The implication being that her degrees gave her a sense of superiority. She hated it.

"Don't start that Jovan. I married you not caring about what you did, so stop trying to make that an issue now. Whatever your problem is, you need to address in counseling. In the meantime, you need to find a way to live in the here and now before it's too late. You are causing severe damage to this relationship and I'm fed up."

He didn't reply. Nia screamed uncontrollably and she hated losing control. She paced around the office, her patience evaporating quickly.

"Look I'm tired of you and your bullshit insecurities," she yelled. "You took something that is very important to me and I want it back." The veins in her neck protruded as she crushingly gripped the phone.

"Yeah, or what? I took the box, so what. You've been sneaking around for months and I knew something was up. Leaving the house and not coming home until late, you think I'm supposed to just live with that shit and not get an explanation? I'm not a fool. I have evidence now to prove I'm not crazy. So who is it Nia? You gonna tell me or do I have to find him myself." His voice cracked as the decibel level increased with every sentence. It sounded as if he had begun to cry.

"You are absolutely out of your mind. You have proof of nothing. I've told you a thousand times there is no one else. What you stole from me is--"

Suddenly, she heard a thunderous explosion through the phone, then nothing. "Jovan?" she called. "Jovan, what happened?"

Nia's lungs felt constricted from anxiety. She listened intently for any noise. A hissing sound rang in her ear. Seconds later she heard someone yelling in the distance.

"Someone help! Call an ambulance, he's not breathing! We need to get him out of here!" the detached voice called.

"JOVAN!" screamed Nia in anguish, knowing what just happened, and fearing the worse.

5

Montgomery Quinn had been rushing all morning after leaving Jovan. Showering and changing cloths at the Smith Center gymnasium on George Washington University's campus, preparing notes for his class, and entering grades from last week's quiz into his spreadsheet. And he was ten minutes late for class.

He returned to his sixth floor office in the Tompkins building after teaching his ten o'clock course on Introduction to Microwaves. He had a small office, but at least he had a window to enjoy a view of the busy D.C. landscape. The morning had a rough start, but he hoped to recover what was left of the day. Time to appreciate a moment of peace.

It was the typical professor's office; shelves filled with books, ungraded exams piled everywhere, and chairs overflowing with papers and academic journals. The wall had two matching African masks bought from one of the vendors at the Foggy Bottom Metro Station near the campus. His favorite picture of Muhammad Ali standing over Sonny Liston, mouth wide open and yelling, after the famous knockout for the heavyweight championship, hung near the door.

On the desk, next to the picture of Gabrielle and his eleven-month-old daughter Eliza, the red light on his phone blinked, indicating he had voice mail messages. But he wasn't in the mood to listen to them just yet.

He took off his glasses and set them on the paper-cluttered desk. He only needed them to see long distances and using them for anything else gave him a headache. He turned on the CD player on top of the file cabinet in the back corner and popped in a Miles Davis CD.

As the only African American faculty member in the Electrical and Computer Engineering Department at George Washington University, Montgomery constantly felt the need to show he belonged. His Ph.D. gave him clout among his family and friends because he was the only one they knew who had achieved such high academic success.

But to his colleagues, he sensed that they questioned whether he was there because of his sharp mind or affirmative action. Montgomery was out to prove to them that he could compete intellectually on any EE theory in the literature. This often led to complete mental exhaustion, trying to outpace them in publication numbers and research.

As the trumpet whined softly from the system, he turned to the computer on the station behind his desk and went to his email. A bite of the stale donut he picked up from the street vendor made him regret the purchase. Although he didn't need it, he was starving and ate it anyway.

The email pop-up window displayed on the flat screen, followed by the simple three-note tone. Montgomery smiled as he recognized the most recent sender: Lila Armstrong. The messages his grandmother sent always uplifted and made him smile.

They had a lot in common and Montgomery considered her the most influential person in his life. He lived to make her proud. Her mentoring drove his decision to become an engineer. She was one of the first black women to receive a doctoral degree in electrical engineering from MIT.

They shared a passion for technology and gadgets. Even at seventy-three, she continued to stay in touch with the latest trends and often told him about technology he didn't even know existed.

He double-clicked on the message.

Subject: Our date
From: Lila Armstrong
To: Montgomery Quinn

Hello sweetheart. Look forward to our date Saturday.

I'm sure you will treat an old woman to a good time. I plan to wear my best dress since I will be with the most handsome man in the D.C. metropolitan area. Give my love to Gabrielle and my lovely great-grand daughter.

Love Grandma

Montgomery flashed a fabulous smile as he chuckled to himself. Lila's birthday was Thursday and they always had a standing dinner date for the occasion. He looked forward to it every year with delight. *I wouldn't miss it for anything, Grandma,* he thought.

A knock on the door interrupted the blissful moment. Montgomery turned to see his graduate student, Donatello Cetronelli. He preferred Donnie. Montgomery never thought to ask why, but he assumed he thought Donatello sounded too feminine.

Donnie looked like Al Pacino, but taller, and told all who would listen that he was 100% Italian to the core. They had built a pretty strong relationship because they had a lot in common.

Donnie also made all-conference as a high school running back in New Jersey. He attended Rutgers on a full scholarship. In the first game of his freshman year, he blew out his knee and had a tough time recovering. Eventually he lost his scholarship and couldn't afford to stay.

Deciding he needed a change, Donnie transferred to historically black North Carolina A&T University and joined the ROTC. Montgomery respected that he had the nerve to jump into an environment where he was clearly a minority.

Although it paid for school, the military commitment he had after graduating never enthused him. It was the early 90s and the U.S. had just begun the fight in the Persian Gulf. He never expected to fight in a war when he signed up.

Somehow Donnie ended up in an Army Special Forces unit, which he rarely talked about. But apparently the experience left a definite negative impression on his outlook on structure, organized bureaucracy, and a general dislike for taking directions.

Donnie left the Army several years ago and decided to work on his Masters at GW full time. Corporate America was not for him and he knew it. He craved flexibility. After graduation he decided that being a professor may work for him so he stayed to pursue his Ph.D. As a thirty five year old first year doctoral student he brought an intense intelligence and seriousness that Montgomery appreciated.

His strong research skills proved valuable to the grant Montgomery had from the National Science Foundation to study waveform advances for satellite data communications. In addition, he had a more than thorough knowledge of the Internet and the ability to find anything on any topic, which saved Montgomery from some of the drudgery of research. Plus they enjoyed each other's company and the jousting about who had the better high school football career.

"Monty, got a new site for you on yoga poses," said Donnie, his broad shoulder seem to take up the entire entrance. His clean-shaven face represented the only remnant of his military career. His long coal black hair was slicked back.

"I'm still trying to get the ones you gave me last week. I'm not that limber yet. Remember, I'm a rookie. You've been at this a while."

"Yeah, I know. It takes some practice, but you'll get it."

"Practice," Montgomery said. "Life's interruptions seem to keep that from happening."

"By the way thanks for the invite to the game last night. I owe you one."

"No problem. Since the Redskins just got Clinton Portis, maybe you can tell some of your mafia buddies to score us some tickets."

"Yuck, yuck. You've been watching too much HBO." In his strongest mafia boss impersonation, Donnie shrugged his broad shoulders, hunched his thick neck, bit his lip and in the thickest Italian accent said, "Maybe I should tell my uncle Pauli about your stereotypical views on us Italians. A fuckin' late night visit to a dump site on the New Jersey shore would show you some fuckin' respect." They both laughed at the awfulness of the attempt.

"So will you be in the lab today?" asked Donnie.

"I may get down there sometime this morning. Feel free to go and get started, I'll catch up with you later."

"Is there anything in particular you want me to finish?"

"Just that paper on broadband Internet access using satellite communications. We need to submit it by next week for the IEEE conference next year. And don't forget we have to work on the semi-annual report to NSF. Its due next month."

"Writing stuff, not my strong suit you know," Donnie smiled, brushed back his coarse hair, and walked away.

"Writing seems to always be a problem for most graduate students, especially engineers. Somehow you don't seem to realize that the bulk of a professor's job is writing," Montgomery called out to him.

He rearranged some of the documents covering his desk but the flashing red light on the phone distracted him again. Montgomery picked up the receiver and pressed the button for the voicemail. He entered his password, listening to the tone of each keystroke.

"First message," said the computerized voice.

"Hi baby, its me. Hope your run went well this morning. I just called to chat since we missed each other this morning. Call me when you can. Oh, and I got another call from Nation's Bank about that credit card. I hope you paid it. Love you. Bye, Bye."

More frustrations. The soft voice on the phone was his wife Gabrielle. Montgomery couldn't remember if he paid the bills or not. An early meeting at her tax law firm required her to leave before he got up. She dropped off Eliza at the day care so he missed seeing them both this morning.

He didn't miss Gabrielle's nagging about their weakening financial situation. They had the normal expenses of a lifetime of education, student loans. But since he'd been in school for so long he eagerly wanted to live a little. The result led to some irresponsible spending, like the new indigo BMW 528i and her taupe Lexus RX330 SUV. But he felt he deserved it after sacrificing for so long to pursue his studies.

A professor's salary didn't quite support a lot of free spending, however. Montgomery's occasional poker losses and Gabrielle's credit card splurges weren't exactly helping much either.

Since he was running late to class, he never got the chance to call about his visit with Jovan. She loved both Jovan and Nia and hated to see their relationship deteriorate as much as he did.

Montgomery pressed the three button to delete the message. "Second message."

"Monty! Jovan's been in a car accident. Oh God, I hope you're teaching today. He's at GW hospital. I'm on my way there. Please call me as soon as you can."

It was Nia. Montgomery felt an instant rush of blood to his head.

What could have happened, I just saw him this morning!

Montgomery smashed the phone down, jumped to his feet and rushed out of his office, slamming the door behind him. He ran down the hall and pressed the elevator button. Looking up, the monitor above the door read '1'. Students often held the thing up and it could take forever to move.

He darted for the staircase to the left of the elevator bank. Running down the stairs two at a time, he finally reached the first floor and bolted onto the sidewalk. As he ran down 23rd street toward the hospital, painful thoughts rushed through his mind.

Montgomery's parents had a car accident his sophomore year of college. Getting from Penn State to Washington, D.C. proved to be the longest day in his life. Paul Lewis, a friend from D.C. volunteered to drive him, because he couldn't afford an airplane ticket.

Well, Paul wasn't really a friend but he understood enough to make the sacrifice. And although they don't talk much, Montgomery sent him a Christmas card every year in appreciation of what it meant to him that day. He had no one else to turn to and Paul responded to his request for help.

They talked sparingly for the entire trip, but all Montgomery remembered is the long periods of silence and the flood of worse case scenarios that bombarded his brain. Navigating the Allegheny Mountains seemed like an eternity.

No one told him about the seriousness of the accident until he arrived at the hospital. As Montgomery rushed down the corridor, the first person he saw was his grandmother Lila with tears streaming down her angelic cheeks as she collapsed into his arms. She told him he was too late; both of his parents had just died.

If I had only gotten there thirty minutes earlier.

He'd live with that thought in his head for all these years. It might not have made a difference in whether they lived, but he always struggled with the fact that he missed their last moments. The pain overwhelmed him for months afterwards. The remainder of the year was lost in a foggy stupor and he almost flunked out.

Now another tragedy, this time his most beloved friend. *I have to get there*, he thought.

As he crossed H Street, he darted behind a car stopped in the cross walk and broke into a full sprint for the two blocks to the hospital. He felt the burning sensation in his lungs and stretched his legs as fast as they would go. He typically ran long distances, which kept him in great shape. Surprisingly, sprinting proved much tougher than he remembered.

He let out a big breath and pushed himself, faster and faster. The starched white shirt stuck to his back from the perspiration. He was oblivious to the noise of the city streets. The hundreds of students crowding the sidewalk appeared as poles to navigate around, like in a video game.

"Dr. Quinn, is everything OK?" someone called out as he passed Kennedy Onassis Hall. Montgomery heard the distant voice but focused on one goal, reaching the hospital as fast as possible. His eyes glared straight ahead.

At the corner of 23rd and I Street, he turned to the left and looked up at the street light, realizing at that point that he had forgotten his glasses. The street signs looked blurry.

He sprinted diagonally across the intersection and into the hospital, ignoring the blaring horn of the car that just missed him.

When he reached the hospital emergency room entrance, he stopped at the reception desk manned by a young blond lady. At first she talked into a headphone, ignoring him.

Acting as if he annoyed her, she finally said, "Can I help you?"

He tried to catch his breath. "I... I need to find... Can you tell me where to find Jovan Givens?" he said.

"Sir, are you OK?" said the nurse.

"A friend of mind was brought here. He was in a car accident. Jovan Givens."

"Hold on sir." She began typing into her computer system. Montgomery wiped the sweat from his forehead with his bright white shirtsleeve.

"Monty!"

He turned and saw a fuzzy image that appeared to be Nia standing down the brightly lit, narrow hall. As she ran closer to him, the frame of her face became clearer and she buried herself in his arms. He could feel her quivering and held her tight, still trying to catch his breath.

"Where is he?" asked Montgomery.

"Monty, he's in a coma," said Nia.

"What happened?"

"All I know is we were talking on the phone and I heard a crash. The police told me he lost control on an exit ramp to 395. That's all I know. He's in surgery now."

Speechless, Montgomery pulled her closely and hugged her tight. *My God, a coma?*

"What are we going to do Monty?" Nia looked up at him, eyes red from crying. The despair gripped him and tears began to run down his cheeks.

6

Several hours passed. Jovan had come out of surgery and the doctors sent him to the intensive care unit. He was in a private room, still unconscious. Other family members arrived and mingled among the relatives of other patients. They all tried to calm one another and wait for any positive news. In typical doctor speech, they were informed that the surgery went "as well as could be expected."

Montgomery sat in the corner of the waiting room trying to steal a moment and collect his thoughts. The large, sterile room had ordinary paintings of fruit and abstract images by unknown artists. Old copies of Sports Illustrated and People magazines sat on the tables. The television was tuned to Divorce Court, the volume barely audible above the rumbling conversation.

He noticed a blurry figure at the entrance walk in and greet Nia. Squinting, he realized it was Donnie Centronelli. The two had met before, once at a barbecue at Montgomery's house and another time when they went to pick up Jovan for a Redskins football game.

Donnie hugged her and gave his sympathies. Looking up he noticed Montgomery and began to walk towards him. He pulled up the leg of his tan khakis, and sat down, adjusting the collar of his yellow polo shirt.

"I just heard the news and rushed over. Damn shame," he said.

Montgomery didn't respond. He knew Donnie and Jovan barely tolerated one another, but he appreciated the gesture.

27

He wasn't in the mood for empty conversation. That's the reason he purposely avoided mingling with the family and friends. He had too much to think about.

Sifting through a copy of the Washingtonian magazine, he tried to read an article about the sale of executive homes in the D.C. area. He marveled at the breathtaking pictures of the magnificent mansions.

After a moment, he said, "You know, me and Gabrielle always ride through these neighborhoods in upper northwest Washington and dream of living in one of these homes. Not a super large one, just a nice brick home with lovely landscape and a big backyard. We might even think about moving to Virginia if we needed too." He kept reading, "Well, maybe not Virginia, but certainly Montgomery County."

Donnie appeared confused and concerned. "Yeah, those are nice," he said.

Montgomery knew the conversation didn't fit the occasion, but that's what crossed his mind. He looked up and saw Nia talking to one of Jovan's uncles. She had on jeans and an oversized tee shirt with FUBU on the front. Her hair was pulled back in a ball and she looked more pale than usual.

Understandably, she didn't spend much time dressing before she hurried to the hospital. The elderly uncle placed his hand on her shoulder, looking as if he was reassuring her that all would be fine.

Nia navigated the crowd and made her way to Montgomery.

"Looks like you need some attention," she said, forcing a smile. He often thought she could have been a model, if she had straighter teeth.

"Absolutely," said Montgomery as he picked up the magazines lying in the slightly worn gray chair next to him.

"I'm going to the cafeteria for a bite. You all want anything?" asked Donnie. The two declined and Donnie got up and walked out the door.

Montgomery and Nia sat quietly in a corner of the busy waiting room holding hands and silently praying that Jovan wake up. A little boy from one of the other families came over to show them his new Power Ranger motorcycle. Nia played with him for a moment and he quickly moved on to the next person simulating the noise of a powerful Harley Davidson.

They tried to comfort one another and keep their distance from the congregation of people gathering. Montgomery looked down at Nia as she rested her head on his shoulders. He rubbed her skinny arms softly.

Strangely, until that moment, he could not recall ever seeing her without makeup. The rawness of her facial expressions seemed to show more emotion than he thought she had the capacity. The heavy makeup she often wore made her appear distant and unattached, almost as if she was hiding behind a veil. Now she looked less impassive, more human.

"Jovan really hasn't been himself lately," Nia spoke softly into Monty's chest, breaking the silence. "We were arguing when he crashed. That may have been what made him lose control of the car."

"I doubt you were to blame Nia. We know how he drove the 'vette. They were designed to go fast, and Jovan often tried to test the limits."

"I guess."

Montgomery could feel the front of his shirt getting damp from her tears. He smelled the scent of apricot from her hair as she nuzzled into his arms. He knew how much Nia loved Jovan. Regardless of their differences, they were soul mates if there ever was such a thing. Volatile, but soul mates just the same. He continued rubbing her arms through the oversized tee shirt. She raised her head and looked up at him curiously.

"I know that look," he said.

"I'm just curious, did you talk to him this morning?" she said.

The inquiry caught Montgomery off guard for a moment. The shift in conversation occurred too quickly for him to adjust.

Finally, his mind responded and he replied. "Yeah, briefly. Why?"

"Did you know what he might've been up to or did he say anything? I mean, I told you he had been acting strange, right?"

Montgomery knew what she was getting at but he didn't fall for it. She knew how close he was to Jovan and that they talked about everything, including the problems in their marriage. Based on what Jovan told him, she could be manipulative and he became wary.

"Yeah, I admit he has been acting a little crazy. But he loves you a lot. And you know brothers, this love thing tends to make us lose our minds on occasion."

She forced a smile.

"Well, he took something very important that belonged to me this morning and I can't find it. They gave me all of his possessions from the car and its not there either."

Montgomery recalled that Jovan had given him the thumb drive and the portable GPS system. He also remembered the last thing Jovan said to him. "By the way Monty, promise me that you won't tell anyone about any of this, especially Nia."

He tried to hide what he thought was an obvious look of suspicion.

"Are you sure Jovan didn't tell you anything Monty? This is important." She peered into his eyes looking for a sign of dishonesty. He tried desperately to hide his lie. He had plenty of practice, having perfected a poker face he learned from his father.

"No, we only talked on the phone for a minute, just before I was starting my work out this morning. He didn't say anything."

Nia settled back into Montgomery's chest and tried to get comfortable. The timing of these questions seemed inappropriate. She should be grieving about her near-death husband not worried about some memory card. Montgomery thought, *Was Jovan right? Is she hiding something?*

"It's between us man," was the last thing he said to Jovan. He had to keep his promise. Now Montgomery was curious. He needed to get the thumb drive from his workout clothes and see what it contained.

7

The car radio played *Killing Me Softly* by Roberta Flack. Her soft velvet voice made the hair on Montgomery's neck stand at attention. He felt a chill run down his spine that made him snap out of his daze. Tears cascaded down his cheeks uncontrollably as he sat in the car in front of his house.

He'd dropped off Donnie at Metro Center so he could catch the redline subway to his home in Arlington. The aimless drive around the city didn't provide any clarity to events of the day. The digital clock flipped to four past eleven.

The lights brightened the corner of New Hampshire Ave and Georgia Ave more than usual. The streets were surprisingly bare. Even on a Monday night teenagers typically hung out on the corner. The only living thing this night was a stray cat chasing something down the sidewalk.

Probably a rat.

Montgomery never liked living in this part of the city but he could only afford the row house on Quebec Place. He could stand in his front yard and throw a rock at the strip club, The House, which attracted many unsavory characters. And the late night brawls that spilled into the street often woke him. He feared Eliza would have to grow up in the surrounding downtrodden neighborhood.

The house needed a lot of repairs that he hadn't gotten to just yet. The previous owners had painted the trim purple which made him cringe every time he pulled up. The wire fence had several links missing and the crooked gate didn't fit, so it often just hung open over the sidewalk. Severe cracks in the steep porch steps made the climb highly risky for the ankles.

He looked up at the house and reflected on the day.

Not one of the best days of my life, he thought.

He left the hospital with Jovan still in a coma. No one knew when he would wake up. Nia and Jovan's family and friends had spent hours waiting for any good news and eventually decided to go home and get some rest.

Montgomery insisted on seeing him before leaving. Now he wished he hadn't. The image of Jovan's battered body wouldn't leave his mind. It was a miracle that he even survived. Broken arm, cracked ribs, and burns on his legs. It seemed that every inch of his body had some damage. The wires taped all over his chest monitored some bodily organ or another. Tubes hung from his mouth and nose. Jovan's swollen face looked like it would pop if touched.

The closest thing to Jovan's condition were the pictures of Rodney King that were plastered all over television after the LA police beat him. He wondered how a body could take any more abuse and still have a beating heart.

The song ended and he took a moment to compose himself. Leaving the BMW parked on the street all night always created lots of anxieties. He had already prepared himself for the fact that it would be stolen one day. Such a nice car deserved better and safer storage. The number one thing on the wish list for the next house was definitely a two-car garage. But there was no other option, so he hit the remote controlled alarm and headed for the house.

Opening the front door, the burglar alarm system chimed and the smell of fried catfish wafted pass his nose. Eating never crossed his mind but his stomach began growling.

Gabrielle ran from the kitchen and grabbed him, holding on tightly. She wore one of Montgomery's yellow Washington Redskins tee shirts, which came to the middle of her smooth solid thighs. Clearly from the cling of the shirt to the contour of her shapely body, she had nothing underneath. She wore a short pixie haircut with tousled layers, long on the crown and tapered in the back. Her ginger colored skin glowed in the dim light of the foyer. Other than lipstick, Gabrielle rarely wore makeup and had flawless skin. Something about her natural beauty always appealed to Montgomery.

She loved to take long baths after the baby went to sleep, so the fresh scent of strawberry from the lotion she used permeated her body. Montgomery inhaled it deeply and just held her. Any other night and this was a perfect prelude to sex. But this was not any other night and they both knew it.

Loosening her grip slightly, she looked up with her almond shaped brown eyes. Montgomery could tell she was trying to assess how he had handled his best friend on death's bed. Throughout the day they'd talked countless times so she had a detailed account of all events.

"I love you Monty," she said. Montgomery loved her smile and just looking at her reminded him about the good things in his life. She wasn't a stunning beauty but she carried herself with an elegance that he always admired. He held her closely, never wanting to let go.

"Any more news?" she asked.

"No."

"I'm sure he'll pull through."

After a moment, she pulled away. Moving to the sofa she abruptly changed subjects

"You know I got three calls from bill collectors since I've been home," said Gabrielle. "Honey, we have to do something about this financial mess. It seems to me that we make plenty of money to not have to deal with this. Did you pay the last credit card bill?"

"Yeah, we make plenty of money," he said. "But WE spend plenty of money too."

"Look, I'm not trying to start an argument." She rolled her eyes and turned away, as if she were studying the cover of the Newsweek magazine on the coffee table. "I know you had a rough day, but can you just take care of it please."

"Or maybe I should let you take care of the bills. I'm tired

33

of having to worry about this shit along with all the other responsibilities I have."

"Responsibilities you have! I guess I don't have any. I work just like you do and make more money."

She was right, but Montgomery hated when she threw that up. As a lawyer in a small tax firm, Gabrielle didn't make the money of the average D.C. lawyer. But it didn't take much to beat a junior professor's salary.

Growing up she lived an upscale lifestyle that he always seemed inadequate to provide. With a successful corporate lawyer as a father and her mother a high-ranking administrator at the Washington Hospital Center, the Brunson's lived quite well in their immaculate Rock Creek Park house.

As a graduate of a prestigious high school in D.C., Sidwell Friends, undergrad at Yale, and Georgetown Law, Gabrielle's pedigree was quite distinguished. Montgomery often felt lucky just to get into the family. Although his accomplishments did help appease her parents some.

He knew the conversation needed to be calmed before it got out of hand. These arguments typically led nowhere good and he was not in the mood.

"Look baby, I'm sorry," he said. "I just left Jovan with what seemed like hundreds of tubes sticking out of his body and barely breathing on his own. Life is too short to have to worry about this kind of crap. All I thought about on the way home was how to start enjoying the fruits of all of our hard work before we get taken off this Earth. Who knows when I'll take my last breath. But whenever it is, I want to say I enjoyed life."

Montgomery turned and walked over to look at the frames of their college degrees sitting on the floor next to the sofa. Somehow they never got around to hanging them.

"I want to get us out of this debt more than anything and get that dream house we talked about. But unless we hit the lottery or something, I don't know when we're going to get out of this mess. I do know this, I didn't get us here alone and we need to work together to overcome this."

"Okay, okay, I'm sorry too. Maybe we should talk about this another time," said Gabrielle.

Montgomery sat down next to her on the teal sofa and they hugged. He hoped she wouldn't suggest that they ask her father for help because that would have started another debate. Pride prevented him from asking anyone for help with personal problems, especially the Brunson's.

Moments later, another subject change, this time one more to Montgomery's liking.

"Eliza took her first steps today."

"What! I knew she was ready. Man, I wished I had seen it." This news brought a welcome reprieve. He loved Eliza more than he thought humanly possible. He vowed to be the best father ever. And he wanted to experience every moment of fatherhood.

"You'll see tomorrow. I think all the walking exhausted her. She was out early tonight." She grabbed his hand and guided him to the kitchen. "Come on, I have dinner ready for you and we can talk some more in here."

"That catfish smells fabulous, I haven't eaten since this morning."

"Then you'll have room for the lemon cake, I guess."

"Girl, you know how to work me when you want to, don't you." They both laughed as Montgomery settled into the kitchen table.

Later that evening, Gabrielle retired to the bedroom. She tried to persuade Montgomery to join her, but he convinced her that he really had to check on something important. He kissed Eliza good night and made his way to the third bedroom at the end of the short hall on the second floor.

The small room had been converted into a shared office. It contained just enough room for a small desk that sat against one wall and a small metal blue file cabinet. Patches of putty blotted the walls, which covered holes left by the last occupants. The to-do list included painting too.

Two small bookcases sat in the closet with all of the reading materials for his research and classes. A daybed with a white linen comforter took up the opposite wall. On nights when Montgomery worked late writing his articles, he crashed there so he wouldn't disturb Gabrielle by climbing into the bed.

He sat down, turned on the desk light and booted up the Dell laptop. An American Express and Visa bill sat on the desk. Both were late, that's why Gabrielle got the call. Now he remembered. He had planned to pay them with their last paycheck, but something else came up, as usual. He hated bills, especially ones that he couldn't pay. With late bills comes late fees and the debt keeps piling up. Compounded interest, but in the wrong direction.

It also kept Gabrielle on his back because she often blamed him for their financial ineptitude. That topic led to the most major battles in their marriage. The end result of many of those fights resulted in him sleeping on the day bed.

He grabbed the bills and placed them in the box with the other notices. He'd get to it on the next payday.

While the computer went through its boot up processes, Montgomery looked up at the picture of himself and Jovan on the wall over the desk. Gabrielle took it the day he got the Corvette. They both stood, arms crossed, leaning on the car and grimacing like two rappers in a MTV video. It was his favorite picture of the two of them. The wells of his eyes began to fill and he wiped them away quickly.

"Alright, enough of this," he whispered to himself.

Reaching in his pocket, Montgomery pulled out the USB flash memory drive and GPS. He set the GPS on the desk, plugged the thumb drive into the computer and double-clicked on the drive. After a second, a single file came up in the window. It was a compressed file named *Crucible* with an unusual looking symbol as an icon.

He didn't recognize it. *No wonder Jovan didn't know what to do with this,* he thought.

He double-clicked on the symbol and the WinZip program opened and decompressed the file. Several spreadsheet and word processor files were listed, along with some program files. Montgomery settled into his chair and began from the top opening them one by one.

Lets see what's on this thing that's so intriguing to everyone.

before making some final cosmetic adjustment to her program. Typical paranoid behavior for most computer programmers is to keep copies of the previous versions, just in case new changes blow up. That way they can always revert back to the status quo.

The fact that her program could be sitting in some ditch waiting for a scavenger to pick it up ten years from now bothered her the most. Hopefully it'll be twenty years. By then the program would be obsolete anyway and she could care less what they found.

Eventually finishing her tea, Nia pulled herself up, set the cup on the table and made her way to the office. On the way there she stopped to look at the gold framed wedding picture of her and Jovan sitting on the end table. She picked it up and stroked it gently with her index finger. That day reminded her of an unforgettable joy.

Jovan wore a white tuxedo with a blue paisley bow tie and cumberbund. Nia's aunt custom made the dress to simulate a design she saw in a French wedding book.

The smiles on their faces showed their deep love for each other on that day. She longed for a return to that moment. A tear rolled down her face.

Nia strolled into her office and sat down. Besides the accident, she still had work to do. She booted her computer and logged onto the Internet to check her email. Spam dominated the list of incoming mail. Nothing else intrigued her enough to spend the time to read it. Opening her programming files, she settled in to begin making the changes she started the night before.

Within an hour, a message popped up on the screen that shocked her.

Alert!
File Accessed
Domain name: Quinn_tesential@hotmail.com
Time: 1:02am

Impossible, she thought, as her eyes opened wide with confusion.

Nia had written a small hidden program that reported to her anytime someone accessed one of her files. She always embedded these in her programs in case they came into the wrong hands. If anyone other than her opened the primary file while online, the program sent an instant message.

She realized that someone must have found the thumb drive and was poking around. She hurriedly went to a website that searched email addresses. She didn't recognize it immediately. Entering the address, the results caused her to stand straight up from the chair. Unable to take her eyes from the screen, Nia glared at the name:

Email: Quinn_tesential@hotmail.com
First name: Montgomery
Last Name: Quinn

Jovan gave the thumb drive to Monty, I knew it, she thought.

She knew that eventually Montgomery might figure out the use of programs and the other files. Especially since the files on the thumb drive were not encrypted, which they should have been.

Now she had no choice. Nia had to rectify the situation after an uncharacteristic comedy of errors made over the last twenty-four hours. She would deal with the embarrassment of her carelessness later.

Reluctantly, she had to call her colleagues and admit to her negligence and the jeopardy she placed them all.

Nia reached for her cell phone and dialed.

The gravely female voice answered after the first ring, "Hello?"

"I have an emergency, we need to talk," said Nia.

"What time is it?"

"I need your complete attention here."

"I heard about your husband. Are you OK?"

"I'm fine," said Nia. "But I have something important to discuss. We have a problem and need a video conference immediately. All of us."

"You know you should not be calling me here." A long pause followed, then the voice finally said, "I'll arrange the conference. You know, this is quite unusual. I trust whatever this is justifies a special session."

"It does."

"I'll get back to you within the hour." The phone went dead.

9

Montgomery Quinn waded through the files on the thumb drive with amazement. *What is Nia into?* he thought.

The folder contained numerous programs written in C and Visual Basic computer languages. He knew both languages and began digging into the code to figure out their function. The first program looked like it was designed to gain remote access to Unix web servers and Microsoft Internet Information Servers, and then take control of computers.

He hated creating computer programs, but had done a paper in graduate school for one of his networking classes on hacking, so some of the code looked familiar to him. Though he was no expert, he knew hackers typically used similar techniques to seize control of institutions computer systems to attack the software applications from within. The more complex the intrusion program, the more it would look like manipulations in the computer system came from someone on the inside when the network administrators investigated. A stealth way to cover ruthlessness.

But why would Nia have such a program? Maybe it was some top secret NSA project.

Montgomery entered another program that seemed to do searches for accounts and use a random generator that created millions of combinations to match passwords. The efficiency of this program startled Montgomery the most. He ran the program and had never seen anything so complicated move so fast.

This program also looked like it created fake accounts once it identified the format within a system. He couldn't figure out all of the specifics because much of the code looked foreign to him. Montgomery recognized the general language, but the complicated use of the processes confused him. Someone more knowledgeable would have to help dissect the intent of all this information.

His eyes glazed over as he stared at the screen and tried to make sense of what he saw. The fact that he may have stumbled on a state of the art program being developed by NSA excited him. His inquisitiveness occasionally got him in trouble. In this case, the program piqued his curiosity and he wanted to delve into this further. Whether it led to something more dangerous was not something he wanted to consider. If nothing else, maybe there was potential for some major research publications. Publish or perish was a reality for a young professor and the constant search for new ideas to write about was preeminent in his mind.

He felt a strain in his neck, his head pounded, and his eyes burned. To no avail, he reached up and tried to massage the tension away. It was time to shut it down. Montgomery made a copy of the entire compressed file on a CD. The symbol caught his eye again but he still couldn't imagine what it was or what it meant.

Sitting back in his chair, he looked up and saw the unsecured air vent in the ceiling with the gaping hole on one side. No heat came through it for the whole winter, making the room ice cold without the electric space heater. It reminded him that he needed to call someone to take a look at it before the summer came. D.C. summers were insufferable without air conditioning.

Tomorrow Montgomery would take the thumb drive to Donnie Centronelli and have him start to dig into it. Donnie had more experience with software and could provide more insight into the program's purpose. For now sleep called.

Montgomery shut down his computer and crawled onto the day bed. He could tolerate the hard and uncomfortable mattress for one night. He stretched out his arms, knocking his knuckles on the wall and buried his head into the pillow. He only had a couple of hours to rest before Eliza would call him and he didn't want to miss seeing her in the morning.

10

Nia's computer had a secure video conference package she had acquired from a small firm in Denver, but of course she had to make some upgrades. The program encrypted each frame coded in a JPEG video and transported them using real time protocol packets via the Internet. The technology permits someone to send and receive live video broadcasts without concern for interference or interception of the feed. Virtual secret meetings were a necessity for this group.

She learned about this from one of her cryptology colleagues at the NSA known as an expert in the technology. A little research and gathering of the necessary technology–cameras, servers, etc.-was all she needed.

The video conference was scheduled to start at 3:30 am. Nia had two minutes to calm herself and get her story straight. Using the reflection of herself in the computer screen she checked her eyes and hair to makes sure everything was satisfactory. Puckering her lips slightly she admired her profile and smiled.

She adjusted the camera on top of her desk and before she could lean back in her chair, a face appeared in a window on Nia's screen.

"Hello dear. You'll have to excuse my appearance. I didn't think I needed to fix my hair and put makeup on for you all," said Paulette Aventis.

"You look fine."

"It's been a while since I've been up this late," said Paulette with a wry smile. "I hope whatever your problem is justifies missing my beauty sleep."

Shortly, two other windows had popped up.

"Hello, Charity here."

"I'm here too. Three thirty in the fucking morning, this better be good." said Sanja.

All were present and thus began the official *baraza* or meeting of Njama's *mzingo zima* or circle of queens. Njama is a Swahili word meaning secret society. The group consisted of African American female scientists, engineers, and mathematicians.

To qualify for membership one had to meet a few criteria. First you had to be African American and female of course. Then one had to have an IQ greater than 95 percent of the general population, a degree in a science/engineering field, a desire to change the world, and the ability to keep your mouth shut. The group ensured the latter through a thorough background check from contacts within the FBI.

The qualifications were simple, but very difficult to reach. This made the membership of Njama unique and limited it to a select population. However, just meeting the qualifications did not ensure membership. The selection process was intricate. You had to prove that you belonged and that you could contribute to the causes. And again, you had to prove your ability to remain surreptitious under pressure.

Njama was organized in levels and one had to prove their dedication to the tenets over an extended period of time to get a promotion or *ukuzaji*. The mzingo zima consisted of members who had reached the pinnacle and their identities were kept secret from those at the bottom of the organization.

Basically, the inner circle developed the strategies and the vision of Njama, while the lower levels implemented them. The lower levels had to trust that their leadership's direction was purposeful and never asked questions.

Their ultimate mission, like the mythical Robin Hood, was to rob from the rich and give to the poor, literally and figuratively. More precisely, Njama ensured that the entities that had long standing reputations for overt racist and sexist behavior were put in positions where they had no choice but to pay those who were wronged by their actions.

In other words, make the bigots so uncomfortable by exposing their closeted skeletons, that charitable contributions were a welcome reprieve. They considered it a win-win: The extremists were brought to their knees and the victims were rewarded for their pain and suffering. In the rare case when they experienced resistance, Njama had potent and forceful ways to make these people see the error of ignorance.

The network of membership was small but powerful. After all, African American women in science and technology make up a small fraction of the population. After weeding out the unqualified, less than fifty women across the country made up the network. Technology expertise and representation in federal law enforcement, corporate boardrooms, government agencies, universities, and countless other areas, provided unimaginable influence.

Paulette Aventis currently led the group and all referred to her as the *amiri*. She was the chief technology officer for NanoTechniqs, Inc. Her company was an innovator in the area of molecular sized robotics devices that allows fabrication of smaller, stronger, and more precise computer components.

With a Ph.D. in Physics, she had risen quickly to the top of one of the most powerful technology firms in the United States at the age of forty-four. The company went public in 2002, adding great wealth with all of her stock options. This on top of her quarter million dollar salary made her life comfortable.

Her colleagues found her one of the most determined, ambitious, and sometimes, overzealous women they knew. Recently, she grew short dreadlocks to give her an edgier look, but some thought it enhanced her gorgeousness even more. Her light brown eyes and flawless dark chocolate skin were soft enough to engage, and many mistook her beauty for lack of intellect and motivation.

That misjudgment proved costly for some, because Paulette competed fiercely and went for the jugular when corporate colleagues took her for granted. She resented disrespect and played hard to make sure no one overlooked her talents.

Paulette started off the meeting. "We are all aware of the tragedy with your husband Nia and I'm sure I speak for all of us, when I say we are here for you."

All of the others chimed in with their condolences.

"I hope all is well with your husband," said Paulette.

"He's in a coma, but he seems to be stabilized. Thank you for your concern." The look of despair permeated Nia's face. She disliked the attention and wanted to move along before she started crying. She'd done enough of that for one day.

Abruptly, Sanja Coston forged forward to the topic at hand. "So Ms. Givens, what is so important as to drag three ladies from their beds in the middle of the night."

Sanja was known to be gruff and had a long history of personality conflicts with everyone in the group. Nia believed it came from years at the Pentagon working on high tech secret projects for the Department of Defense. Hanging around those military types made Sanja think she had to talk to everyone as if she were commanding troops.

Now at forty-eight years old, Sanja had become the Director of the Information Technology Division at the Federal Reserve Board of Governors. Several years ago some African American professionals threatened a discrimination lawsuit over promotion policies at the Fed. Being the conservative entity that they are and always trying to avoid negative publicity, the Governors agreed to become more proactive in their promotion practices. As a result, the plaintiffs dropped the suit.

This action cleared the way for Sanja to become the first African American director of a major division at the Federal Reserve Board. However, she resented the fact that the promotion wasn't based strictly on her own merits. Having a doctorate in information systems should have been enough, along with her years of experience at the Department of Defense.

On top of that she was the lowest paid director in the entire agency. Even the director of support services – the person managing the janitors and security guards – made more than she did. Nia believed this affront contributed to Sanja's bitterness, among other personality flaws.

Nia went on to explain her predicament starting from the beginning, after she left the meeting they had the night before – the lost thumb drive, Jovan's accident, the coma, and her discovery that Montgomery Quinn now possessed the drive. She emphasized the gravity of the situation and apologized for the carelessness that led to this point.

"So how well do you know this man, Quinn?" asked Paulette.

"Well, he and my husband were best friends. I mean ARE best friends."

"A little Freudian slip there, huh?" said Sanja with a smirk on her face.

"Very tasteful Sanja," said Charity. She rolled her eyes.

Of the four, Charity Newhouse had the least capricious personality. Her round cheeks, green eyes, and caramel skin color provided an unarming allure. She normally wore a straight shoulder length flipped haircut, but she had pulled it back and pinned it in a ball on top of her head.

A computer scientist, her expertise was in electronic surveillance for the FBI, but her charm and worldliness reached far beyond just technology. Growing up the only daughter of two career Air Force officers, she had traveled the world before she graduated from high school.

This experience forced Charity to become comfortable in any situation and with anyone. She could communicate with the Director of the FBI just as easily as the homeless people at the shelter she volunteered her time at once a month. Her maturity made her appear much older than forty-two.

Charm and intelligence made Charity a prime candidate to become one of only one hundred twenty African American female agents of the eleven thousand in the entire FBI. Njama noticed her success immediately and brought her on board. She easily rose through the ranks.

Charity provided the conscience that Njama often needed

during frequent catfights among a group of highly intellectual females.

As often is the case, Sanja ignored Charity and continued with her abrasive badgering as if she were a prosecutor questioning an uncooperative witness.

"So, due to your lack of respect for protocol and totally irresponsible actions, we find ourselves in a murky situation. What are the chances he will figure out that the software is used to hack into banks?" she asked, playing with her side swept ponytail twisted in double strands.

"Since he is an EE professor at GW, I would guess not long. It may take him awhile to put everything together though."

"Shit! When you fuck up you really go all out don't you," said Sanja, leaning forward into the camera. "If you were smart enough to plant a tag on the software to alert you, why the hell didn't you encrypt it."

"Go to hell Sanja. I told you I was working on the damn thing and just made a copy for a backup!" yelled Nia.

"Okay, that's enough. Looks like cooler heads need to step in here," said Paulette.

"That's why you're the amiri," said Sanja.

"That's right, so show me some respect, Dammit!" Paulette glared into the camera, directing her gaze at Sanja. The audio on the call seemed to die as all of them sat silent for what seemed like ten minutes, but was more like twenty seconds. Sanja looked down like a puppy hit on the nose with a rolled up newspaper, surprised by Paulette's outburst. Nia smiled slightly, welcoming Paulette's intrusion into their exchange.

Finally, Paulette broke the stillness. "Nia, you said you asked this Dr. Quinn whether he had the USB thumb drive and he denied it?"

"Well, I asked him indirectly whether Jovan gave him something and he denied it"

"What are the chances that he would return it if asked directly, assuming that he hasn't figured out what the program is and how to use it of course."

"Knowing how close he and Jovan are, I would guess that

he's hiding it for Jovan and will never give it up."

"Then we'll make him give it up," said Paulette. "We can't let this one event jeopardize our operation. We're working on a deadline here. We need this program to infiltrate the bank accounts of those bastards and take back money that they acquired illegally, or at least immorally. So this is what I think we should do--"

"Madam amiri, let me interrupt. I want to voice my opposition to this strategy once again. This was not the intent of our founders. We are not thieves and this is not the mafia. Our priority has always been to *pressure* these wicked people into making contributions to the appropriate charities by exposing their corrupt activities and immoral deeds. I think we need to rethink--"

"Sister Charity, we've been through this already. Your opinion has been noted before, and you have decided to abstain from these particular activities, and I respect that. We have the majority on this one, and we still need your help, so lets move on shall we," said Sanja.

"I just want to make sure you are all aware of my position." Charity looked away, showing a glimpse of disgust on her face. She never wanted any part of this extortion scheme and wanted to stay true to the tenets of the original purpose of Njama.

The whole process of hacking into others' bank accounts made her uncomfortable and almost ashamed that they had started down that road. But Charity was committed and loyal for the long term, so she would let this one go. She just knew the next outlandish plan required stronger resistance from her to keep everyone focused on Njama's original purpose.

"We understand your position my sister," replied Paulette. "This is a new era, Charity, and we must find new ways to achieve the same goals our founders established for us. But first, let's take care of this crisis."

Paulette cleared her throat and developed the look of someone who knew how to take control.

"So Charity, can you find out anything and everything you can about this Dr. Quinn. We may need to take an aggressive stance and we could use some background information on him. Family history, friends, finances, vices, etc."

"I'll take care of it."

"In the meantime, maybe we should pay a little visit to the good doctor to see if we can convince him to hand over the software and keep his mouth shut," said Sanja.

"Maybe. Nia, contact Quinn again and this time be more direct. Let him know we are aware he has something that belongs to us. In the meantime, lets do some background work and see where we go from here, agreed?" said Paulette.

The other three responded in agreement.

"We need to move fast on this before he learns more than he does already. I want to get some answers by end of day tomorrow. If we don't have the software back by then, Dr. Montgomery Quinn will have to answer to some pretty angry women, and his life will never be the same." Paulette chuckled a little, like she enjoyed the thought of potentially destroying another man's life.

"One day we need to talk about how to get these men in our lives in check. Right now, I'm losing it," Sanja said, then yawned. "I have a meeting tomorrow, I mean today, and need to get some sleep. Plus, my boyfriend should be waking up soon and if he sees I'm up, his hands will be all over me. Are we done?"

Paulette laughed at Sanja's plight. "One more thing. Sanja, could you get one of our kizushis to keep an eye on Quinn so we know what he's up to," said Paulette.

Kizushis, also known as newcomers, referred to the ladies at the lower end of Njama. Sanja acted as the liaison between them and the mzingo zima and provided the directive to them on the missions. They were often eager to demonstrate their worthiness, so getting them to help was never a problem.

"I'll make a call."

"For now, lets call it a night. We'll reconvene sometime tomorrow," said Paulette. "Timiza ahadi, ladies."

"Timiza ahadi," the others replied, as each disconnected from the call.

Timiza ahadi is Swahili for "to keep a promise." The mzingo zima always ended their baraza with this phrase to remind each other of the eternal promise to the Njama. Their commitment to the canons of this organization superseded all others and they were to never speak of their alliance.

Nia sat back in her chair and thought about what just happened. She regretted that Jovan had gotten Montgomery involved and wished he would just hand over the thumb drive when she asked about it. But she was committed to following the leadership of Paulette, so all she could do was wait to see what would happen.

11

Five minutes after the conference call, the phone rang at the fifty acre, colonial estate home of Paulette Aventis. She stood in the country style kitchen drinking a glass of water before returning to bed. Flustered and surprised, she rushed to pick it up quickly; already knowing whom it was from the caller ID.

"Yes?" Paulette whispered anxiously.

"You know this could cost us a lot of money," said Sanja Coston.

"Are you out of your mind? Why are you calling me here? We will deal with this efficiently and effectively before any losses. And don't call me here again."

"I know, but this is a major fuck up and I didn't want to talk in front of the others, especially Charity. We've worked too hard on this to let it all go down the toilet. I'm gone, but you and I need to talk. Soon." And Sanja hung up.

Paulette looked around the corner into the hallway, hoping she didn't wake her husband. There was complete stillness in the house. Sanja often displayed misjudgment, but she knew better than to initiate unsecured communications from personal residences.

Nia had imperiled Njama, but Paulette saw nothing insurmountable about the situation. Most important was keeping everything under wraps. They would deal with Montgomery Quinn like they did all of the others who threatened their mission. The fact that he was black would have no bearing on her decisions.

All she had to do now was think about a strategy to pressure him to comply. Charity's FBI connection would provide all the information they needed to expose Montgomery Quinn's life to the fullest. They just needed to use their intellect and resources to exploit him. Easy enough.

Paulette poured a cup of orange juice from the refrigerator, walked to the kitchen desk and pulled out a pad and pen. She pulled up a barstool to her brownish granite counter top, sat down, and began to jot down some notes. Ever the strategist, she had to devise a plan.

No use in going to sleep tonight, she thought.

8

A long day had finally come to an end. Nia worried that Jovan might not survive and the thought of becoming a widow at thirty-two made her ill. His accident scared her and their last conversation left her feeling conflicted.

Nia had changed into a pair of beige silk pajamas and stood in the kitchen pouring hot water to prepare some cinnamon spice herbal tea. Steam rose from the cup as she added some sugar and took a sip, inhaling the aroma. She moved to the family room just as the eleven o'clock news had ended.

She turned the television to the smooth jazz cable music channel and settled into the blue oversized chair in the corner to reflect on the day's events. Grover Washington's version of *Take Five* wailed in the background as the pressure from the day began to drain her body. Worn out by the constant throng of family and friends at the hospital, finally she had a moment of peace. She didn't realize how much she needed to just be alone.

Nia looked at the manila envelope on the coffee table. It contained all of Jovan's belongings from the car. Everything was there: his watch, wallet, gold necklace and bracelet, keys, even the black box he took from her desk. But it was empty.

Trying to remain optimistic, she thought that maybe it fell out of the car and still sat on the side of the highway. At least she hoped for that possibility.

If so, maybe she wouldn't have to tell anyone that she lost the thumb drive. It only contained backup files that she saved

12

Marvin Gaye's *What's Going On* rang out from Montgomery Quinn's cell phone, startling him. He had just climbed into his comfortable bed to get a couple of more hours of sleep after seeing Gabrielle and Eliza off. Tuesdays meant no class and, barring any meetings or research projects, a day to relax. Three hours of sleep on the lumpy daybed provided a pain in his back.

The red LED display on the clock read seven forty. He threw off the comforter in disgust and reached for the cell phone sitting on the nightstand.

Jovan's Home, the display read.

Montgomery snapped out of his groggy state and pressed the button to answer, "Hello."

"Monty, this is Nia."

"Hey, how're you doing over there? You headed to the hospital?"

"Shortly, but we need to talk."

Montgomery knew that anytime a woman used that phrase, what followed meant nothing good for men. He sat up and braced himself.

"Okay, what's up?" he asked.

"Monty, I need that thumb drive back."

"What drive, I'm not sure what you're talking about."

"I know you have it so stop trying to play stupid. I know Jovan gave it to you. You're about to find yourself way in over your head, so don't fuck with me Monty."

How did she know this, he thought. Her aggressiveness and anger caught him off guard. Montgomery pulled the phone from his ear and stared at it in bewilderment.

As far as Nia knew, Jovan had the thumb drive. Reverse psychology was not going to work. Montgomery was sticking to his story. Like Jovan always said, 'deny everything, even if they see you doing it.' Plus he had a commitment to his friend.

"Nia, I don't have anything that belongs to you and I told you I did not see Jovan yesterday. Just calm down, maybe you misplaced it or something." Although insulted by her threat, he hoped his composure would prevail. Maybe she was still upset about the accident. Montgomery wanted to give her the benefit of the doubt, but he wasn't sure how long he would take any further verbal abuse.

"Alright Monty, no problem. We'll talk again ... soon." And Nia hung up.

Shocked, Montgomery looked at his phone again to make sure she had really hung up in his face. *Now what was that about?*

Crazy images flooded his mind. He'd never had this kind of interaction with Nia. Now he wondered whether he really had stumbled onto some secret NSA operation. He quickly dismissed the notion that some covert federal outfit caused Jovan's accident as too bizarre. Jovan's state of mind was the only possibility for crashing the Corvette. Or was it. Montgomery couldn't be sure about anything anymore.

Emotions began to run together. Anger, fear, sadness, all seemed combined into one gut wrenching feeling. He certainly didn't need anymore stress in his life, especially from the federal government. He had enough problems with the government in his interactions with the IRS. He didn't want to add NSA to the list of those out to get Montgomery Quinn.

Montgomery debated whether to just give the thumb drive back to Nia, but convinced himself not too. Not yet. Jovan wouldn't have wanted that. And he was determined to keep his word, at least until Jovan came out of his coma. Besides, now curiosity had gotten the best of him and he wanted to get to the bottom of the program's intent.

He ran to the computer in the office and picked up the thumb drive. He thought it might make sense to hide the backup CD he made until he could figure out what to do next. Quickly glancing up at the vent, Montgomery figured it would make a perfect storage place. He stood on the chair and reached his long arms into the hole to place the CD on top of the ceiling dry wall in the crevice. He also placed the GPS Jovan gave him up there too.

Montgomery sifted through the cell phone directory to find Donnie Cetronelli's number; then he pressed send. Donnie picked up on the first ring.

"Sup Doc, you up kinda early for a Tuesday."

"Donnie, I need you to look at something for me. Can you meet me in the lab in an hour?"

"I've started the articles and I think they're close to completion. The research is going--"

"Not that Donnie, this is something new that I'm sure you can help with.'

"Sure, Monty. What is it?"

"I'll tell you when I see you. One hour."

"Yeah, uh... I'll be there."

13

After hanging up on Montgomery, Nia felt nauseous. She sat at her desk with her head buried in her hands. She dreaded what the day had to offer. The image of Jovan on that hospital bed haunted her and she had difficulty not blaming herself for the accident. After all, if she hadn't been arguing with him at the time, maybe he wouldn't have crashed. But it was just that, an accident. Reckless driving by Jovan caused the crash, nothing else.

Now she had to deal with Montgomery and get back that thumb drive. She felt a headache coming and walked to her office to find some Advil.

Staring at her computer, Nia tried to think about her next move. Sitting behind the desk, she opened her laptop. She went to her email encryption software and typed an untraceable message:

Subject: Dr. Quinn
From: Nia Givens
To: Paulette Aventis, Sanja Coston, Charity Newhouse

I contacted Quinn and he denied having the thumb drive again. I don't know what he is up too, but we need to move quickly. Hopefully everyone is following up on what we talked about a couple of hours ago. I will wait to hear from you before taking any further action. Please get back to me as soon as you can.

Timiza Ahadi

She reread the message and clicked send. Making her way upstairs, she prepared to head to the hospital. Nia went to the closet to find something quick to throw on, nothing fancy. A simple blouse, faded jeans, but makeup was still necessary.

Thirty minutes later, after she showered and dressed, she checked her email and saw responses from everyone. Charity responded first, saying she would complete the background check by 12 noon and send it to everyone. Sanja stated that she already had one of the kizushis on the job who would track Quinn until further notice. Someone very reliable, she noted.

Paulette suggested that after they received Charity's report, a face-to-face meeting was needed. She emphasized that they deal with Dr. Quinn swiftly and forcefully. No more mistakes.

Conflicted. That word expressed Nia's emotions the most. She felt terrible for placing Njama in such a crazy situation. After more than thirty years why was she the one to potentially bring harm to such an important network?

At the same time, she felt bad for Montgomery Quinn. These women knew how to destroy a person's life and took no prisoners in the process. Nia wished it wasn't him, but now this was bigger than her and she couldn't stop things. She wasn't even sure if she wanted to at this point. There was a lot at stake; tradition, unwanted exposure, and money. Montgomery Quinn was just a speed bump in the middle of a major highway. It was all about damage control now.

And now she had to go to the hospital to check on a husband that she loved dearly, but hated for putting her in this position. Looking in the foyer mirror reminded her about the missed hair appointment, and the massage. Nia grabbed Jovan's Baltimore Orioles baseball cap hanging in the pantry and headed out the garage door.

Conflicted.

14

Aphone call from the bank about his late payment on the BMW reminded Montgomery to write checks for some overdue bills. The rude and forceful tone of the person from the bank made him want to just get them off his back. Now he knew how Gabrielle felt having to deal with annoying bill collectors.

He spent a few minutes writing checks and balancing the books. As always, not much was left when he finished. That's why he hated doing it because it reminded him about how little discretionary income they had.

Late for his meeting, Montgomery showered and threw on the first thing he found in the closet, which wasn't the normal dress when he went to the office. He thought a crisp shirt and tie received more respect from the students than the polo shirt and khakis preferred by his colleagues. So people rarely saw him on campus without business attire. Today would have to be an exception. He didn't plan to stay long anyway. Montgomery wore blue khakis, Nike sneakers, and his Penn State football t-shirt.

The BMW rushed down Georgia Avenue toward downtown. The D.C. traffic was miserable as always, but luckily this was a rare event. Typically if he left the house this late in the morning he would catch the subway. Even as a native Washingtonian, he never acquired a tolerance for rush hour traffic.

Nearing the convention center Montgomery realized that he had enough time to make a quick stop at his favorite Starbucks on the corner of H and 7th Street for a cup of chai tea.

It stood in the heart of China town, which always buzzed with the new revitalization going on in the area. The MCI Center built for the Washington Wizards was near by, new restaurants had opened, and hundreds of new upscale condos priced at more than five hundred thousand dollars were within blocks.

Years ago, people rarely walked the streets there. Crime and other conditions of urban plight had made the area run down and deplorable. Now it seemed like midtown Manhattan, people walking everywhere, day and night, enjoying the new cleanliness of revitalization.

Luckily he noticed a metered parking space on the street in front of the restaurant two doors down. This rarely occurs in D.C., especially just before nine. People often grabbed a meter and sat in their cars to wait for nine o'clock to roll by, so they could park legally and then leave for their offices. Parking enforcement had a notorious reputation for its efficiency. It wasn't unheard of to get a ticket at 8:59.

Montgomery parallel parked in the space and made his way to the Adams National Bank for a quick twenty-dollar withdrawal from the ATM. He then walked briskly down the sidewalk, savoring the smell of fresh blueberry muffins drifting from the Starbucks.

Four people waited in front of him at the counter. He hoped this wouldn't take long, but it was never a good sign when teenagers worked the cash register. The young woman taking the orders looked about eighteen, talked with a lisp through her braces, and walked slowly. Urgency never topped the list of the priorities for teens in restaurants, or any other service-type environment for that matter.

Ten minutes later he finally made it to the counter. His affinity for sweets caused him to eye the muffins, but he decided against it. Skipping breakfast also helped keep the waistline from expanding out of control.

After paying for his tea, Montgomery impatiently turned toward the exit. Donnie was waiting and, looking out of the café window, he could see the rush hour traffic starting to pick up. A line of cars jammed the street outside the window, blocking the BMW.

A silhouette in the door, framed by the morning sunlight, took him aback. It looked almost like an apparition.

The hourglass figure provided an internal pleasantness that caught him off guard. Early in his marriage, Montgomery had trained himself to not gawk at women, having been caught by Gabrielle a couple of times and receiving many slaps on the back of the head.

This time he was alone and he wanted to soak in this view. The woman had a certain allure that reminded him of his bachelor days. The shapeliness of her calves struck him first. Enhanced by the canary heels, the long legs flowed effortlessly as if she was rolling on a walkway like the ones at the airport.

As his eyes worked their way up her thighs, they were interrupted midway by a lemon sundress. Continuing the journey up her shapely body to her dark skinned face, he stopped in his tracks as their eyes met. Her brown eyes were small, but captivating. She wore a rounded bob cut with bronze highlights that framed her face perfectly. Something about this woman seemed familiar.

"You are one fine man, but are you deserving enough to wear a shirt from my alma mater," the woman said, breaking into a smile so broad that it showed all of her glistening white teeth. Montgomery snapped from his trance, looked again, and saw the cute gap in her front teeth. He immediately knew this was not a stranger.

"Carmen Underwood? Damn girl I haven't seen you in years."

Carmen and Montgomery had a history. They met during fall semester of their junior year at Penn State in an electronic circuits class. There weren't many African Americans who majored in electrical engineering so they formed an alliance and began to support one another and study together. She was the most intelligent woman he had ever met.

Needless to say, college students give in to a lot of lustful thoughts at wee hours of the morning after intense studying.

One thing led to another and they ended up dating for a year.

Born in South Carolina, Carmen had a southern charm that attracted everyone. Men especially loved her flirtatious accent and bubbly personality.

A body that equaled Halle Berry's didn't hurt either. And although all the men on campus envied him, Montgomery grew tired of the advances he had to endure whenever they went out. It also became clear after a year that a long-term relationship interested neither of them. They agreed to break up but remained close friends and study partners until graduation.

That meant no more sex, but Carmen had no problem sharing the intimate details of all of her escapades. On the one hand Montgomery didn't mind, he loved the stories. On the other, he fantasized about being those other guys and often wondered if he had made a mistake.

Carmen went off on a full scholarship to Stanford for her Masters degree and he stayed to do his at Penn State. They eventually lost touch, although he would hear about her every now and then from some of their classmates at homecoming games. And he thought about her more than he would admit.

"Boy, I haven't seen you in how many years? I know you missed me, didn't you." Carmen reached out and hugged Montgomery. She hadn't lost the accent.

He savored the feel of her soft breasts against his chest and fell into a moment of lustful memories as he wrapped his arms around her small waist.

"Time has definitely been good to you baby. Last I heard you were working on some special NASA project in Texas or something. What brings you to the chocolate city?" he asked.

"NASA is old news. You know I don't have much patience for nine to fives. Those stuffy folks at NASA got on my nerves quick. I left there a couple of years ago. Now I work for a small wireless firm in Connecticut. I came here to the TechWorld show they're having at the D.C. convention center."

Montgomery realized he'd forgotten to shave and his dress would certainly not leave a good impression. He felt the need to hurry the conversation along, although he really didn't want to.

"I hear you're a big time professor now," said Carmen.

"I don't know about how big time it is, but true."

"I knew success was in the cards for you Monty."

"Well, you know," he cleared his throat, feigning embarrassment. "So, how long you gonna be here?"

"The conference ends Wednesday, but I took some vacation time to stay until Friday. Wanted to check out the city, see some of my girls, and hang out a little bit since I haven't been here in a while," Carmen winked and rubbed Montgomery's arm softly. "You know, I could use a handsome escort."

Her flirtation caught him off guard and words escaped him.

He felt the eyes of all the men in the Starbucks on Carmen, a feeling he knew all too well from past experiences.

Finally, he spit it out, "Well, uh, I'm on my way to the office now to meet someone, but maybe we can get together for lunch."

"Sure your wife wouldn't mind." Carmen giggled and pointed to the gold wedding band.

"I don't see why not, married men gotta eat too don't they."

"Alright now," she said. "Go ahead and try to act like you the man with everything under control. But I ain't tryin to be no home wrecker and I didn't come here to get shot either." They both laughed.

"No problem at all, you got a cell phone? I'll call you when I finish up this morning."

Montgomery pulled out his cell phone and entered digits as she gave the number. He had to remember to erase it later. One thing he did not need was Gabrielle finding an unknown woman's number in his phone. They had a trusting relationship and she never snooped, but caution was still important. Anyway, this was just a lunch with an old friend, he thought.

"Man, you just don't know how good it is to see a pretty face after the last couple of days I've had. But look, I really have to meet someone, so we'll hook up for lunch," said Montgomery, reaching for another hug.

"Okay, I look forward to it." Carmen turned and walked toward the counter to order. "I think I'll have a chocolate brownie frappuccino," she told the teen at the counter.

Montgomery bit his lip as he eyed her pear shaped bottom swerving under the sundress. She looked back and smiled, aware of his gaze. He waved and turned away and she waved back. Two men walking out of the Starbucks behind him nudged him as he stood in the door.

"My man, that woman there is fine as hell. I wanna be like you when I grow up," said one of the men.

Montgomery smiled. For a brief moment he'd forgotten where he parked his car. It was nine thirty and he was supposed to meet Donnie a half an hour ago.

Lord knows I can't let this woman get me in trouble, he thought. He found his car and jumped in, heading for his office.

15

onnie Centronelli sat at the computer in the research lab playing a golf game. The large room had gray, cloth cubicles filled with old computer equipment, research projects at various stages of completion, and paper everywhere. Graduate students scurried around trying to meet the graduation deadlines for completing their thesis or dissertations.

Donnie noticed Montgomery coming toward him.

"You're an hour late Doc. You know after leaving the military, getting up this early is not my style. Man, you better be glad we've become close or I would have to--"

"Yeah, yeah, I know." Donnie went into his mafia boss impersonation again, but Montgomery wasn't in the mood.

"I gotta show you something, but you have to keep it between us." Montgomery pulled a chair into the cubicle and sat next to him.

"What is it?" Donnie whispered, looking around. "You got some more sexy pictures of Serena Williams. I can keep a secret." He burst into laughter.

"That's funny." Montgomery smiled, but returned to a more somber mood. "But seriously, I stumbled on to something I think you can help with. Jovan gave me this."

He handed Donnie the thumb drive. "He got it from his wife. I looked at it last night and need some help understanding it."

"Oh shit, not some top secret NSA program." Donnie took the thumb drive and plugged it into his computer.

"How is Jovan by the way?" Donnie asked as he prepared to look at the contents of the drive.

"I don't know, I'm on my way to see him after I leave here."

"I hope he pulls through. I'll try to go over myself this afternoon."

Donnie clicked on the drive and the symbol popped up.

"What the hell is that?"

"I don't know. I haven't figured it out yet. But once you click on it, it decompresses to some strange set of programs. I think it allows you to hack into some sort of system, but I couldn't figure out exactly what. There are some other files on there too. I need you to look at it and make sense of it for me."

"Hold on man. If she was working on some secret NSA project don't you think we should give this back. Take it from me; you don't want these government people breathing down your neck. Especially with all this Iraq and bin Laden crap going on."

"Jovan didn't want to give it back to her, and--"

"Wasn't he on that jealously thing again?"

"Yeah, but now its beyond that. Nia called me this morning trying to get me to admit to having the thumb drive and kinda threatened me, but I denied knowing anything. Now I'm curious as hell about what this is all about. There may be some state of the art technology here that could lead to some research for us. You know I need to get my publications up to qualify for tenure. I may just give it back, but lets look at it first."

Donnie sat back in the chair and stared at the symbol. "This is a reach. I can't see how we can relate this to your research."

"I'm not talking about the intent of the program. I'm referring to the software itself. You have to check on the sophistication of the code."

"You know what they say about curiosity and the cat?" Donnie asked.

"Yeah, but they say cats also have nine lives. If I lose this one I'll still have eight left." Montgomery smiled wryly. He knew Donnie was hesitant about getting involved, but he also knew he needed help. Finally, Donnie looked at him.

"Look man, I'll do this for you. But you need to be careful here. All of the dealings I've had with these people have never been good." He stood up and looked over the cubicle to see if anyone was listening. No one was around.

Donnie continued, "I know this guy who was in Desert Storm with me in the special unit I told you about. He's a serious computer wizard. He's hooked up with some underground hackers. They're all pissed about their military experiences, like me. Always trying to get into government systems to keep an eye on what the military, NSA, CIA and people like that are doing. I'll send it to them."

"Hold on," Montgomery interrupted. "I don't want anyone else involved with this."

"Don't worry. These guys don't care about any academic high tech research projects. They do this for kicks. They'll never say a word because they don't want to be uncovered. I wouldn't be surprised if they don't already have a copy or at least know about this software. I certainly can't break this thing down by myself."

"Alright. How fast can we get something from them?"

"He lives over in Fairfax with his brother. His brother's a computer geek too. If I get it to them this afternoon, I'll bet they'll know what it is within twenty-four hours. I just have to make contact and they'll tell me how to send it."

"Okay, cool. Let me know what they say as soon as you hear back. I'm headed over to the hospital." Montgomery got up from the chair and walked towards the door of the lab. His stubbornness in this case prevailed.

Donnie grabbed his arm, and said, "Be careful. These people have no problem with fucking you up."

"I will, don't worry."

He trusted Donnie would get what he needed. Now he needed to turn his attention to his friend's health.

16

Nia Givens sat in the wooden chair watching the various signals cascade across the monitors. Incessant hisses, beeps and buzzes from the devices reminded her that machines kept Jovan alive.

He still had not regained consciousness. Family members wandered in and out of the room to check on his status, but she hadn't left the seat since arriving at eight o'clock. Two hours later and she still couldn't take her eyes off the monitors, even with the dull headache that she'd had since yesterday.

Some of the swelling in his face had gone down, but he still looked like he'd been through hell. She reached out and held his hand, caressing his wedding band.

"Jovan," she whispered, "I'm here baby, waiting for you."

The nurses told them to continue talking to him; he may be hearing every word. No one knows what happens to the brain when a person enters these states. People often awoke with vivid memories of conversations heard while comatose. Nia wasn't convinced that was true, but anything was worth a try at this point.

"I love you Jovan."

She sat back in the chair, entranced again by the dance of the signals on the machinery.

"Can I get you anything Ms. Givens?" asked the nurse, entering the room for the routine check of the equipment. The round, elderly white women had strawberry hair and bifocals hanging from a string around her neck. Nia didn't recognize her from the day before and wondered how she knew who she was.

"No, I'm fine. Thank you."

"We changed shifts, so if you need anything, I'll be out at the nurse's station."

"I'm okay for now."

The nurse left Nia in the room and entered the one across the hall. Among the other bells, buzzers, and pneumatic wheezing sounds, Nia heard a faint, but familiar ringing. It was her cell phone in the black leather Coach purse. She reached inside, looked at the phone and saw an unfamiliar number.

Nia never answered the phone if she didn't recognize the number. She waited. Seconds later, the message signal popped on the screen. The text had a phone number followed by 1969. The mzingo zima always sent the code number 1969, the year Njama was founded, to initiate contact. That was her sign to call back, but not from her line.

She took one last look at Jovan and left the room in search of a pay phone. In the corner of the visitor's lounge, she noticed one, but a middle-aged, chubby Hispanic woman in a loud, checkered blue shirt was talking into the receiver in Spanish. As Nia walked toward her, she finished her conversation.

"I'm waiting for someone to call me back," the woman said rudely in a thick Spanish accent.

"Well, sorry, last time I checked this was a public phone." Nia stared up into the woman's dark eyes, waiting for any excuse to punch her in the mouth. On any other day, the woman may have taken her, but after what she had been through the last twenty-four hours, the fat woman had no chance. The women turned and walked away, whispering something under her breath in Spanish.

"Yeah, whatever, you better take your ass on," Nia yelled, feeling confident.

She picked up the receiver, entered a quarter, and dialed the number displayed on her cell phone.

Paulette Aventis answered from a service station pay

phone in Upper Marlboro, Maryland.

"Everything alright over there?" Paulette asked.

"No change. I have a major headache, my back hurts, and my eyes are glazing over."

"What about your husband?"

"Oh, he's still in a coma," Nia answered, slightly embarrassed at her selfishness.

"We're praying for him." Paulette paused for a second, appearing to gather her thoughts.

"Well dear, we'll have our report within the hour. We are meeting at the Cajun Cuisine for lunch to discuss. We'll understand if you can't make it."

"I'll be there, don't worry."

"Twelve noon, Okay?"

"That's good, see you then."

"Stay strong, sister."

Nia hung up the receiver. She erased the number from her cell phone and slipped it back into her purse. She needed to go home and get herself together. Going to the hospital dressed like a bum was one thing, but the Cajun Cuisine was another.

It was a small upscale lunch spot where many downtown lawyers and politicians dined. She needed to look her best to walk around K Street.

Leaving the visitors room she gave an evil stare to the Hispanic woman and walked back toward her husband's room. Jovan's mother sat next to the bed looking at her son.

"Mom, I have to go take care of something."

"Go ahead honey. I'll be right here watching over my baby."

"Please call me if anything changes. I should be back in a couple of hours."

"Alright."

She kissed Jovan on the forehead, adjusted the Orioles cap, turned and left the room. Walking down the hall toward the elevator, the bright florescent lights made her feel light-headed. She pushed the elevator button and entered the car as it arrived.

Minutes later, Montgomery's elevator reached the third floor and he exited looking around for room 343. He turned left, following the signs. As he made his way through the intensive care unit, he noticed an elderly white man alone in the second room on the right, hooked up to numerous devices.

The old man looked like he could have been one hundred years old. His body was wrinkled, pale, and frail. He appeared peaceful, but Montgomery knew he wasn't, especially with all of the tubes in his nose, mouth, and arms.

Montgomery remembered how much he disliked hospitals. The smell just brought back bad memories. Most visits occurred because someone had died or was dying. He had never been to a hospital and heard good news, except the birth of Eliza. Even that day, he remembered as he wheeled Gabrielle into emergency, an ambulance was bringing in a teenage boy who was shot in the chest.

Walking slower, he turned and stood in the door, frozen by the sight of his best friend's battered body. Hazel Givens sat next to the bed, stroking Jovan's forehead and singing "Amazing Grace" softly.

He thought about turning around and walking away. But he couldn't; he just stood there. Finally, his vocal cords became unconstricted; he wiped the tears forming in his eyes and entered the room trying to gather himself.

"Mama Givens, how is he?" Montgomery reached down and kissed her on the cheek.

"Hey baby, only the Lord knows, I've put everything in his hands," she responded in her deep Alabama accent. After living most of her life in D.C. she never lost that southern drawl.

"Yes ma'am. I hope you got some sleep."

"Yep, I went home and slept a little, but I was here first thing this morning. I need to be here in case he wakes up. I want to be the first one he sees."

Montgomery smiled and grabbed Ms. Givens hand.

"You just missed Nia. She said she was going to take care of something. Poor thing, she's taking this pretty hard."

Yeah I bet, thought Montgomery. His phone conversation

with Nia that morning erased the little sympathy he had for her. He continued smiling.

"Sorry I missed her."

"You know Monty, Jovan told me they were having problems," Hazel whispered. "I've noticed she's been acting pretty strange lately. You notice anything?"

"No ma'am."

"I never really liked her much anyway you know." Ms. Givens lean over, touching Montgomery on the arm. "A person that wears all that makeup is definitely hiding something."

Montgomery smiled and looked over at Jovan. He had never seen anyone so swollen. If Jovan's mother were not sitting there, he probably would have thought he had the wrong room. This person didn't look anything like the man he had known most of his life. Montgomery didn't know how long he could stand there watching Jovan labor to take each breath.

"Its okay Monty, you can talk to him. I know he can hear you."

"I'm not sure what to say Ms. Givens. My heart hurts so bad." A tear rolled down Montgomery's face.

"I know baby," said Hazel Given. She reached over and held Montgomery's hand. "But you two have been friends forever it seems. You shared so much, I'm sure you'll find something. Let love direct your tongue."

She paused for a minute, smiled and said, "Why don't you talk about that time you both stood on the roof of Mr. Peterson's garage and threw tomatoes at cars going down South Dakota Ave."

"Now you know that wasn't us Mama Givens." Montgomery chuckled, knowing it was a lie. *Deny everything.*

"I ain't no fool Monty, one day I'm gonna get you two to admit to that and all the other foolishness you did." They both laughed. It was needed to break up the tension.

"Anyway, I'll leave you two alone. I have to go to the ladies room anyhow." She got up and slowly disappeared into the hall.

Montgomery looked around, unsure of what to do. His eyes

returned to Jovan once again.

"Jo, its Monty. I'm here for you man." No response. Montgomery wasn't sure why he expected one. He wasn't sure what to expect. This feeling of despair hadn't been felt in many years, but the pain was familiar.

Jovan Givens was his closest friend since middle school. They met at a video game arcade playing Pacman. The two hit it off quickly and just began hanging out at each other's house. In high school, Jovan played fullback, opening all of the holes that made Montgomery a second team all-city tailback.

Montgomery's mind flashed to one football play in their senior year. He only needed eight yards to break the school record for yards in a season.

Jovan, the fullback, walked up to him in the huddle and whispered, "Follow me Monty, you got this bro."

The ball sat on the twenty-three yard line and the team trailed by three points in the fourth quarter of the last game of their high school career. As the quarterback handed Montgomery the ball on the sweep left, he did as Jovan suggested and followed his lead. Jovan hit the linebacker coming up from the outside on the kneecap and the entire sideline squealed from a crack that sounded like an ax splitting a log.

Montgomery darted inside and sprinted to the end zone to win the game. And he broke the record. Some may think a football play is not a big deal, but that moment cemented their relationship forever.

During the summer they often hung out at Hains Point with all of the other teenagers, leaning on their cars, playing music loudly and trying to talk to every girl that passed by. Football brought them a sort of celebrity status they both enjoyed.

Just recently, they played at the Hains Point golf course. And ironically the last time they talked was at that same place that brought so many memories.

They'd shared so much together that he felt closer to Jovan than anyone he knew, other than his grandmother.

The two even shared a room at Penn State, until Jovan dropped out after their sophomore year to become an electrician.

Montgomery felt disappointment with his decision, but it worked out for the best. He developed other relationships that made him grow personally and socially. Yet, coming back to DC after school, their bond picked up right where it left off.

Just talk, he thought.

"Jo, you left me in some shit this time brother. That package you gave me yesterday has Nia all pissed off. She called me this morning and threatened me. It looks like it has some secret or illegal stuff on it. Since I promised you, I'm holding on to it. I got your back this time." He looked up at the dancing signals on the machine. "But you need to wake up soon so you and Nia can work this thing out. I can't cover for you forever. I hope you aren't using this coma thing so you can get out of this mess. If so, when you wake up I'm gonna kick your ass." Montgomery laughed.

"Look bro, I'll keep you posted on what's happening. Stay strong and get back to us soon. It's only been a day, but I miss you man. I'm gonna be here everyday for you. Maybe you'll get tired of me harassing you and eventually wake up."

"Excuse me."

Montgomery turned, startled to see the wide-bodied nurse standing behind him.

"I'm sorry sir, but we're going to change his dressing now. Can you step outside for just a moment?"

"Sure."

Montgomery squeezed Jovan's hand and left the room.

In the hall he talked with Hazel Givens and some of the other relatives for about thirty minutes. One of Jovan's cousins on the police force had stopped by earlier to assure the family that there was no apparent foul play in the accident. The telephone argument with Nia provided the primary distraction and he just skidded off the road into a concrete barrier. They were lucky he survived because, at the speed he was traveling, that brief lapse behind the wheel could have cost him his life. Based on the condition of the car, he should have been dead.

Montgomery remembered he needed to go home and get ready for his lunch date with Carmen. He excused himself and headed for the elevator. Somehow, he knew Carmen would bring some joy to a dreadful day. And he anxiously wanted to see her again.

17

The Cyber Division of the FBI investigates criminal activity involving the Internet, computer systems, and the information infrastructure. Charity Newhouse was a member of a task force responsible for monitoring cyber crimes and tracking the known people responsible for them. She'd worked in several capacities in the agency over the years, but found this one the most interesting.

Charity sat in her small office at the headquarters multitasking work related activities and the report on Montgomery Quinn. Most of the background information was easily obtainable from the many databases available within the agency. She needed help, however, on gathering some of the data because she didn't have access to certain secure systems.

Heightened security placed a lot of emphasis on only obtaining data on a need to know basis. Charity's access was limited to those systems pertaining to cyber-crime investigations, but she had relationships within the agency to get all she needed on Dr. Quinn.

The electronic world made collecting a history on someone easier. People used credit cards to buy everything from gasoline, groceries, books, music, clothing and even cars. Every time someone applied for credit they report some information about who they are, where they live, and what they do for a living.

Telephone and cell phone calls, Internet usage, all provide some information about a person's likes, dislikes, habits, and relationships. Everything is stored somewhere in a database, making the FBI's life easier when trying to build a profile.

As Charity cut and pasted data into a usable report format for Njama, Chuck Royce poked his round head in her office. He was one of the few men she trusted in the department.

"Charity, got the history on your man," he held up the manila folder and brushed back his unkept, thinning hair.

"Thanks Chuck, you came through for me again."

He dropped the folder on her desk. "Anything for the most beautiful woman in the agency. Just trying to help out. What are you doing for lunch today?"

Chuck always tried to hit on Charity. She found it flattering and disgusting. Although she was a little overweight, mainly due to her addiction to double-stuffed Oreos, white guys were just not her type. Especially short, round, and balding, white guys. Some of his comments bordered on harassment, but he always came through when she needed him, so she tolerated him.

"Not today, I have another appointment. Thanks anyway, maybe another time?"

"How about definitely another time?

"Okay, definitely."

"Promise?"

Charity forced a smile. Chuck annoyed her with his persistence, but she indulged him. Just then the telephone rang.

Thank god, Charity thought.

"I really have to take this Chuck, I'm expecting a call. We'll get together one day this week."

"I'll hold you to that." He waved and backed out of the door into the hall.

"Hello, this is Charity Newhouse."

"How're we looking?" said Paulette Aventis, calling from a pay phone in Arlington.

"I'll have it done, are we still on?"

"Yes, same place we decided earlier, see you there." Paulette hung up. She never entertained long conversations, especially on Washington lines. She assumed that all calls were being taped by one of the myriad alphabet federal agencies. Charity thought this was probably a good assumption.

She placed the phone on the receiver and picked up the manila folder. Charity told Chuck that Montgomery Quinn was a victim of Internet identity theft and she wanted to get his background to try and track down the potential suspects. She knew it was a stretch, but it was the best she could come up with at the time. Chuck would never question it anyway. The fact that she asked for the favor made him happy.

She flipped through the sheets. Briefs on his time at Penn State and his research work at George Washington, his financial management inadequacies, and his gambling habits were all rather interesting but nothing earth shattering.

She delved further. Wife worked for a small tax law firm, one daughter, parents died in a car accident. Charity drifted through more mundane history. She'd seen thousands of similar reports so she knew what to look for. She flipped to the next sheet.

Closest living relative, grandmother: Lila M. Armstrong, retired FBI employee.

Charity dropped the folder and stared at the sheet. Lila Armstrong?

Oh my god!

Charity couldn't believe what she saw. Lila Armstrong was Montgomery Quinn's grandmother?

She took a moment to make sure that what she saw was accurate, and then Charity picked up the phone and dialed. She listened intently for the other line to pick up.

"Hello?"

"Lila? This is Charity."

"Well hello dear, long time no hear from. What do I owe this pleasure?"

"I have something important to talk to you about. We need to meet soon."

18

Paulette Aventis sat in a semi-closed room in the back of the Cajun Cuisine restaurant on Connecticut Ave. She appeared distinguished and beautiful, dressed in a crème tailored business suit. Her posture exuded confidence and power.

Her flawless makeup enhanced the beauty of her dark chocolate skin tone. And the dread locks were impeccably kept. Others in the restaurant may have thought she worked in marketing or fashion. She looked like an executive of some sort, just by the way she carried herself. Or maybe a lawyer? No one would guess she led one of the most respected technology firms in the country.

Paulette loved the contrast her look provided. It kept people off balance. They never knew how to approach her, often underestimating her ability. This gave her an advantage in more ways than one and her competitive nature exploited it at every turn, especially in the boardroom.

As she waited for the meeting to begin, the soft sounds of the Joshua Redman trio played softly from the ceiling speakers. She tapped her fingers on the gold trimmed glasses to the rhythm, and glanced at the Picasso renditions hanging on the earth-toned walls.

Lunch in public was highly unusual for Njama's *mzingo zima*. However, this type of emergency certainly called for a face-to-face. Paulette chose the place hoping that four black professional women eating and talking business wouldn't appear unusual.

81

Some of the tables were a little close for comfort, but since she knew the owner, they reserved the small enclosure near the back. It was near the kitchen so the scent of the spicy New Orleans dishes smothered the air.

A couple at the table just outside the door of the enclosure discussed some business meeting they planned to attend after lunch. Something about a legal case gone awry. They tossed around potential excuses to a Judge for missing a court deadline. Paulette tried to ignore them, but they talked loud enough to make that impossible.

She reflected on what Sanja wanted to discuss. Going against the traditional methods of Njama, Sanja suggested a scheme that may now have gone too far. Sanja had planted one of the kizushis in a company called ElecCheck Processing, Inc., also known as ECPI.

The primary target was Frank Hill, the CEO of ECPI.

Hill made millions in North Carolina forcing African American landowners to sell him family-owned property, which he then used to build upscale condominiums. Many of the families had owned the land for years and Hill often took advantage of their naivety. He manipulated them to sell for much less than the property value, in some cases using physical force or coercion. Some of the blacks were too poor to relocate in the state with the meager earnings from selling to Hill. They eventually moved further south.

Charity had also uncovered from FBI sources that Hill secretly funded an underground sect of the Ku Klux Klan. Several extremist leaders in North Carolina had accounts with banks that used ECPI.

Wall Street recognized ECPI as a major new player. They had contracts with several mid-sized banks, credit unions, and brokerage firms to process online bill payments and electronic wire transfers. Its stock rose even in the midst of an economic downturn and Hill held the majority of the stock. He used the money from his shady real estate dealings to start the company.

Sanja's contact worked in the information systems

department at ECPI and could provide a back door into the company's computer system. After accessing the ECPI's web server, Nia and Sanja had been monitoring the way transactions were processed for several months.

Njama's plan was to create fake customer transactions and authorize movement of money from the accounts of selected people to those set up by Njama at various other locations.

Sanja had convinced everyone that this was a double take down. Paulette trusted that she knew what she was talking about. First, in Sanja's opinion, the banking system needed to be taught a lesson because of its practices against hiring and promotion of minorities. It was personal for her.

Second, they'd deal Hill's business a major blow and he couldn't say a word. If he challenged them, his secret alliance with the KKK or the fact that his computer systems weren't secure would find its way to the Washington Post, the New York Times, and every major news outlet in the country. The result would be a severe downturn in the stock price and a vanishing of Hill's financial empire. They all knew he would do anything to prevent that.

The tactics of Njama had changed over the years but the end result stayed the same. Hit the enemy where it hurts them the most, and then get them to comply with the demands of Njama.

Njama loved the thought of destroying the career and the wealth of a closet racist. They initially planned to divert major account holder's money to several nonprofit organizations serving underprivileged groups. If Hill balked, Nia would inform the press of the security infringement, and Njama's knowledge of his personal relationships with some unsavory organizations.

Eventually greed took over and Paulette, Nia, and Sanja devised a strategy for diverting some of the money to personal accounts. Instead of just exploiting the problems of ECPI and forcing Hill to support their causes, they also planned to profit from the plan themselves.

It was so much money, they figured no one would miss it.

Plus a little payment for their services was long overdue. The three knew Charity would never participate so they kept her out of the loop regarding this slight alteration.

This was a one shot, get rich quick deal. And everything thus far had progressed as planned. But now Nia had turned a smooth operation into a fiasco.

Paulette didn't need the money, but went along reluctantly. She now began to have second thoughts.

Coming out of her daydream, Paulette looked at her watch and it said eleven-ten. Sanja had agreed to meet at eleven so they would have an hour to talk before Nia and Charity arrived. She was late, and Paulette detested tardiness.

Paulette sipped her water and looked up as Sanja walked in the door. She dressed in a navy blue business suit that highlighted her curvy feminine figure. The high heels made her stride long and graceful like a runway model. Sanja took professionalism seriously, and it all started with dress in her opinion.

"Drinking that D.C. water may keep you from getting through the airport metal detectors," said Sanja, smiling as she approached the room. She grabbed the linen napkin and pulled out a chair, setting her Louis Vuitton bag on the floor.

"What?"

"You don't know. They've been having problems with lead in the drinking water in the city. You need to read the paper more often."

"Whatever. I read the paper. You have to die from something." Paulette took another sip. "Where the hell have you been?"

"Sorry I'm late, you know how it is trying to park down here."

The waiter walked over wearing a crisp white shirt, black bow tie, and apron. He was a young man in his early twenties. He looked Hispanic, but could have been mixed with Native American.

"May I get you something to drink?"

"Yes, do you have any bottled water?" asked Sanja.

"No, sorry. We have Perrier."

"I'll have a Sprite, no ice, unless your ice machine has a filter on it."

"Uh… I'm not sure, let me go check."

"Forget it, just the Sprite, and no ice."

"No problem. Can I get you ladies an appetizer to start with?"

"We'll let you know when we're ready," said Sanja rudely, turning to Paulette.

"Girl, you have some real issues," said Paulette, rolling her eyes.

The waiter walked away. Sanja leaned across the table.

"So, Ms. Amiri. What are our plans now? Your girl Nia put us in a bind and we have little time to fix it."

"Yeah, I know. What did your source at ECPI give us as a drop dead time?"

"Friday at midnight. Let me bring you up to speed real quick." Sanja settled back in her chair, scooted it closer to the table, and looked around to make sure no one was listening.

"At your place on Sunday, after we finished planning the induction ceremony for Wednesday, I gave Nia the changes to the program. My contact told me we needed some updates to access the system more efficiently. Presumably, that's what Nia was doing when she got careless. It was late when we left and I could tell then she was exhausted."

"What was the change for?"

"Our kizushi found another weakness in their software and network. The company is upgrading to a new version of the transaction software that may correct the weakness. The installation is scheduled for Saturday, that's why we have to do this by Friday."

"Have we set up all the other accounts to capture the transactions?"

"Everything is a go. We have commercial accounts at five different banks around the country. They were all set up with fake IDs and social security numbers by our trusted kizushis. They don't have a clue and will do anything to win us over.

Once we get this shit straightened out with Nia, we can move."

"Honestly Sanja, I'm feeling very uncomfortable with this program floating out there. We may have to postpone this until another time."

"The time is now Paulette!" Sanja slapped the table firmly. She looked around to make sure she didn't bring attention to them.

"Who the fuck do you think you are talking to?" whispered Paulette trying to stay under control. She was losing her patience with Sanja's overbearing nature.

Leaning forward Sanja gathered herself. Then she said, "I'm sorry, but we've been planning this for six months. We have a window here and we have to jump through it. Three days from now, we go in, create transactions to divert Hill's money to our accounts and the others, clean up so ECPI will never know we were there, and collect maybe five hundred thousand or more, just like that."

The waiter returned to the room, "Have you ladies decided on an appetizer while you wait for your other guests?"

Sanja looked at the waiter with hatred in her eyes, "When we're ready, we'll call you. Now please leave us alone, thank you."

The waiter turned and nervously left.

"That was absolutely unnecessary. What the hell is your problem?" asked Paulette.

"These people just get on my nerves with all the interruptions."

"Well, you need to get it together quick." Seconds later, Paulette asked, "So how do we get the money out of the commercial accounts?"

"First the money will be transferred to a Swiss Bank. I opened an account there when I went to an international central bankers meeting in January. I deposited twenty thousand dollars to open the account by the way. But you can thank me later."

"Twenty thousand? Your own money I suspect?"

"Yeah, but I plan to get a pretty good return on it. It cost one hundred thousand to open a numbered account, but I didn't think we would need that much secrecy," Sanja smiled. The waiter returned with her Sprite and left quietly. She waited for him to completely leave the room, took a sip and continued.

"If they do trace us, getting the Swiss to talk is like squeezing juice from an onion. After we confirm the money is there, we have the Swiss bank do a wire transfer to the commercial accounts. Then we just have to withdraw it in small increments over time to make sure we don't raise suspicions."

"I guess you have it all figured out."

"Working at the Fed has some advantages in knowing how banks work."

"So lets focus our attention on Nia and Dr. Quinn."

"Listen, I have some old military friends from my days at the Pentagon. One call and they'll swoop down on Quinn before he knows what hit him. They can grab that thumb drive, get out, and leave him with a few knots on his head for good measure."

"Don't you dare! You're getting way out of control. We are not about violence and I will never approve of that. Do you hear me?" Paulette's temper slowly reached an apex. Sanja made outrageous statements sometime, but this one brought a bead of sweat above Paulette brow. After this ended, Sanja had to be reigned in quickly before she single-handedly destroyed Njama.

"Just a suggestion," Sanja replied nonchalantly.

"We'll hear what Nia and Charity have to say and make a decision. One that fits within the context of our mission. No violence."

"I hear you."

They sat silently for several moments. Finally, Sanja said, "Maybe we should get an appetizer. I missed breakfast." She looked around for the waiter.

"Yeah, and I need a strong drink," said Paulette, rubbing her temples.

19

Montgomery Quinn felt more nervous than the first time he had sex with Marva Jefferson in her parents' basement. He had spoken to Carmen earlier and they agreed to meet for lunch at the Market Inn in Southwest Washington. It was a small place and sort of out of the way. He thought it was unlikely anyone he knew would see him there.

He had the opportunity to go home, shave, and change into something more suitable. A nice beige polo shirt with blue slacks and black leather square toed shoes. Montgomery knew Carmen would notice the shoes, she always believed that the accessories made the man.

Montgomery pulled the BMW up to the curb and handed the valet his keys. He felt uneasy and warm. Closing his eyes, he took a deep breath and hoped not to do something he would regret. The image of Carmen in that sundress played over and over in his head. But he had a wife and child now.

Do not fuck up, he told himself.

Entering the place, his eyes adjusted to the dim light inside. He noticed Carmen sitting at the bar. She had changed into a pair of tight jeans with a low cut crimson blouse. She still had on the high heels.

"Excuse me miss, are you waiting for someone? You look a little lonely."

Carmen turned and looked more radiant than Montgomery had remembered that morning. Age had definitely made her more beautiful. Not a strand of hair looked out of place and the small hints of makeup accented her high cheekbones. And of course that cute little gap in her teeth. He felt the hair stand up on the back of his neck.

"Not anymore, I think my date is here." She turned and they hugged. He didn't want to let go, she felt so soft.

"Lets get a table," he said.

The waitress directed them to their small table in the far corner. As they walked, he couldn't take his eyes off the roundness of Carmen's bottom, filling the jeans like an overstuffed feather pillow. He pulled out her chair.

"Still a gentleman I see. Thank you," she smiled and sat down.

"I try. But you make it pretty easy."

The waitress handed them menus and went through the specials for the day. Carmen ordered an apple martini and Montgomery a cherry coke.

"You know I liked that sun dress this morning, but the jeans topped that."

"Just for you Monty. I knew you would like it," she winked. "I finished early this morning so I went back to the hotel to change." She sipped her drink. "It's been so long, Monty. We have so much to talk about. You need to tell me everything happening in your life. Wife, kids, work, everything."

They went through the years, chatting about all that had transpired since Carmen left for Stanford. Montgomery talked about Gabrielle and Eliza, his job at GW, all the friends they shared, where they were, and what they had accomplished. He even told her about Jovan's accident. She vaguely remembered him from college.

They ordered and Carmen told him about Stanford, her travels and her job with the wireless company. They laughed and talked just like old times. And Carmen flirted, just like old times. Not that Montgomery minded.

After an hour it was like they had never been apart. Carmen slid her hand under the table and rubbed Montgomery's knee. He felt a rush of blood to his lower extremities and started getting excited.

"So Monty," she said, "I think you really missed me. How come you never tried to look me up?"

"You know, I'm not very good at keeping track of old friends. I need to get better at it. This time, I promise to keep in touch."

"You better, I'll give you my number before we leave. If I'm lucky maybe I can convince you to join me for dinner also," she looked up with a gleam in her eye and a sly smile.

"Maybe tomorrow. I have a standing dinner date with my grandmother. We go out on her birthday every year and tonight's the night." He knew that was later in the week, but he needed a lie to get out of this. Gabrielle would never buy a last minute dinner appointment on a Tuesday.

"How sweet. Oh, well. I would never interfere with that. I know I'm way down on the pecking order of the women in your life now. But maybe before I leave I can impress you enough to move up a notch. You think that's possible Monty." She leaned forward and grabbed his hand, rubbing it softly with her thumb. Montgomery anxiously took a sip of his soda.

"So do you want dessert?"

Carmen laughed, "Am I making you nervous, boo?"

"You always did baby, you know that"

"Well we'll have to do something about that won't we?"

Montgomery fanned himself with his napkin and Carmen giggled softly. He needed to get out of this before he did something he would regret. The plunging neckline on her blouse distracted him the entire lunch as he tried his hardest not to stare at her ample cleavage.

"I do hope we can see each other again before you go." He couldn't believe he just said that. But he meant it. *What am I getting myself into?*

"I'm here for the rest of the week, we can arrange that, don't you think?"

20

In Northwest D.C., Njama continued their strategy meeting. Nia and Charity had arrived at noon, ordered their meals, and finished their lunches. The idle chitchat had ended; it was now time to discuss business.

Charity passed around her profile on Montgomery Quinn. She'd made one copy for each woman and cautioned everyone that it should be destroyed immediately after the meeting.

It contained his entire life in twenty-seven pages. Included were basic items like education, wife's employer, childcare, outstanding debt, house, cars, and bank accounts. More detailed information such as what restaurants he dined at according to credit card statements, his salary and other income, and even his blood type. Some things Charity omitted. She had her reasons. But for the most part, it was all there.

Everyone had a long look at the report during the meal, looking for points of attack on Quinn. Paulette picked up her copy after she ate and glanced at it intensely.

"So, any suggestions, " she said, wiping her mouth with her napkin, smudging it with red lipstick.

"Looks like he has some suspect financial management skills," said Nia. "I say we hit him there. Make his finances such a mess that he appears to lose everything. That should pressure him into giving up the thumb drive once he sees the power we have to control his life," said Nia.

"I like it. Anyone else," asked Paulette.

"I still think we need to be more forceful. We don't have

a lot of time for this subtle bullshit. Lets either just hire someone to go into his house or wherever and get the thing," said Sanja.

"I said no violence or other criminal activities," said Paulette forcefully. Sanja ignored Paulette and took the last bite of her blackened catfish. She had her own agenda and she grew tired of Paulette's cautiousness. Someone else needed to step up and make a move. Just then, Sanja's phone rang and she reached in her purse to look at the number.

"Excuse me, one of our girls is calling." She left the small room and went outside to find a pay phone.

"What we are doing here is criminal," said Charity, shaking her head in disgust.

"You've been in Njama for a long time so you're embedded in this as well. Everything we do is borderline criminal, unethical, and immoral. But the end result is the greater good. Don't try to play coy with me now like you all of a sudden are riding the moral horse," said Paulette.

Charity looked at Paulette blankly, but said nothing.

They've had a good relationship for years, and Charity initially looked up to her. Now Charity had lost all respect for Paulette. She knew more about their secret activities than they were aware and Paulette's lack of leadership deeply disappointed her.

Charity felt betrayed and refused to participate in the decision to enter this high tech hijacking. Although she made it clear from the beginning that she disapproved of the plan, they secretly continued without her approval. Charity expected more from the amiri and Paulette failed to live up to the title in her mind.

"Look," Nia interrupted, "Attacking his personal life can be effective and quick. Within the next two days his life can be a mess. I predict by Thursday Monty will be throwing the program at us to take it and give him his life back. I'm suggesting a full assault."

"How fast can we get things moving, ladies," asked Paulette.

"As soon as we leave here I can get the ball rolling," responded Nia.

Sanja returned and sat at the table.

"Good news. Seems our boy decided to tip out on his wife."

"What do you mean?" Nia was shocked. She never thought Montgomery would do something like that.

"We've got pictures. And don't be so surprised. He is a man after all." Sanja smiled at the delight of trapping a man in this way.

"I guess you would know Sanja, you've had you're share of them," said Charity, beginning to reach a boiling point with her frustrations.

"And fuck you too Charity!"

"You're not all that tough Sanja!"

"Ladies! We have work to do here, lets get back to business, shall we?" said Paulette.

"I'm tired of her shit. Always acting like she is above all of us and pushing this ultra moral stance. If you don't like what we do, then leave," said Sanja

"I don't like what you all are doing and I don't plan to leave. But if you continue in this direction, be assured that you might find yourself gone," said Charity, sitting on the edge of her chair and pointing her finger at Sanja.

"Oh really?" Sanja smirked.

"Yes, really."

"Enough! Silence!" Paulette said forcefully, but softly. Charity and Sanja rolled their eyes at each other and sat back in their seats. Things were getting out of hand and Paulette had to reign them back in. People still dined and the rising voices attracted attention. Nia sat in her chair in amazement. No one had ever seen Charity lose her cool like this.

"Looks like we have more than enough ammunition," Paulette said. Sanja, lets take the pictures and use them to our advantage. Use your own judgment on how to do this. Nia, start the strike on the finances. Charity, keep collecting information on Quinn. The more we know the better. I'll also make some other calls to see if we can pressure him in some other ways. We need to get going immediately, today. Time is running out. Are we clear?"

They all agreed. The women of Njama broke up their lunch and left the restaurant one at a time, heading in different directions.

21

Carmen and Montgomery stood at the entrance of the Market Inn waiting for the valet to bring his car. The bright sun complimented the spring breeze and it felt glorious. Time flew by and the lunch went a little longer than either expected. But it was well worth it, at least according to Montgomery.

The two reluctantly broke up the reminiscing because it was two-thirty and Montgomery had to pick up Eliza from day care. Most of the lunchtime crowd had made their way back to the office, so few people mingled on the street. The location of the restaurant was perfect, at the end of a street, under a highway overpass in southwest D.C. Not an ideal tourist spot, so few people noticed the couple.

Montgomery found the lunch delicious, both the food and the company. He never expected sex to happen though. He was happily married, most of the time at least. However, since the baby came, he and Gabrielle's sex life was miniscule at best. Feeling deprived, he basked in the attention, and welcomed the flirting.

Carmen chatted about the conference dinner scheduled for later in the evening, but Montgomery heard nothing. He focused on her full lips as she seductively put on her reddish orange lipstick. Everything seemed to slow down as he watched the stick glide and his imagination spiraled.

The valet pulled up and Montgomery gave him a two dollar tip.

"Professor's salaries must be better than I thought," said Carmen as she eyed the car sparkling in the afternoon sunlight.

"We do alright, but I could always use more." They walked together toward the car.

"Sure you don't want a ride, the closest Metro stop is a little walk from here."

"Naw, I don't have to be back downtown until five o'clock so I'm just gonna walk around and enjoy the sunshine. Maybe I'll do a little shopping and sight seeing."

"Don't get yourself in any trouble," said Montgomery, smiling widely.

"You know me, I only go for the good kinda trouble."

Montgomery reached out and embraced Carmen tightly.

"I gave you my cell phone number so you better call me later, Monty. I'll be waiting. I hope you'll find time for an old friend sometime this week."

"I'll find time, don't worry."

They separated and Carmen reached up and planted her soft lips on Montgomery's. The kiss was long and passionate. He didn't expect it, but he didn't resist.

At that moment, a petite brown skinned woman in a sky blue dress, holding a brief case, stood at the entrance of the restaurant, her cell phone against her ear. She went unnoticed by Montgomery and Carmen, who stood a short distance away saying their goodbyes. As they kissed, the women held up the phone and snapped a picture of the couple. She checked the digital display to make sure she got the shot.

Perfect, she thought. *This is better than the ones I got inside.*

She placed the phone in her purse and headed down the sidewalk.

Montgomery felt an instant rush of guilt. Although, he had hoped for the kiss to happen, he was married, and he had never done anything like that before. He looked around suspiciously, hoping no one saw what just happened. The only people around were the valet and the lady heading down the sidewalk in the short blue dress. He got in his car, rolled down the window, and waved goodbye to Carmen.

"You're going to cause me a divorce, girl." He looked in the rear view mirror and wiped off the lipstick.

"Never that Monty, I just want to have a little fun. You know me."

"Yeah, that's the problem, I know you too well."

She blew a kiss as he pulled off. Looking in the mirror he saw Carmen heading down the street, knowing that some man in her path would eventually fall victim to her seductiveness. He noticed more lipstick on his lips and reached for a napkin in the glove compartment to wipe it off. Gabrielle would kill him if this got back to her.

But for now, he was safe. And the devilish grin on his face showed his mind was drifting into a place of pleasant fantasy.

22

Donnie Centronelli stood at the entrance of the Foggy Bottom metro, on the George Washington University campus, waiting for his old friend Billy Yow. The crowd of students, government employees, and homeless people heading in and out of the metro appeared unusually large. Donnie blew it off as an anomaly. Maybe the nice spring day brought everyone out early.

Donnie and Billy served together in the Persian Gulf and became close companions. Both graduated with degrees in engineering and served in the ROTC. Donnie graduated from North Carolina A&T and Billy from University of Indiana

While Donnie grew up in urban New Jersey, Billy was raised on a farm in rural Ohio and had little exposure to other cultures or populations other than his white family. Even in college he limited his relationships to whites, feeling uncomfortable socializing with other ethnic groups. Meeting Donnie, a high energy Italian from the east coast, opened Billy to a world he never knew and a friendship he cherished.

Donnie's outgoing personality made it difficult to avoid, particularly in the confines of basic training. Plus it's difficult to discriminate in war. Swift decisions are all that count when it comes to saving another soldier's life in the heat of a battle. There is no room for color or cultural biases.

Donnie and Billy became members of the Special Forces Operational Detachment – Alpha, otherwise know as the green berets or the A-Team.

Donnie was the engineering officer responsible for perimeter defense weapons, burst transmission devices, night-vision devices, and electric demolitions. Billy was the communications officer responsible for tactical satellite communications, high-frequency radios, and global positioning systems. Both were ranked lieutenant in the alpha unit. They were deployed together on several assignments and grew very close, braving many life-threatening situations.

Of the many things they now shared in common, one was their distaste for their Army experience. They both felt bitter and resentful about their treatment by commanding officers. The final straw occurred during one of the last operations in Iraq in the early 1990s.

On one assignment their Detachment Commander mistakenly led them into a hostile situations where they were ensnared by enemy fire and almost lost several members of the unit. The commander, eager to transfer responsibility to someone else, suggested to higher ranks that Billy caused them to get trapped because he provided the wrong coordinates. He implied that Billy neglected his duties as communications engineer and requested a replacement.

Knowing the commander had lied, Donnie stood up with Billy against the corrupt officer and they both were removed from the unit for insubordination. They knew after that incident that their days in the military were numbered.

How they dealt with their feelings afterwards illustrated the difference between them. Donnie decided to walk away, forget about as much as he could, and leave it all behind. Billy decided to seek revenge and wreak havoc in his own way. He began secretly accessing military, government, and commercial computer systems, uncovering corruptions, and leaking his findings to the press.

It was never about fame or fortune for Billy; it was all about bringing the dirt to light. He was a wiz with computers and decided this was a good way to use his talents.

Billy had already exposed a high-ranking Army captain for his role in the cover-up of a sexual harassment case and a Congressman who failed to report sales of his book to the IRS. His current project consisted of gathering information on a Navy officer known to frequent illicit gay escort services. He was trying to access the officer's credit card records, hoping he was careless enough to charge the transactions. He did all of this while he worked for Hasmith, Inc., a subcontractor to the Department of Defense. He was bold, but very careful.

Donnie called Billy about the program Montgomery had given him. He could tell it excited Billy by the anxiety in his voice. He agreed to take a look at it.

Donnie walked toward the Pennsylvania Avenue traffic circle trying to look as inconspicuous as possible. As he turned to head back to the subway station, he was startled by Billy's pale face standing right in front of him. His lean body made the brown three-button suit look too big. The tan silk designer tie fit neatly into a Windsor knot around his thin neck.

"What's up Don?" said Billy as he smiled, glowing in the satisfaction that he had caught Donnie with his guard down.

"Billy, how the fuck are you? You dress up pretty nice, boy." They shook hands and Donnie slipped the thumb drive into Billy's palm. Billy dropped it in his brief case without anyone noticing.

Donnie felt his hand pulsing from Billy's crushing grip. His Tae Kwon Do training made him deceivingly strong.

"Still trying to play college student I see." Billy looked around the campus. "I know its just so you can keep your eyes on these young ladies." His eyes followed the behind of one of the young female students as she passed by.

"Still trying to be a playboy, huh. You're getting too old for that don't you think," said Donnie.

"Never too old man, these young girls know how to take care of us, if you know what I mean." Billy winked and nudged Donnie's shoulder.

"So are you gonna be able to help me out with this program? I'd really like to help out this friend of mine."

"Some secret shit, huh," he said. "I'll take a look. You know it's my pleasure to bring the government assholes to their knees."

"Good, get back to me tomorrow"

"No problem. By the way, you can make a lot more money if you join me over at the firm. They have an opening. You have to be broke as hell trying to become a professor."

"Not my speed man. I'm happy right where I am. Thanks anyway."

"Just let me know if you change your mind. You know I owe you so it wouldn't be a problem."

"You don't owe me Billy, and I'm cool."

"Alright Don, I've gotta go. I'll be in touch soon."

The two men shook hands, and quickly went in different directions, Billy headed back to the metro and Donnie to the office.

23

Before heading over to pick up Eliza from the day care, Montgomery Quinn figured he had enough time to check in on Jovan. His condition hadn't changed, not that Montgomery expected anything different. He walked from the hospital to his office at George Washington University to check phone messages and email.

There were two voice mail messages, one from a student offering an excuse for missing the last homework assignment. She requested an extension because she had some allergy problems. The student left a return number, but his syllabus states that no late homework is acceptable, so Montgomery deleted the message. He would deal with the student when he saw her in class.

The second call reminded him about a committee meeting for the University honors program next Monday. The location changed, so he wrote the room number on a note pad and stuck it on his desk.

Montgomery removed his glasses and logged into his email system. He deleted several recognizable spam messages immediately. He scanned the other messages to see if anything required his immediate attention.

The first three messages were jokes sent from old friends. He wasn't in the mood, so he would get to those another time. The last message caught his attention. Intrigued, he double-clicked on it. Leaning toward the screen, he read the message, slowly.

Subject: Montgomery, you are in trouble!
From: Nashiha Msiri
To: Montgomery Quinn
I want to help you. To learn more about the computer program you've obtained, your must first learn about the people you got it from. Contact Dr. Erin Kelley in the History Department at American University. Ask about Njama. THIS IS EXTREMELY IMPORTANT.

Montgomery thought for a minute about whether he should take this seriously. *Who or what is nashiha msiri?* he thought. *And why would this person want to help me?*

He went to American University's home page to see if a Dr. Erin Kelley really existed. Once on the history department web page, he found her name among the list of faculty. She had a home page.

He sifted through the list of her publications and saw that she specialized in history of conspiracies and secret societies. Her biography stated she had recently made an appearance on the television show Prime Investigations discussing the Illuminati and the Skull and Bones society at Yale University, rumored to have membership in pretty high places, including former Presidents, Senators, executives, lawyers, and other famous and powerful men and women.

Montgomery was skeptical about what this had to do with Nia and the thumb drive Jovan gave him. But he was curious. He reached for the phone and dial the number on the web page to Dr. Kelly's office. She picked up on the first ring. "Dr. Kelly," she answered, sounding rushed.

"Hello Dr. Kelly? This is Montgomery Quinn over at GW in the School of Engineering. Have I caught you at a bad time?"

"Well, I'm preparing some notes for my class tonight." Her voice sounded older and strained. "Quinn did you say?"

"Yes, Dr. Quinn. I won't hold you, but I was told by a source to talk to you about something called Njama. Do you know what that means."

"Njama, ah yes. Who did you say referred you to me?"

"I couldn't tell you. It was an anonymous message."

"Of course." There was a brief silence.

"Well, Dr. Quinn. Should I dare ask you why you want this information?" Before he could answer, she interrupted. "Never mind. I'll gladly give you a brief history of Njama, but not now. I'm not a big fan of discussing such things over the telephone. I will gladly meet you after my class tonight if you're available. It usually gets out at seven."

Montgomery had to pick up Eliza and see if Gabrielle would get home in time to meet at seven. He looked at the email on his screen again. The last line, *This is extremely important,* jumped out at him. He would make the sacrifice.

"Where do we meet?"

"Just meet me here in my office."

"Thank you. See you at seven."

Montgomery hung up the phone. He shut down his computer and grabbed his glasses as he made his way out of the office. He was late picking up Eliza and had to hurry to avoid any late fees from the day care.

24

Montgomery expected Gabrielle home from work at any minute. She had a late court appearance scheduled and some small things to rap up, but she was on her way. Montgomery informed her of the last minute meeting at American University, though he didn't explain to her its purpose.

He fixed Eliza a snack, watched Rugrats, and played nerf basketball with her on the toy hoop. Montgomery loved the time they spent alone. Realizing how little sleep he had gotten the night before, he managed to sneak in a quick power nap while Eliza watched her favorite movie *Finding Nemo*.

After getting dressed in his black slacks with crème crew neck shirt, he placed his favorite mahogany four-button blazer on the sofa by the door. He was prepared to meet Dr. Kelly and anxious to see what she had to say.

Montgomery grew a little restless with Gabrielle's tardiness because he had hoped to stop by and see Jovan again before his meeting. It was a little after six and by the time he finished with Dr. Kelly, he may miss visiting hours. If so, he would have to go tomorrow.

The kitchen door swung open and Gabrielle entered, heading straight for Eliza.

"Hey little girl, Mommy's home. Come give me a hug."

"Mommy!"

Eliza waddled to Gabrielle and jumped into her arms. Montgomery smiled at the two of them kissing and loving one another, then he walked over to the door and put on his blazer.

"Hey babe, I'm running late." He said, walking over and kissing her and Eliza.

"You look pretty nice. Sure you don't have a date?" Gabrielle smiled and softly brushed Montgomery's cheek, then stroked his manicured mustache.

"Yeah right." He had a flash back to his lunch with Carmen. He hoped his face didn't disclose any hint of deceitfulness.

"By the way, did you take care of those bills we talked about?"

"Uh, how was your day honey? Did you work hard?" Monty replied sarcastically.

"Very funny." Gabrielle smiled and hugged Montgomery. "Enjoy your meeting."

"And yes I did pay them."

"Okay. You did good."

"Alright, I love you both."

Montgomery left the house and headed for the BMW. After settling in and turning the ignition, he noticed something on the windshield. It was an envelope. Montgomery got out and took it from under the windshield wiper and flipped it over. The front of the envelope contained the same image from Nia's computer program.

He sat for a moment and stared at the symbol, still not sure exactly what to make of it. He then wondered why Nia would put it on his windshield. *Did she know for sure that Jovan had given me the program?*

Although, Montgomery still wouldn't have admitted he had it. With all of the other events in the day, Montgomery had almost forgotten that he had given the drive to Donnie.

Montgomery set his glasses on the passenger seat. He turned over the envelope and ripped it open to reveal a letter, typed in an elaborate script.

You have something that belongs to us. Either return it before 7:00pm tonight or your life will change forever.

Montgomery looked at his watch, it said six twenty five.

Pulling out the cell phone from his jacket pocket, he went through the phone list to find Jovan and Nia's home number.

He hesitated to hit the send button. "What would I say?" he said aloud to himself. Montgomery dropped the phone on the passenger seat and looked out onto the busy Georgia Avenue strip as rush hour began to wind down.

He felt uneasy, a little scared. Why? He didn't know. Anger even entered the mix of emotions swirling all over his body.

Shaking his head, Montgomery gathered himself and decided to just think about the next step during the evening. In the meantime, there was a meeting that deserved his undivided attention. He turned on the radio to the smooth jazz station in the middle of a Bob James tune.

Nia would get a call later tonight when he got home. Either an apology was in order or a good cursing out. But, certainly, they could work out this problem without resorting to threats. That was the second time in the last twelve hours, and Montgomery was determined to put an end to this nonsense.

He entered the mixing bowl of traffic heading towards upper northwest D.C.

25

After settling in from a long workday, Gabrielle felt exhausted. She and Eliza ate dinner together and she went through the mail, hoping not to find more delinquent payment notices.

They made their way upstairs and she bathed Eliza. Afterwards they settled into the second floor master bedroom for the night.

Winnie the Pooh characters were scattered around the bed while they sat and looked at the pictures in some children's books. The light from the television sitting on the dresser flickered in the dim room as the network evening news wrapped up. Gabrielle took a moment to close her eyes and reflected on the hot bath waiting for her once Eliza fell asleep.

The ceiling light hadn't worked since they moved in the house and a small halogen lamp sitting in the corner provided the only source of light. Montgomery had asked Jovan to come add a light and ceiling fan, but he never got around to it. Now they may have to pay someone to check it out.

Gabrielle wondered if they would ever move up to something better, more suitable for the lifestyle they both deserved. She agreed to buy the fixer-upper but didn't realize the time or cost it would take to make it comfortable. Now she was saddled with regrets, a house she hated, and a husband that didn't know how to manage money.

Hoping to feel a little better, Gabrielle decided to go to the Internet and fantasize while looking at some houses for sale. She often did this, hoping that their move to her dream home was closer than it seemed.

Picking up Eliza, she walked down the hall to the small makeshift office. Turning on the computer and logging on the Internet, she checked her email and bounced around to a couple of real estate sites. Eliza crawled around at her feet, chasing her toy Piglet and Roo.

After forty minutes, Gabrielle stumbled onto pictures of a beautiful house in a quiet suburb of Prince George County that mesmerized her. It had everything she wanted, hard wood floors, gourmet kitchen, finished basement with recreation room and a wet bar, a nice backyard, and most importantly a large master bedroom suite with whirlpool bathtub. And the price looked like something they could afford.

She sat and looked at the pictures of the interior and waded through the specifications. The clock on the computer read almost eight, time to get Eliza settled in for bed. But she wanted to save this page to show Montgomery later.

As she made her way to the bookmark menu, the computer played the musical chime indicating an instant message had been sent and a window popped up on her screen. It was from someone called *Mesenja*. Gabrielle didn't recognize the address, but the message intrigued her.

From: Mesenja

Click the link below to see your husband, Montgomery, at his best.

Montgomery Quinn's Best Moments

Who would be sending me a message about my husband? she thought. She dismissed it as some kind of joke or maybe someone selling something. She had no time for games. Gabrielle closed the instant message window, bookmarked the real estate site, and reached down to pick up Eliza.

She turned off the lights and as she got to the door of the hall, she heard the chime again. Gabrielle glanced over her shoulder to see the instant message window in the middle of her computer screen again. Walking back toward the light of the computer, she glared at the message, which read: Gabrielle, your husband is cheating on you. Take a look.

What? How would they know my name?

She set Eliza down on the floor, and slowly eased into the chair. Her stomach churned. The light from the computer screen smothered her face. The frown deepened as she tried to determine whether to ignore the message. Was it a farce? A bad joke? If it was, it was far from funny.

Gabrielle reached for the mouse and placed the arrow on the screen over the link. She slowly leaned in and read the message again, and again. Finally, she clicked on the link below the message.

Several white boxes appeared on the web pages, apparently for pictures of some sort. Gabrielle leaned in closer to the screen as the first image began to form from the top down. Their outdated computer took several seconds to download images. The delay made her nervous and sick. The top third revealed nothing but the top of a man's head standing or leaning near a car. She couldn't tell where he was or when it was taken. She squinted to get a better look. It wasn't a clear picture, but she could make out most of the image.

By the time half the picture formed on the screen, Gabrielle knew exactly what she was looking at. The man was Montgomery and he was locked in an intimate kiss with another woman, standing by his car.

Is this a joke?

Gabrielle stood up in disbelief and looked again. *Are these fake pictures?*

The computer indicated that the download was finally complete. She scrolled down to find more pictures. One of Montgomery smiling and laughing with the woman at a restaurant table. Another of them holding hands. It was definitely him. There was no doubt. She went to the instant message window and typed: Who are you? Where did you get this?

She clicked reply, but no response. The person had logged off.

"You son of a bitch," she whispered to herself. Tears slowly cascaded down her cheeks as she stared fixated at the image of her husband's lips locked with this other woman. "Why would you do this?"

She wanted to scream, run, crawl in hole and die. The man she loved, trusted, and shared a child with had been unfaithful. And for what reason? Was it just sex? Did he love this woman?

Gabrielle felt her heart pounding faster and her hands started to tremble. The tears fell uncontrollably onto the keyboard as she just sat, staring at the light of the computer screen. Eliza pulled on her leg trying to stand up, which brought her back to reality. The baby had been crying and she hadn't heard anything. She picked up Eliza and hugged her firmly.

Now what do I do? she thought.

She deserved an explanation. Gabrielle ran to the telephone to dial his cell phone number. After the first five digits, she hung up and slammed the phone down. She needed to talk to somebody, but whom. The thought of discussing this with anyone was too embarrassing.

Anger had taken over her and she felt a sense of rage. She had to calm herself down. Taking deep breaths, she took Eliza to her room, set her on the bed and wrapped her arms around her baby. Eliza started whining and Gabrielle's head began pounding.

One thing was certain. As soon as Montgomery came home tonight, he had some questions to answer and hell to pay.

26

The halls of Battelle-Tomkins Hall were empty. Except for an occasional outburst from a classroom of students working on some group project, no one else was around. Montgomery Quinn wandered the halls of the first floor looking for the History Department and Dr. Erin Kelly. He found the directory, and headed for room 137.

Through the crack in the door he could hear the pecking of a keyboard. He knocked twice.

"Come in," the tiny voice said.

Montgomery slowly pushed opened the door and peeked his head through. The smell of a blackberry aroma candle filled the small office. It appeared much messier than his. Books filled the shelves that spanned the entire back wall, illustrating signs of a professor that had been around for a while. Papers and manila folders spilled over the side of her desk.

"Give me one moment." Never turning around, Dr. Kelly continued typing with her back turned, as if working on something so intense that she couldn't break her concentration. A petite woman, she had silver dread locks down to her waist and wore a flowing brown, yellow, and orange multicolored dress.

Montgomery stood at the door awaiting some recognition of his presence. It reminded him of being a student on a professor's time. He glanced at some of the books on her shelf. The titles covered every area of conspiracy imaginable: *AIDS and the Government Coverup, The West Nile Virus and the CIA, Was the Columbia Disaster Intentional, Secrecy of the Jehovah's Witness, The Illuminati and the Committee of Three Hundred, The Secrets of the Federal Reserve* and several books on African languages and symbolism.

Finally, she turned slowly. "Dr. Quinn?"

Startled, Montgomery stepped into the room, "Yes, Dr. Kelly, nice to meet you."

She extended her small, frail hand. The strength of her grip surprised Montgomery. Dr. Kelly appeared in her seventies, with a small body frame, but good physical condition. She wore eyeglasses that appeared too big for her face. Her eyes sagged slightly at the corners, as she smiled broadly and pointed to a chair for Montgomery to sit.

"So, you want to know about Njama?" she started off with an almost wicked smile.

"So I've been told." He held out a copy of the email he received and she read it.

Dr. Kelly laughed, "You look a little concerned. I'm not going to hurt you. Relax."

"Things are a little eerie for me right now, so it's tough to relax just yet. I got this anonymous email saying I needed to talk to you, but I have no idea why, what Njama is or what I'm doing here to tell you the truth."

"Sounds about right. Most of these people love to operate in mysterious ways. You must have tweaked them in some way for them to contact you."

"Apparently so." *These people*, Montgomery thought. *Who are these people?*

"At least you have a friend." Erin smiled.

"How so?"

"Your email. Nashiha msiri means sincere friend and confidant in Swahili."

"Good, I need one these days."

Dr. Kelly sat the note on her desk and settled back into her chair. She stared directly into Montgomery's eyes and asked. "So, what do you know about Njama at this point?"

"Nothing to tell you the truth. Today is the first time I've heard the word."

"Is that so? I'll be glad to share with you what I know. Which isn't much myself to be honest." Dr. Kelley stood slowly and reached for several books from the middle of the shelf abutting the corner. With her back turned to Montgomery, she began talking.

"Njama has been one of the hardest secret societies to get information about. They are good at keeping their business to themselves. I've gathered some insight over the years from insiders, but none who have gotten very high up in the organization."

"Anything you can tell me would be great. I guess I'll have to figure out what to do with the information later Dr. Kelly,"

"Lets first start by suspending the formalities. Call me Erin, if that's alright with you Montgomery." She turned and set some books on her desk on top of the other papers. Then she leaned back in her high back black leather chair. The chair seemed to engulf her small body. "That's fine, call me Monty."

"Okay, let me start from the beginning.

Montgomery settled back in his chair, and the envelope from his windshield peeked from under his jacket. He glanced down, remembering the books on symbols he saw on Erin's shelves. He reached in his jacket pocket and pulled out the envelope.

"Before you start, do you know what this is?"

Dr. Kelly took the envelope in one hand, and grabbed a bottle of spring water with the other. She looked at the symbol for a moment and raised her left eyebrow slightly. Setting down the bottle, she began to open the letter.

"Do you mind?"

"No, go right ahead."

She slowly opened the letter and read it.

Montgomery studied her face and could tell something was on her mind. He kept silent as she read the two-sentence letter. After a few seconds, she exhaled, folded it back up and placed it back in the envelope. Dr. Kelly looked at Montgomery and pointed to the front of envelope.

"Any idea who sent you this?" she asked.

"I have a hunch," replied Montgomery.

"Could you close the door please," she said. Montgomery got up, closed the door and returned to his seat. He sat on the edge of his chair waiting for her to share her thoughts.

Erin opened a tattered book on African languages and handed it to Montgomery. He began reading. He saw the exact same symbol on the page in front of him.

"That is the Adinkra symbol for a chain or link, known as Nkonsonkonson. It represents unity or that the individual is an important part of the group or society."

Montgomery sat back in the chair, his eyebrows raised and mouth open.

"So what does that mean?" he asked as he continued to read.

She ignored his question and responded, "I can't address the contents of your letter, but let me tell you a story Monty. Hopefully it will shed some light on your predicament. How much time to you have?"

"As long as it takes, Erin."

27

Billy Yow and his younger brother Gene shared a small two-bedroom apartment in Fairfax, Virginia. The furnishings were limited: a sofa, television on a small wooden cabinet, and a kitchen table with two chairs. They shared one bedroom with bunk beds and the other was packed with computer equipment and related supplies.

They spent most of their time in the evenings developing various programs. Both were familiar with several languages, C++ and Java being their favorites.

Although they had a firewall, paranoia prevented them from going online unless they were checking sports scores, weather, or other insignificant data. Gene in particular always accessed networks from home cautiously, aware that anyone could gain remote access to a system and determine what you were doing. They had another more secure location where they stored the most important programs and other activities.

For about an hour, they had been digging into the program that Donnie Centronelli gave Billy. The sophistication and elegance of the program impressed them both. But it wasn't anything they hadn't seen before.

"Looks like it gains root access to the host computer," said Billy.

"Who's the target?" asked Gene.

"Some company that processes banking transactions."

"Figures. People always want to go after the banks."

"That's because most of them won't admit to being attacked. People won't keep their money where someone like you can access it." Billy laughed while Gene rolled his eyes and smiled.

"I need a break," said Gene. "You hungry?"

"Yeah, go get the number for Papa Johns. I'm gonna keep looking at this a little more. It's pretty impressive the way it's written."

"Not really." Gene left the room headed for the kitchen.

Billy determined that the program accessed files on the ECPI network, which identified what external networks were trusted to connect to critical ports. Through telnet, it then set itself up as one of those trusted external hosts, allowing a person to roam around ECPI's computer system unnoticed. This strategy let someone bypass firewalls and filters set up to secure the network.

When Gene returned with the phone to discuss the pizza toppings before ordering, Billy explained what he found.

"Interesting," said Gene. "But that only works if you have someone inside who can provide a back door to gain root access."

"They must have someone then."

"Let me look at that. You call the order in."

Gene took over the chair and dived into the program while Billy ordered the pizza. Gene had more experience with this, having been involved with several underground hacking groups over the years.

Gene looked up to his brother and always wanted to follow in his footsteps. After he graduated sum cum laude from Columbia University with a degree in computer science, he tried to join the Army Special Forces. He and Billy were built similarly, tall and thin, but fit. Though Gene was a bit more aloof. Unfortunately, Gene's bad eyesight prevented him from passing the physical.

He bounced around several jobs, but never found satisfaction with the safeness of corporate networks management. He spent most of his time patching holes in the system to keep hackers out. He felt his intelligence and skills were wasting away and wanted more excitement.

Some old friends from Columbia began developing scanning programs to check corporate networks for security vulnerabilities. His experience provided him with an insight into where to look and what to look for in the systems.

It didn't take long for them to develop some very sophisticated programs that could penetrate almost any system. The word got around in the underground world of hackers. Ultimately, his success brought a number of secret clients and a more exhilarating way to make a living. Their first client, a large pharmaceutical company, hired them to steal some research and development data from one of their competitor's systems. The team accessed the network and got the data within three days.

The large pay off and the thrill gave him a major rush. He never looked back. Thus began his venture into high tech industrial espionage.

Billy joined the team once he left the Army, changing their focus slightly to accessing defense contractors looking at sensitive classified military data. He had his own agenda. And he was learning from his brother as he went along.

"This is pretty good work," said Gene, "I could have done it better though."

"I'm sure, little brother," Billy smiled, impressed by his brother's arrogance.

"At least they've taken some steps to hide themselves. See." Gene pointed to the screen. "This part bounces through some 800 numbers before connecting to an Internet service provider using a random account. That way if they're caught, it hides their true IP address. Pretty old technique."

"I even know how to do that," said Billy.

"Sure you do." Gene said with a smirk. "I'm gonna take a ride. While I'm out I'll get us some beer. Don't eat all the pizza before I get back."

"Go ahead, I'm gonna take a break and check the email."

Gene headed out the apartment for the liquor store, while Billy went online to check on the score of the Baltimore Orioles and the New York Yankees.

He logged on to a website to get a real time feed of the game and sat back to listen while he continued to work. Billy was less careful about accessing the Internet in an unsecured manner. He saw the merit in cautiously protecting their activities, but he always thought Gene was a bit too paranoid.

Once he logged onto the Internet, Billy unknowingly initiated Nia's tracer program. While he listened to the bottom of the eighth inning, with the Orioles leading seven to five, a hidden message navigated his DSL line and into cyberspace.

28

Nia returned home from the hospital and entered the kitchen from the garage. Jovan's condition had not changed. He had a lot of swelling, burns, broken jaw, ribs and arm, and lost a couple of teeth, but the doctors said there was nothing life threatening. She felt a sense of relief that he would be fine. He just hadn't come out of his coma, which concerned her deeply.

The day was long and filled with more stress than she had ever felt. She planned to go straight to bed and rest. She dropped her purse on the kitchen counter, kicked off her shoes, and threw her jacket on the barstool.

Reaching in the breadbasket on the counter she grabbed a bag of pretzels and headed to the family room. The house was dark and the only glow came from the night light in the office.

Nia walked in and picked up the phone to check the voicemail for messages. There were none and she felt relieved. She turned on the laptop to do a quick scan of the emails to make sure there was nothing that needed her immediate attention. While she stuffed her mouth, she noticed a message on the screen.

Alert!
File Accessed
Domain name: Comin_at_ya@anony.net
Time: 7:22pm

"Now what the hell is Monty up to?" she said through the mass of pretzels.

She recognized the domain name as one of the anonymous addresses people sign up for when they want to send emails without being identified. She did a search of the email address to find a name attached to it, not expecting anything to come back.

Email: Comin_at_ya@anony.net
First name: Unknown
Last Name: Unknown
Location: Unknown

Nia knew it would take some digging into to identify this person. Although this was not uncommon, she wondered why Montgomery was all of a sudden using an anonymous email address. Or was someone else helping him? Nia opened her email encryption software to send an untraceable message and began to type. She wanted to send this latest news to the mzingo zima, and then she was going to bed.

Subject: new news
From: Nia Givens
To: Paulette Aventis, Sanja Coston, Charity Newhouse

I got an alert that Quinn tried to open the program again. He is now using a different email address:

Comin_at_ya@anony.net

The account is set up by one of those anonymous servers to protect emails so I cannot identify who it is right now. I'm not sure what he is trying to do, but I'm confident he won't get anywhere. I will follow up tomorrow. All other efforts to pressure Quinn are in action. Please advise if you want any other action taken.

Timiza Ahadi

Nia sent the email, and closed the laptop. She had no energy to try and track down an email address tonight. She grabbed her bag of pretzels, left the office, turned on the burglar alarm and headed up the stairs. Her eyes felt heavy and she wanted nothing more than to lay her head on her feathered pillow and sleep. Everything else could wait until tomorrow.

29

D r. Erin Kelly had pulled down several more books from her shelf to help prepare her impromptu presentation for Montgomery Quinn.

"As you may have guessed from my hair style and the gray, I'm a product of the 1960s."

"I like natural hair and it's not necessarily a sixties thing as much as it is a realignment with your self and history."

Erin smiled, "I'm impressed Monty. That's pretty profound coming from an engineering professor."

Montgomery laughed, "Well, we get to read more than just numbers and formulas on occasion."

"That was a pretty volatile time for us black folks, as I'm sure you are aware. You ever heard of COINTELPRO, Monty?

Montgomery nodded enthusiastically, "Yeah, wasn't that some operation to bring down the Black Panther Party. I think I read about it in history."

"Partially, but it was more than that. The FBI had been involved with harassing civil rights leaders throughout the sixties. In 1970, Congress approved what was called the Huston Plan. It proposed a collaborative effort by the FBI, CIA, DIA, and NSA that advocated wiretapping, break-ins, stealing mail, whatever it took to expose, disrupt, or neutralize organizations considered threats to the United States. It put a stamp of approval on what the FBI was already doing."

"As if they needed any reassurance," Montgomery shook his head and kept listening. History was kind of a hobby

123

for him and he often found himself stopping on the History Channel, when flipping the channels. On occasion, when they weren't showing a World War II documentary, which is what he found most of the time, Montgomery would be absorbed by the complex lives of others in the past.

"COINTELPRO was an FBI operation that started with an attack on communists, and Hoover used the Huston Plan to focus his attention on organizations who were fighting for civil rights. They went after all of them, King and the Southern Christian Leadership Conference, Stokely Carmichael and the Student Nonviolence Coordinating Committee, Cesar Chavez and the United Farm Workers, the Nation of Islam. So it wasn't just the Panthers, it was all of them."

"I didn't know about the farm workers, but I'd heard of Chavez before. So I guess this was the operation that had the secret tapes of King in the hotel rooms and all that."

"That's right, among other things," she said. "So during that time, there were a few Black folks in the intelligence related government agencies, and some outsiders, who were recruited and pulled into this. They used these people to infiltrate the organizations, plant devices, do surveillance, you name it. They were convinced that they were doing a service to our country."

"A service to the country? How could they come to that conclusion considering the hell black people were catching everywhere?"

"Remember Monty, when you're in the middle of a tornado, it's easy to lose your bearings. You're looking back with a much clearer perspective."

"I guess you're right."

Erin opened another book and handed it to Montgomery. The book dealt with the blacks used to infiltrate organizations and the harm they caused. Montgomery tried to read and listen to her at the same time.

"Black women were heavily recruited, because they could get inside of these organizations without appearing threatening or suspicious. I've been told there were some intelligent women involved with designing and planting some of the electronic bugs. The whole operation was to gather information that would show involvement in criminal activities, drugs, and so on. The goal was to gather anything that would get them in legal trouble or could be used to turn them against each other."

Monty became concerned. He wasn't sure why Erin was taking him on a history lesson on the ruthlessness of the FBI and civil rights. How did all this relate to Njama? Or for that matter, how did it relate to him? He decided to indulge her for a few more minutes then try to get back to the purpose of the meeting. After all, the conversation interested him.

"As I remember, the FBI's mission worked pretty good. Wasn't that why Huey Newton and Eldridge Cleaver started feuding, which began the destruction of the Black Panther Party?" Montgomery tried to show some of the knowledge he retained from his own reading. During his undergrad years, he and some friends got pretty heavy into reading about sixties revolutionaries, so he had a good knowledge of the events. But he still hoped they would get to a point of discussing Njama soon.

"Very good, Monty," Erin smiled and again nodded with approval. "At the time most blacks lived either in the deep south, or cities where there was extreme segregation, like Boston. Some were pretty naive about civil rights and the movement. The blacks that worked for the government thought they were doing the right thing by bringing down some of these so-called radicals. Most of them were sheltered, educated people and felt some of the organizations were just causing too many problems for black folks and needed to be shut down. Now we know that they were brainwashed into believing that they were doing the right thing."

Erin took a break and sipped from her bottle of water. She sifted through some more books looking for references to the events of the 1960s. "I was one of the few blacks who worked in one of those agencies at that time, so I know the culture they operated in. I did some work for the FBI from 1963 to

1966. We kinda got caught up in the politics trying to balance working and civil rights issues."

Montgomery looked at her surprised. Then looked down at the books, wondering where this was all going.

"What's the matter Monty, I don't look like an FBI type?" She said with a chuckle.

"I can't say that you do Erin. I have a hard time trying to imagine you in a business dress, heels and permed hair."

"Time has a way of changing all of us, my brother. We can only hope its for the better." She laughed heartily and Montgomery felt obliged to join in.

"Anyway, from what I understand the last straw for a lot of black people in those agencies was the Fred Hampton murder. You remember that don't you?"

"Vaguely, it was a little before my time. But wasn't he the young brother who the police shot in Chicago? I think he was a Black Panther too, right."

"Yeah, that's it. December 1969. Shot down in his home, no weapons, defenseless." Erin shook her head and looked down as if the memory still pained her.

After a few seconds she continued, "Well, when the rumors started swirling that the FBI and the Chicago police had set him up, I was devastated. There was a teletype that came into the FBI office detailing the whole event. One of the blacks got ahold of it and spread it around. He was such a young fella, probably twenty or so, and he was doing some good things with the breakfast programs for the kids in Chicago. A friend of mine met Hampton once and she told me how great of a young man he was."

Montgomery was losing focus and becoming impatient. He finally felt the need to interrupt and get back on track. "Sorry Erin, but I'm not seeing the connection to all of this and Njama."

"We're almost there Monty. Hang with me a few minutes more," she said. "So, the story goes that there was a group of black women who found out that some of the devices they had designed had been used to pin down Hampton's movements in that house. And they were pissed."

"So what did they do?"

"My understanding is that they requested to be removed from the operation. But they were bitter about how they were manipulated into participating in all of these activities. Things were beginning to come to the light by the end of 1969. Assassinations, negative images, lies, deceit, they were convinced it was all in the name of justice. But it wasn't. We know that now."

She sat up in her chair and glared at Montgomery.

"These women wanted to do something to make up for their involvement in all those things. They realized that the people most hurt by all of their activities were the lower class blacks who lost so much when these organizations were torn apart. And the perpetrators appeared to get away unscathed. So they started an organization of black women scientists and technologists."

She paused for effect and looked at Montgomery curiously. "It's called Njama, meaning 'secret society' in Swahili. They organized a small group of highly intelligent women and used their intelligence training and technology skills for their own missions."

"What kind of missions?" Montgomery asked, his interest rejuvenated.

"The same missions those white men used on us, except they reversed it. Mostly using surveillance to gather information on the ones committing cruel acts on the helpless people of society, then using that data to convince these men that they need to make amends."

"Forgive me Erin, but this sounds a little out there," Montgomery said with skepticism in his voice.

"Again, most of this is unsubstantiated. I hear that the first case was a wealthy District Court Judge in North Carolina in 1971. They planted electronic bugs and revealed that he had been a member of the KKK in the 50s. He also had two children by a black woman who was a former maid in his house. None of this he wanted to get out to the public. So Njama secretly presented him with what they knew and convinced him to contribute large donations to several non-profit organizations that helped down and out blacks in North Carolina. He didn't like it, but he did it."

"Since 1971? And no one ever reported it or found out about it?"

"Remember most of these people don't want their dirty laundry aired out for public scrutiny, so they typically won't report anything. They just give the money to make it all go away."

"You would think somebody would have gone after them by now though."

"They tried. But the membership grew to include women in most every agency in the government and some corporations. They held a lot of influence and they are all sworn to secrecy. More importantly, they believe that what they do is valuable and sacred. They're always one step ahead of any investigation or effort to find out who they are. And they know the tricks of the trade about how the government tries to infiltrate and mess with you. Over time they've become good at ruining people's lives if they don't cooperate, mostly through the use of technology."

"I guess that would be pretty easy to do now since our whole identity and world is so digitized."

"That's exactly right, Monty."

"So Erin, if I may ask, how did you find out about them," he said, looking directly at her with a frown of suspicion.

Erin smiled mischievously.

"No Monty, I am not a member of Njama. Over the years I managed to contact a few women who have been involved. But like I said, none of them ever reached the highest levels. They are mistrusting and hard to penetrate. My research tells me there are three levels or *usawas*."

She opened a Swahili-to-English translation dictionary. "The new recruits are called *kizushi*, which means newcomers in Swahili. They are recruited to carry out small surveillance and information gathering tasks. But they are never told what the ultimate mission is. They have to prove themselves worthy."

"So if they don't prove themselves worthy then what, are they tortured to keep quiet," said Montgomery, sounding a bit smug.

"Not exactly. In fact, when they are initiated, I was told that they are blind folded and escorted around various locations for hours. On the last stop, they are stripped naked, and searched, probably to check for any wires, then couriered around for another several hours. They finally end up at an initiation ceremony where all of the other high level members are dressed in masks and flowing black capes. No one knows who they are."

"Sounds like a Hollywood script."

"Yeah, but its effective," said Erin. "That's why you can't figure them out. Once they are finished, the women are given a drug which knocks them out. Then they wake up the next day in some out-of-the-way motel naked in bed, with their clothes folded neatly next to them. They may not get their first assignment for up to a year after that."

Erin turned the pages of the dictionary. "The second level, known as the *kati*, gets more responsibility. But they still are not privy to the secrets. At the top is the mzingo zima or the circle of queens. No one knows their identity, not even the lower two levels. That's how they maintain their secrecy."

"And this is still going on?

"Yes. Which brings me back to where we started tonight."

"Which is?

"You know that symbol on the envelope you showed me?"

Erin picked up the book on African symbols and languages again and pointed to the symbol.

"Yeah."

"That is the symbol used by Njama."

30

Sanja Coston sat in the master bedroom of her small row house in Adams Morgan, one of the eclectic multicultural neighborhoods in D.C. She drank peach flavored herbal tea and tapped on the laptop sitting on the bed next to her.

The sparse room contained little furniture. After the divorce, she kept only a small television sitting on top of a wood grained dresser, one side table with a crystal lamp and royal blue shade, the queen-sized bed, and an ab-roller. She wanted no reminders of the dreadful life she had with her husband, so she let him have everything. That was four years ago and replacing furniture never became a priority.

The move to Adams Morgan was an attempt to get back into the single life. However, times had changed while she was married. The people in their twenties hung out there and only wanted to get drunk. The dancing had shifted from high-energy fun to lewd grinding. In her forties, Sanja quickly realized that she had outgrown the new singles atmosphere once she stepped in the first club.

So she searched for other outlets of entertainment. The Internet chat rooms became her new source of meeting people. Sometimes it was difficult to filter who people really were through the crap they spewed. But it was better than sitting in a crowded nightclub, yelling at the top of your lungs to a man while the music left you near deaf by the end of the night.

Sanja talked with some strangers in a chat room titled

Divorced But Not Dead about the downsides of being a black, single professional woman. The conversations were often nonsensical, rude, obnoxious, and silly, but Sanja found it entertaining none the less. It made for more entertainment than the latest reality television show.

Over the years she had established relationships with some of the regulars and even went on dates with a few of the men she met online. None of them ever worked out well. While Sanja looked at the date as an opportunity to meet a new friend to go to movies and dinner, the men often regarded it as sure-shot sex. It wasn't long before she realized that meeting men this way was never going to lead to anything significant. But she still couldn't pull herself from the rooms. She felt like an addict.

It was getting late, and she had to get up early to host a meeting with the vice presidents from several of the Federal Reserve Banks to talk about issues related to upgrading their check processing servers. Often she was the only female and only African American in these meetings and even though they never mistreated her, she despised the thought of having to educate them on these issues.

As an officer at the Federal Reserve Board, the Reserve Banks never had to do anything she suggested, and most times they didn't. They simply tolerated her so they wouldn't upset the Governors. Often times they ignored her advice altogether and did what they wanted at their regional locations.

Sanja had come to hate her job immensely and most of the people there. The Federal Reserve officers knew banking and economics but they had little knowledge about technology and she hated having to address their ignorance. She needed all the sleep she could get to maintain her energy levels as she sat and held her tongue in frustration in these meetings.

Sanja said her goodbyes and signed off from the chat room. It was a little after nine o'clock. Checking her secured emails one last time before she logged off, she noticed the message from Nia.

"This shit has got to be put to an end," she said to herself, shaking her head in disgust as she read.

Now, Sanja felt the need to take matters into her own hands. Paulette was not being aggressive enough in her opinion and time was ticking away. If they wanted to attack ECPI's systems by Friday, they needed to get that program back from Quinn tonight.

Not that they couldn't do the job anyway.

Nia had already made the changes they needed. But just the thought of this program floating around out there made everyone uneasy. Quinn was a loose end that needed severing. And Sanja knew exactly how to do it.

She opened a window on the computer screen to type an encrypted email message. She had already talked to Ted Jacobson, one of her former colleagues from her days working at the Pentagon. He was known for his involvement in dubious activities.

Subject: Our agreement
From: Sanja Coston
To: Ted Jacobson

Ted, I told you earlier I might have a job for you. Well, I definitely do now. This is extremely sensitive. I need you to get the drive we talked about earlier today and return it ASAP. The person who has it used this email address less than an hour ago: Comin_at_ya@anony.net

I'm not sure if it is Montgomery Quinn or someone else. It is an anonymous email address so, please use whatever sources you have to identify this person as soon as possible. I mean ANYTHING. Find this person and get the drive back, TONIGHT! You will be rewarded according to what we discussed, when you deliver.

And I trust you will keep this between us.

SC

Sanja dated Jacobson briefly a few years back and knew he had been trained in military tactics for surveillance, torture, and other warfare things she was not privy to know. Most of the details, she never wanted to know about.

Ted also used his skills to make money doing undercover

jobs, including everything from harassing the husbands of jealous wives to providing techniques to drug dealers on how to torture rivals. As long as she'd known him, he kept his dirty secrets to himself, except for the occasional name drop of his clients when he wanted to impress her.

Ted would sell his soul for the right price. And she knew he would do anything to get back in her pants again. Of course he wanted to get paid as well.

31

Montgomery wandered around the American University campus for another hour after he left Dr. Kelly. Then he drove around D.C. for another hour. He had to clear his head from all of the things she told him.

A secret society? Now they were after him.

Deciding what to do next was all he could think about. He even considered contacting Nia and just giving the thumb drive back.

Erin made him promise to keep her abreast of anything he uncovered about Njama. For research purposes she said. But he wanted no trouble and was ready to fold his hand.

Just after midnight he parked the car in front of his house and headed to the front door. Montgomery quietly turned the key, opened and closed the door slowly, turned off the alarm and took off his shoes. Gabrielle was a light sleeper and he didn't want to wake her.

The house was dark, which was unusual because they always kept a lamp on in the family room. As he turned, he noticed a small candle sitting on the coffee table. The light flickered, showing a silhouette of Gabrielle's face looking right at him as she sat on the sofa. She had watched him the entire time without saying a word and he hadn't noticed her initially.

"Hey babe, what are you still doing up this late?" Montgomery asked nervously. He flipped the light switch on the wall and could see the frown on her face and the tear stains on her cheeks.

Gabrielle stood and walked slowly toward him. She said nothing.

"What's wrong?" he asked. He'd never seen this look before.

She gazed right into his face for the entire stroll, never letting her eyes stray. She handed Montgomery several sheets of paper and looked intently at him waiting for his response. He recoiled slightly, his eyes darting from the papers to Gabrielle.

Montgomery's eyes widened slowly and his mouth opened. He snatched off his glasses and glared at the picture of him and Carmen engrossed in a deep kiss. The next picture showed Carmen's hand on his leg under the table. Another of them smiling and flirting.

Oh shit! he thought.

"Gabrielle, I can explain. This is not what it looks like… she…"

Gabrielle stood back and in one fluid motion slapped Montgomery across the cheek with everything she had in her body. The swift move caught him unexpectedly; he never saw it coming. He had never been slapped across the face before and the pain felt extremely intense. Montgomery grabbed his cheek as the sting shot straight to the top of his head. His nose began to bleed and blood oozed from a cut on his face.

"Fuck you and your bitch," said Gabrielle as she turned and walked away.

"Wait Gabrielle, she was just an old friend from school. This is nothing. She means nothing to me. Come on baby, listen to me."

Montgomery grabbed Gabrielle's wrist and she swirled around and punched him in the eye with her right fist, knocking him onto the sofa.

"Shit Gabrielle," he said as he grabbed his eye, moaning in anguish.

"Monty, I have nothing to say to you right now," she said,

rubbing her knuckles to sooth the pain from the punch.

"You betrayed me you asshole! How could you do this to me! We have a baby, dammit!" She broke down and the tears flowed uncontrollably. Covering her face, she ran up the stairs and slammed the master bedroom door.

Montgomery sat up on the couch and looked down at the pictures. *Where the hell did she get these?*

They looked like they were printed from a color printer so they had to be in some digital form. He stared at the picture, flipping through them over and over again. The images burned into his mind.

This was a big one, the mistake of his life. Montgomery knew he had messed up this time and had to make it right. But he had no clue how.

Why did I kiss her? Who took these pictures? Why did they send them to Gabrielle? Who would do this to me?

The questions kept coming but no answers followed. His mind was spinning. Montgomery closed his eyes and tried to breath, slowly taking the air into his nose and exhaling out of his mouth. He had no answers.

He picked up the tissue box from the coffee table and grabbed one to dab his nose and the blood stains on his shirt. He threw the pictures down on the floor and cradled his face in both hands and tried to think.

Now what? The only thing that came to mind was the pain in his face. And that he had to spend another night on the day bed.

32

The doorbell rang and Billy Yow went to answer it.

"Hold on a second," he said.

He grabbed his checkbook and opened the door. A large black man stood there, dressed in army fatigues and empty handed.

"Where's the pizza?"

Just then the man punched Billy in the nose, sending him back into the apartment against the wall.

"Shit!" he yelled, grabbing his face. "What the fuck are you doing?"

Two men barged into the apartment, the first one holding Billy's arms behind his back while the second, Ted Jacobson, closed the apartment door behind them.

"Where is the thumb drive?" asked Jacobson.

The question was deliberate and without emotion. He was dressed in fatigues also. Jacobson clearly worked out, based on the bulging forearms that strained the rolled up sleeves of his shirt. He had the barreled chest of a middle linebacker. The grimace on his face indicated that he was in no mood for a long conversation.

"Who the fuck are you?" Blood oozed from Billy's nose.

"Just answer the damn question," Jacobson replied in a deep bass. Then he drove his fist into Billy's stomach. "Where is the thumb drive?"

Billy took a minute to catch his breath, his lungs feeling like they had collapsed completely. Jacobson walked around the den area of the sparse apartment while the second man held Billy up.

Ted returned to Billy and stood face to face with him.

"I'm not fucking with you man," said Jacobson. "My time is critical. I'm only gonna ask you one more time. Where is the – "

Before he could finish, Billy kneed him in the groin and head butted the man behind him sending him into the wall. He kicked Jacobson in the face and he fell to his back in agony. Then he used an open handed punch to the chest of the second man, sending him into the wall again. He grabbed Jacobson's left arm and twisted until he heard a loud crack. He screamed and collapsed to the floor.

"You fucked with the wrong guy tonight, my brothers," said Billy, bending over Jacobson. "Who sent you here?"

Just then he felt hard metal pressed against the back of his head. He realized it was a gun.

"Get the fuck up bitch," said the second man, holding his mouth with his other hand.

Whatever was going on, Billy knew he wasn't ready to die for it. He stood with his hands raised and backed up. Jacobson rolled on the floor in anguish.

"Look man, take whatever you want," said Billy. "Just don't kill me." He tried to sound scared, but he really wasn't. He could take the gun and kill the man in two moves, but he didn't. He just wanted them to leave.

The man held the gun on Billy, and then went to help Jacobson off the floor.

"The drive is in the back bedroom."

Jacobson fell down on the sofa, contorting. With the gun in his back, Billy led the man to the bedroom. He pulled the thumb drive from the computer and handed it over. Billy then put his hands back in the air and tried to collect himself.

"Okay, you got what you wanted. Now just leave me alone."

The man said nothing. He backed out, keeping his eyes and the gun on Billy, and his left hand on his bloody mouth.

He helped Jacobson up, his face bleeding and his arm dangling from his side. They headed for the door. From the bedroom, Billy could see all of their movements.

As they headed out, Jacobson said, through his clinched teeth, "I'm coming back to fuck you up for this punk."

Go for it, thought Billy. *I'll be right here waiting*. The two men slammed the door.

Billy collapsed into the chair, as the sharp pain in his mid section became more intense. He wondered what had taken Gene so long to return. The blood from his nose trickled down his shirt. He didn't know what kind of mess Donnie Centronelli had gotten him into, but he no longer felt he owed him anything.

33

Wednesday morning the phone rang. To Montgomery it sounded much louder than usual, like he had his ear pressed against the school bell as it rang indicating recess time. He was sprawled on the daybed, hanging off the side in nothing but his boxer briefs. The night had been unseasonably hot, making the unventilated room sticky, and unbearable. And his back felt like someone had stood on it in nine-inch heels.

He slowly pulled himself up from the bed, cringing with every movement and groaning like a man twice his age. His face felt swollen and painful. The effect of Gabrielle's right hook had begun to set in and it felt worse than a hangover.

Most of the previous night, Montgomery had sat in the window looking out at the busy street trying to figure out how to explain his unfaithfulness to Gabrielle. He hoped she would listen to him today. When he finally attempted to sleep about three in the morning, the unbearable heat made it impossible. Two hours may have been the sum total of his rest with all of the tossing and turning. When he awoke, he noticed his sweating had soaked the bed sheets.

The second ring seemed louder than the last. Montgomery hoped Gabrielle would pick it up. He was in no mood to talk to anyone. It kept ringing and Montgomery put the pillow over his head to deaden the sound. Finally, it stopped.

Montgomery looked over at the clock and it read six-forty-six. He wondered why Gabrielle didn't get the phone, then rolled over to get back to sleep. He briefly thought about getting ready for his yoga and workout routine, but somehow, it wasn't a priority this day.

The phone rang again.

"Shit!" Montgomery yelled.

He jumped up and walked briskly to the master bedroom.

"Hello!" he said angrily.

"Damn Doc, kinda early to be so pissed off, don't you think."

"Who the hell is this?"

"It's me Donnie. We have a problem."

"Not now Donnie, I'll deal with it when I get to the office, alright." Montgomery looked around the bedroom, realizing that Gabrielle had left.

"It's about that thumb drive you gave me."

"Yeah. What about it?" He headed to Eliza's room. She was gone too.

"I gave it to my buddy yesterday and somebody went to his house and jumped him. Fucked him up pretty good. They took the thing. Nia must have some pretty vicious connections."

Fully awake now, Montgomery walked down the stairs. He peeked out the door to see if Gabrielle's SUV was still parked out front. The space was empty.

Realizing that Gabrielle and Eliza had left without saying goodbye, he dropped to sit down on the bottom step with the phone to his ear. He flashed back to the night before and the conversation he had with Dr. Kelly.

Njama. What have I gotten myself into, he thought.

"What the hell happened?" Montgomery asked.

"I talked to my friend Billy's brother Gene this morning. They were looking at the program last night. He said it was some pretty good shit. Nothing top notch, but good."

"Come on Donnie," said Montgomery. "Get to the point."

"Alright, alright. Anyway as they were breaking down the code, Gene decided to go out to get some beer. While he was gone, Billy gets a knock at the door, thinking it's the pizza delivery and opens up. Two assholes bust in and start to kick the shit out of him, asking about the drive. At this point, Billy is trying to figure out who these guys are and how they found him."

"Is he alright?" Montgomery got up and made his way to the kitchen to pour a glass of fruit juice.

"Yeah, he's cool. Got a broken nose. May have some bruised ribs, but he'll live. He got his licks in too. Billy's trained in Tae Kwon Do, so he left his mark on those dudes. He broke at least one of their arms. Green berets don't take beatings without giving something in return."

"So how did they get the drive?"

Montgomery wanted to get Donnie back to the story. He tended to drag these kind of things on. In that way, Donnie and Jovan were just alike.

"One of them pulled out a gun and Billy gave in. Then they took off. By the time Gene got back with the beer and found Billy they were long gone."

"Damn," said Montgomery, "Now what?"

"I told you these intelligence people are some beasts. I say leave this alone and be lucky they haven't come after you."

"Believe me, after last night, the thought has crossed my mind."

"What happened last night?"

"Never mind, I'll tell you later. Did your boys say anything about what the program did?"

"Yeah, Gene said it hacked into a company that did banking transactions. I think he said something about it takes over account names, captures transactions, allows people to wander around their system unnoticed. Something like that. I think they even ran the program and went into the system last night to see how it works. I guess Nia and whoever could be trying to move some money around. For what, I don't know."

Montgomery had a flashback. He remembered he had made a copy of the program.

"Donnie, meet me in the office after my class this morning. Eleven o'clock. Do you think your boy Billy will still work with us?"

"I don't think so. He may be incapacitated for a couple of days. His brother Gene might help though, but he would want to stay more undercover than Billy. They don't want any trouble. But I'm warning you doc, you might want to leave this alone."

"Don't worry Donnie, just meet me at eleven."

"Alright, later."

Montgomery hung up the phone and noticed a note on the kitchen counter. He picked it up.

Monty, you hurt me terribly and have a lot to explain to me. I'm not sure if I can ever forgive you. I plan to stay at my parents' house for a while with Eliza. I'll call later and we can arrange a time for you to spend with her tonight.

Montgomery wasn't sure what to make of this. He felt a sense of desperation. Was he losing his family? And for what?

While thinking about his options during the night, he'd concluded that Njama was probably behind the pictures. Who else would have done such a thing?

Montgomery felt stupid for even being in that position in the first place. It could have all been avoided if not for his lustful thoughts of Carmen. He needed to talk to Gabrielle soon. To explain, to apologize, to beg, whatever it took. He did not want to lose his wife and daughter.

He took the note, headed up the stairs, and placed it on the bed. Running down the hall to the office, he stood on the chair and reached into the ceiling vent for the CD with the program. He also pulled down the GPS system Jovan had given him.

As he climbed down from the chair he glanced out the window and his mouth dropped wide open. He squinted and looked again. A tow truck had hooked up chains to his BMW.

"Hey! What are you doing?" Montgomery yelled, ignoring the fact that the window was closed and the driver couldn't hear him. He banged on the window, but the man kept moving, trying to get it hooked up as fast as he could.

Montgomery bolted out the room, down the hall, down the stairs and out the front door. He ran out to the tow truck driver.

"Hey, what the hell is going on? This is my car!"

"Yeah, and its being repossessed." The driver held an ax handle in one hand and scratched his bloated belly with the other. He grinned with a jagged smile, revealing his brown tobacco stained teeth. His beard was dirty and he wore a beat up Florida Marlins cap covering a stringy mullet haircut.

"You've got to be crazy," said Montgomery. "Repossessed? For what?"

"All I know is I got a call that the note ain't been paid and I was told to take the car. You need to call your finance company."

Montgomery knew the man probably never finished high school, especially the way he butchered the English language. Montgomery had a habit of correcting people who spoke incorrectly, something he picked up from his grandmother. But this was not the time. Regardless of the man's education, he had the power. Montgomery wasn't going to challenge a man with an ax handle and chains hooked to his BMW.

"Shit, this must be a mistake, I've never been behind on this note."

"Don't know what to tell you buddy." The driver kept hooking up chains and pushed the lever on the side of the rusted truck, raising the car off the ground. He looked at Montgomery out the corners of his eyes.

"Wait man, shit." Montgomery paced in front of the tow truck trying to think about what to do.

"Look, can you wait right here while I call the finance company? This is a big mistake."

"Okay."

Montgomery ran in the house and picked up the portable phone from the base in the family room. He ran up the stairs to the office looking for the phone number to the finance company among the dozens of papers on the small desk. He found it and began dialing the number.

Peering out of the window, he saw the tow truck rolling down the street and turning north on Georgia Avenue at the corner. His car tagged along on the back.

"Hey! Wait!" Again yelling at the closed window. "Shit, asshole liar!"

Montgomery flopped down and navigated the maze of menus on the phone system for Banker's Financial. Press one for English, press two for questions on your account, and on and on. Finally, press zero to speak to a customer service representative.

He pressed zero and waited while the automated voice told him his wait time was five minutes. He listened to the bogus instrumental version of *Sitting on the Dock of the Bay* and fumed.

In about three minutes, a voice came on.

"Hello, may I have your account number please?"

Montgomery gave the account number.

"And what are the last four digits of your social security number."

Montgomery quickly reeled them off.

"How may I help you Mr. Quinn?"

"Yes, a tow truck just took off with my car saying it was repossessed because I missed payments. I've never missed a payment and I need to know what the hell is going on."

"Just a minute sir. I'm checking our system."

"Fine. I know I've been late a couple of times, but I've never missed a payment."

"Sir, according to our records, you are six months behind on your payments. We show your last payment was... October."

"That is impossible! I just sent a payment yesterday and I have made every payment up to that point."

"Well, I'm not sure what to tell you Mr. Quinn, I'm looking at my computer and it shows--"

"I don't give a damn what your computer says. Look, let me speak to your supervisor."

"Hold on sir. Let me transfer you."

Back to the music. Montgomery knew someone there had made a mistake and planned to talk to everyone in the company until he got his car back.

34

Driving along Route 4 in Maryland toward Washington, D.C. Paulette Aventis' listened to national public radio. The guest discussed the increased population growth in Florida seaside resorts. Her mind drifted to her vacation home in Nags Head, North Carolina and she wished she were there.

Her cell phone interrupted the peaceful thoughts. Paulette reached down and checked the number. The number indicated that one of her Njama colleagues wanted to talk. She pulled into an Exxon gas station. A woman using the pay phone glanced over at her tan Mercedes S500 as she pulled up and parked.

Paulette wanted to rush the woman so she pulled as close to the phone as possible. "Excuse me," she said. "Will you be a while?"

The woman appeared around forty and unkept, dressed in house slippers, a bandana, and long blue Mickey Mouse shirt that hung under a tattered blue jean jacket. She turned her back to Paulette and continued her conversation. Paulette rolled up her window and waited, letting the engine run hoping the fumes would become intolerable.

Moments later, the woman turned, looked at Paulette, and said something she could not decipher, but she knew it was unpleasant. Paulette smiled and started to extend her middle finger, but decided against it. The woman walked to her rusted old Buick LeSabre and drove off.

Paulette pulled out the can of disinfectant spray she kept in her glove compartment. She went to the phone, sprayed it, and dialed the number.

Sanja answered on the first ring.

"I got it," she said.

"Got what?"

"The key, I got the drive."

"How the hell did you do that?"

"I have my ways."

Paulette paused briefly to let a jet taking off from Andrews Air Force Base pass by so she could hear.

"Sanja, what did you do?"

"Don't worry, the good Dr. Quinn was unharmed. One of his buddies just got roughed up a bit."

"Fuck, Sanja! I thought I said no violence."

Paulette's tolerance with Sanja's maverick proclivities evaporated fast.

"Look Paulette, we have the damn thing, what's your problem."

"The end doesn't always justify the means. You ever heard that saying before?"

"Yeah, and I don't believe it," she said. "So what?"

Several seconds passed by as each woman tried to calm herself and figure out what to say next.

"So you paid somebody to get the drive back?" asked Paulette.

"Well not completely. I made a down payment, but I still owe some uh... personal favors, you know. Its an old friend and hard to explain."

"Venturing into prostitution now too, huh?"

"I got the job done. You should be thanking me!"

"Whatever. Are you sure you have the damn thing?"

"I'm holding it in my hand right now."

"Alright, just keep it and let Nia know. We need to get off this line." *I'll deal with you later,* Paulette thought. She hung up the phone.

Paulette sat back in her car and flopped her head on the headrest. Paulette needed to reign in Sanja's uncontrollable behavior before she destroyed everyone. But how? Paulette put the car in gear and continued on to work. She would have to develop a strategy later to bring Sanja back in line or remove her from the mzingo zima.

35

The subway train was Montgomery's only mode of transportation since the finance company towed his car and Gabrielle wasn't answering his calls on her cell phone. Hiding his bruises with dark prescription shades, he walked the few blocks to the Georgia Avenue-Petworth station. He took the redline train to L'Enfant Plaza, transferred to the blue line train, and took that to Foggy Bottom-George Washington University. He had forgotten how long it was to get to the university by train.

By the time he arrived, his boiling point had been reduced to a simmer. The jog to his building from the metro eased some of the stress. But it didn't matter, he was still twenty minutes late for his ten o'clock class.

The students had waited the customary fifteen minutes allowed for professors, then dispersed. Only three remained in the classroom when he arrived. He sent them on their way and would resume the lectures on Friday.

The conversation with the finance company went nowhere. The customer service representative insisted that he hadn't made a payment in six months. Now he had to go to the bank with cancelled checks, demonstrating his payment history, to get his car back.

In the mean time, Montgomery sat in his office, staring at the picture of Eliza on his bookshelf and engrossed in thought. The department secretary startled him when she knocked on the opened door.

"Dr. Quinn, the Dean just called and wants to see you in his office."

"Thank you Ms. Hawkins, I'll head over."

Montgomery found this highly unusual. The Dean rarely spoke to him. The serious demeanor of Dean Benjamin Orson demanded respect. At six foot five, two hundred and fifty pounds, the former University of Arkansas lineman towered over most people in an intimidating way. His size often prevented him from having to deal with any confrontation over his management of the School's affairs. Faculty just let him do what he thought best. He didn't bother them and they didn't challenge him.

Montgomery grabbed a pen and pad and made his way to the Dean's office, wondering all the way the reason for the summons. Dean Orson's secretary waved him in. He knocked and peeked his head in the cracked door.

"Dean, you wanted to see me."

"Come on in Monty, have a seat."

The wrinkles on Orson's forehead pushed back the gray on his receding hairline. He looked and sounded a bit like former President Lyndon Johnson. Montgomery found him difficult to read because the expression on his face never seemed to change, regardless of the circumstances.

Montgomery sat as Dean Orson shuffled a few papers on his organized desk and pushed the do not disturb button on the phone. Oversized furniture filled the office. Awards, plaques and family pictures covered the massive glass top desk. A perfect view of the campus landscape and the morning sky framed his back wall.

The Dean sat in the middle of the desk, erect and appearing as serious as ever. He looked at Montgomery, noticing the black eye. He frowned and took another look, but never said anything about it. Then he exhaled and shook his head.

"Monty," he said, "you have a problem."

"Yeah, I have a lot of those lately. You might as well throw another one on the pile."

This was definitely not the typical way to talk to Dean

Orson, but Montgomery didn't care at this point. His day, or even week for that matter, couldn't get any worse.

Orson looked at Montgomery curiously for a second, then continued. "I just got a call from the National Science Foundation. It seems they have an issue with your grant."

"What kind of issue?"

"Someone over there decided to do an unscheduled audit of your budget and found some disturbing spending patterns. They're suggesting that you may have used money from this grant for personal uses."

"That's a damn lie!" Montgomery stood up to defend himself. "Sorry Dean, I meant no disrespect."

"Calm down Monty, take a seat." Dean Orson looked up at him from behind his desk, waiting for Montgomery to gather himself. He settled back down into the brown leather chair slowly.

"It could just be an error with their records," Orson continued. "But they want to take a more in-depth look. In the mean time, they want to suspend any further transactions until they finish their investigation."

"Investigation! So am I being accused of a crime here?"

"Monty, this is a lot of money. What is it? Three million dollars or so."

"Yes."

"I don't want to lose this any more than you, you know that. All of our grants allow us a lot of flexibility with research, facilities, supplies... everything. You're a good man. I believe you but I don't want to piss these people off and not get any more money from them. I'm sure you understand."

"Dean, that grant pays my salary for the summer. The spring semester is almost over. Where do I get money from now?"

"Let's just see what happens. Maybe it won't take that long for them to discover their mistake. If it does, we'll work something out. But I can't promise you it will be anywhere near your entire summer support."

"Dean, this is unbelievable." Montgomery shook his head and looked down at his blank pad.

"Monty, I'll try to make some calls to see if we can straighten this out sooner than later. I'll get back to you."

Montgomery knew that was his sign to leave. He stood and left the office without saying a word. He shuffled down the hall, past the offices of his colleagues, dejected and nauseous.

Before he realized it, he was standing on the stairs in front of the building. He kept walking. He needed to think and maybe the fresh air would help. His head felt like it would explode.

36

The tourists ambled along the path of the Vietnam Memorial in a solemn trance. Although nearby Constitution Avenue bustled with traffic and the steps of the Lincoln Memorial that towered above contained a rowdy set of teens, visitors always respected the war memorial. A silent appreciation for the thousands of names etched in the wall.

Nia Givens sat on a park bench watching the parade, always amazed at how visitors reacted to the wall. She'd been there dozens of times, but the emotional impact never seemed to dissipate. She focused her attention on two young women rubbing a pencil across a piece of paper along one of the names. She felt a presence.

Sanja had joined her silently. The Federal Reserve Board building stood directly across Constitution Avenue, so Sanja had asked Nia to meet there at eleven. Sanja's meeting had a brief break before she had to host the visiting Reserve Bank officers at lunch. They sat for about two minutes without a word, watching the young ladies finish their imprint of the name.

"Amazing isn't it," Nia turned and said to Sanja, not expecting any response of sensitivity.

"I have an uncle on that wall. My mother's brother. I must have done the same thing they're doing at least ten times." Sanja's voice trembled. To see such raw emotion from her surprised Nia. She never expected that Sanja had the capacity.

They both turned and looked again at the two women as they made their way up the path toward Lincoln.

"I got the thumb drive," said Sanja, holding it in her open palm on the bench next to them, out of sight from anyone else. Nia looked, then calmly reached down, grabbed it and put it in her jacket pocket.

"How did you do that? I just sent the email last night." Nia tried to act unsuspicious and hide her astonishment.

"I have my ways," Sanja said. "You can thank me later."

Nia knew any further questioning would lead nowhere and she had no energy for verbal wrestling. Nia just looked at Sanja as she stared into the distance. Two squirrels jolted by and stood, waiting to be fed. Sanja shooed them away with a kick of her feet.

"Don't worry, your boy is safe." Sanja stood and looked down at Nia. "I have to get back to work. You can take care of our program from here right?"

"Yes."

"Good, we'll talk later." Sanja walked away up the path toward the street. After a couple of steps, she stopped and walked back.

She bent down and whispered to Nia, "Oh, and by the way, since we have the drive back, we've called off the dogs on Quinn. We can't stop what's already in motion though. But I'm sure that'll make you a little happier. I must admit, we screwed him pretty good." A sinful smirk crossed her face as Sanja turned and walked away.

That was good news. Nia felt relieved that the assault on Montgomery had ended and remorseful for what he had gone through. She watched Sanja reach the light and jog across Constitution Avenue toward her marble office building and disappear into the crowd of vacationers, joggers, and business attired government workers.

37

Four blocks away, on the campus of George Washington University, a major migraine made Montgomery's eyes water. He rested his head on the desk. The world seemed to have come to a stop, but his life was spinning out of control.

During his walk, he found the campus brimming to capacity with students sitting on benches, standing in line at the street vendors, playing Frisbee in the limited green space of a city landscape. He meandered with no preconceived destination for an hour.

Thirst finally directed him to the student union building to grab a bottle of juice. There he realized he needed to get some money from the ATM machine. After entering the card in the machine, punching in the PIN number and requesting a forty-dollar withdrawal, the machine report insufficient funds. Thinking the machine must have malfunctioned, Montgomery tried another machine on campus. The same message displayed.

His paycheck should have been direct deposited just that morning. Making his way back to the office, he called his bank. His gut told him to expect the worst. Bad news seemed to be the theme for this day.

The bank officer told him the computers showed that his account was overdrawn. *Of course it is; Damn computer,* he thought. He found no need to argue. The migraine came instantly after he hung up the phone.

Njama, he thought over and over.

The cell phone tune vibrated against his waist. Montgomery reached down and flipped it open without lifting his head.

"Yes." His voice trailed off into an echo under his desk.

"Monty, what's up baby? Got off to a rough day?" The cheerful voice sounded familiar to him, but his brain wasn't making any connections.

"Who is this?"

"How soon they forget. I thought I left a pretty good impression on you yesterday boo."

"Carmen!" Montgomery lifted his head, instantly alert. "Girl, you will not believe what the hell happened."

"What's that?"

"Somebody sent my wife pictures of our little kiss after lunch, along with some other shots.

Carmen was silent.

"Gabrielle fuckin' left me because of that shit. And I won't bore you with how the rest of my life is unraveling. Do you know anything about this Carmen?"

"Monty, I'm sorry. I don't know what to say. I ..." Her voice fell to a whisper as she searched for the words to console him.

"Monty, we need to meet," said Carmen finally. "Maybe I can help fix this."

"I think you've done enough."

"Monty, let me help. Please."

"I need to get my wife and my life back. You can't help with that. I don't blame you, but I can't see you anymore Carmen."

He hung up the phone. The words stayed with him. *I need to get my life back.*

He reached in his bag and pulled out the GPS and CD and looked at them. *Think.*

He realized he needed to do something, but nothing came to mind. A hard knock on his office door broke the spell.

"Who is it?"

"It's me doc. Donnie." Montgomery looked at the clock on his desk. It said eleven fifty-eight. He got up and opened the door.

"I told you eleven," said Montgomery. "Where the hell have you been?"

"Calm down man. I came by at eleven and you weren't here. So I went to run a couple of errands. I called and left a message saying I'd be right back." He looked Montgomery in the face and said, "Whoa, somebody kicked your ass."

Montgomery covered his purplish face, looked over at his phone and saw the red light flashing, signaling a voice mail message. He hadn't noticed it until now.

"Never mind. Sit down." Montgomery closed the door and moved to his desk.

"You have to help me man." Montgomery shared the events of Tuesday evening and that morning. The note on the car, the meeting with Dr. Kelly, pictures with Carmen, Gabrielle's punches, the towed car, the visit with the Dean, and the overdrawn bank account. The words came fast and no parts of the narrative seemed connected. The more he talked, the more unreal it appeared. He could see from Donnie's expression that the story sounded more fictional than a Grisham novel.

"Damn." That's all Donnie managed to utter when Montgomery finally took a breather. Montgomery showed him the CD and the GPS.

"I made a copy of the thumb drive."

"After all you've told me, I would think you'd had enough. I warned you, whoever these people are, they play for keeps. You've only seen a taste in my opinion and look where you are."

"Well, I'm in now. I need to fix this shit. We are going to run this program, with your boy's help."

"I'm not sure how they tracked Billy, but it must be something on that program. Before you run it again, you probably need to find a secure and isolated environment. Billy's brother Gene may be able to help with that."

"Okay, lets call him. But first we need to take a ride. Jovan gave me this GPS for some reason, whether he knew it or not. I don't know if it'll help, but I need to see where Nia went Sunday night. They seem to have access to everything in my life and it might start out there. These bitches are not taking me down without a fight."

"Who are you talking about?"

"Nia and her crew."

"Crew?"

"I'll explain later. Are you with me?" Although he didn't know why, somehow he knew he might need Donnie's green beret training on this excursion.

"You know me, I enjoy a good rumble." Donnie smiled an evil grin, rubbing his hands together.

"Good. Can you get a car from somewhere? We're going on a field trip to Calvert County."

38

Donnie went home and returned with a bold yellow Chevy Camaro. From his insistence on using public transportation, Montgomery never knew Donnie owned a car. Turned out nothing pissed Donnie off more that driving in D.C.

When Donnie first moved to town he found the streets confusing and ended up in some pretty seedy areas. Not a good thing when you're driving a loud, bright sports car. Once, on a traffic circle, a couple of teenagers in a beat up Dodge ran into him, scratching his rims. From that point on, Donnie kept his prized sports car in the garage of an elderly neighbor. He only drove it on the weekends in Virginia.

Navigating the traffic through southeast D.C., they finally got to Route 4 heading east through Prince Georges County and into Calvert County. Montgomery used the GPS device to track Nia's exact route.

Along the way, Montgomery brought him up to date on the recent activities in his unraveling life. Afterwards, Donnie tried to engage in conversation about the Baltimore Orioles, the upcoming Prince concert, and satellite imaging software. Montgomery's responses to these topics were minimal. His eyes focused on the device and his words were reserved for telling Donnie where and when to turn. The trip moved from the inner city plight of D.C., through the busy suburbs, to the rural farms of Calvert County, Maryland.

They drove for more than an hour. Without warning Montgomery had dozed off, mentally exhausted. A nudge by

Donnie awakened him. Donnie had grabbed the GPS after it fell onto the seat and continued the journey without his direction. Montgomery looked up, surprised to find them coasting along a barren rural highway.

"We're almost there," said Donnie, eyes dead ahead on the road.

Montgomery noticed the signs as they passed by. They were on Route 521.

"Where are we?"

"Hell if I know," said Donnie. "I haven't seen a living human being for twenty-five miles. Plenty of cows though. Based on the GPS we're close."

They finally turned off onto an unmarked road with signs pointing toward the Patuxent River. After a short distance, they crawled to a stop at the entrance to a gravel driveway with white painted stone pillars on either side. Large shade trees bordered the entrance on both sides, making everything up the driveway nearly invisible.

"This is a pretty mysterious place," Donnie said.

"Looks like an old plantation. No name on the mailbox," said Montgomery.

"Somebody lives here. Those shrubs along the fence are manicured. Let's drive around along the road and see if we can catch a better peek."

Donnie pulled the Camaro slowly along the main road following the edge of the property. Behind the trees in the distance they saw a large colonial estate sitting on a hill. Other smaller buildings were scattered around within walking distance.

They came to an intersection and turned right. Compared to the properties in the city, this place seemed massive to Montgomery. Another building sat behind some trees and shrubs, but neither of them could tell exactly what it was.

"This place is huge. With all of these trees, I can't tell what's out there though," said Montgomery. With the sunroof open, they could smell water in the air and soon realized they were close to the Patuxent River.

"I don't think we should wander around here too long. I'm sure this car stands out with all of the country people out here," said Donnie.

"Alright, lets take off and try to think about what we do next."

They turned around and headed back by the house, slowing down to take another peek. Donnie entered the main road and turned back onto Route 521.

"What do you think Nia was doing way out here?" asked Donnie.

"I don't know. I assume she knows whoever lives there. Lets stop at this store and get some chips and soda. I'm starving."

Donnie treated, after Montgomery reminded him about his bank problems. Walking out of the store, they sat in the car and tried to figure out their next move.

"Do you think we can get on that property and look around?" asked Montgomery.

"What for?"

"Maybe we can find some computers or something. They had to use something to access all those computer systems, like my car finance company."

"That's a stretch, but we can't go in there in broad daylight. It would help if we had a layout of the place. Then we could probably at least look around at night."

"How can you see anything at night."

Donnie smiled and said, "There are ways." Montgomery remembered Donnie's special forces training, nodded and took a sip of his juice.

"We can get the layout from satellite imaging data. Our remote sensing database should have this place. If not, we should be able to get it from the county government. Somebody's always doing flyovers out here and taking digital photos along the Chesapeake Bay watershed. They have all of that stuff online now. Shit, we can even find out who lives there from the public records."

"That's true, it may cost you though if it's not in the county system. But that should be pretty easy to get."

"We'll find it," said Montgomery. "Once we do, we can download it into the geographical information system software and create images that'll give us all we need to know. The data should tell us where all of the buildings and structures are on the entire property."

"That'll help. Then if we come back at night, we'll know exactly where to go. Sounds like a plan. You sure you up for this?" asked Donnie.

"Hell yeah. What have I got to lose at this point?"

"We need to get back to the office to get the satellite data. I also need to go home and pick up a few things. We'll come back tonight." Donnie started the car and put it in gear.

"Cool, lets get out of here. I need to see my daughter and hopefully my wife will talk to me." Montgomery doubted it, but realized he needed to try.

39

Ladies, your journey begins now. You have proven yourselves worthy of induction into our bond. Take a taxi to the Thomas Jefferson Memorial. A black Lincoln Towncar will be waiting there to pick you up. The sign in the window will read FREEDOM. Get in the back seat, put on your blindfold. Do not talk to each other. You will be taken to your next destination from there.

Sanja Coston recorded the message into the ASV-VC1 portable telephone voice changer, adjusting the pitch and octave to make it sound childish. She would send the message to the three potential inductees simultaneously from a pay phone on the way out. They all waited by the phone in separate cheap motel rooms around the area, ready to become new kizushis.

By four o'clock Sanja had returned home from a long day of meetings. She had hoped to leave her office early to catch a nap, but it didn't work out that way.

By the time the towncar picked them up, drove them around awhile, transferred them to a cargo van, got them blind folded and naked, and drove around some more, it would be midnight before they got to Paulette's. All in an effort to confuse them, make sure no one followed them, and protect the identities of the inner circle.

Paulette's husband had left for a business meeting in Atlanta earlier in the day. Nia arrived at Paulette's house to prepare for the ceremony and make some minor upgrades to the hacking software. Charity would get there a little later, due to some other commitments.

One of the *katis* was to leave the van full of recruits at a beach near the Chesapeake Bay at eleven. Then Sanja would drive the van over to Paulette's still making sure no one followed.

If she hurried, there was a little time to get to the house before Charity had to meet them. Anxious to see what Nia had done, she changed her clothes, grabbed a banana and a coke, and rushed out the door.

40

Sitting in his office, Montgomery reflected on his earlier discussion with Gabrielle. Looking up at the fluorescent lights, he sighed and tried to think of ways to convince her of his innocence.

The conversation with Gabrielle had been useless. Montgomery could say nothing to prove to her that nothing happened with Carmen. They had met back at the house and he told her about everything, including Njama and how they were out to get him. Her only response was telling him about a message on the phone from the IRS questioning their tax return from last year.

He never listened to it, but assured her it was all part of the conspiracy to get him. She took the opportunity to berate him for his irresponsible financial management.

Exhausted by the whole experience, Montgomery sat on the bed, watching Eliza roll her Barbie sports car on the Sponge Bob Square Pants blanket. No words would come out. Gabrielle looked at him like he had idiot stamped on his forehead while she packed a small suitcase. He knew she thought it was all made up.

At any moment he expected her to blacken the other eye with a straight left. Finally, he gave up and moved down on the blanket to play with his daughter until they were ready to leave. He focused on spending quality time with Eliza since he had no idea when he would see her again.

So far, Montgomery had failed at winning back Gabrielle's

trust. But he was not giving up that easy. He would try everyday until he succeeded.

Gabrielle drove him to the subway station without looking at him once. He said his goodbyes to Eliza and tried to kiss Gabrielle on the cheek. She immediately turned and pushed him away. Montgomery jumped out of the car. He stood and watched the truck turn the corner, and then he jumped on the subway headed for his office.

Once he arrived, Montgomery sat in the research lab surfing the web and waiting for Donnie. He went to the State of Maryland website and clicked on the Department of Assessment and Taxation link. While looking for homes, he and Gabrielle discovered this site and used it to get information on homes suspected to be in foreclosure.

With an address, a person could get just about everything he needed to know about who owned a home through state and county records, including who had the mortgage and how much they owed.

From the drop down menu Montgomery selected Calvert County. He entered the street address. Up popped the names Harold and Paulette Aventis. Among other data, the page said that the home was built in 1930, stood on more than fifty acres, and the Aventis' purchased it in 1990 from a Mr. and Ms. Reginald Unser for $695,000. Montgomery printed the page.

Through the NSF research grant he had access to a number of databases that contained satellite images from either the LandSat or SPOT systems. With the address or some other coordinates, he could get images of anything.

He'd used satellite mapping technologies for data modeling and other analysis to get color photos with a resolution of ten meters.

Working with the biology department, he even used the multi-spectral bands of LandSat to show where different types of vegetation, creeks, dams, and fence lines were located to help them analyze environmental impacts on habitat in coastal areas. Because of the assistance he provided them, they shared some aerial photos that could provide even more detail, down to one meter of resolution, although they were a little more distorted.

With Maryland being a coastal state and the push to keep the Chesapeake Bay clean, there was always some entity flying over the rivers, streams, and creeks taking photos and logging them in a database. It was just a matter of finding them, but luckily Montgomery knew generally where to look.

More importantly now, he could get pictures of where certain buildings were located on a property, the fence lines, and even underground pipes or wells. Montgomery went to the database that contained satellite images for sites across Maryland, Virginia, and D.C. Entering the Aventis' property address and some other coordinates, it took the database two minutes to provide a clear view of the entire property.

As the computer churned, Donnie walked into the empty lab, dressed in all black, including polished army boots. Holding a half eaten apple, he sat down next to Montgomery.

"Ready for a quick and dirty education in strategic reconnaissance?" Donnie appeared overly excited about the opportunity to use his special forces training, although he would never admit it.

"You sure you still remember anything? I've never heard you talk about your training in all these years. Now you show up looking like Rambo?"

"Believe me, the way this gets embedded in you, it's never forgotten."

Montgomery believed him and didn't want to ask about any of the details.

"I've got the images," said Montgomery, pointing to the monitor.

Throwing the apple core in the trash, Donnie studied the images.

"Got a few buildings out there. Who knows what's in them. It's a pretty big place so it's going to take us a while to navigate it."

"I think I have everything that's available in the databases. Can you think of anything else we need?

"No, lets print these images. We can study them on the way. It's going to be pitch black and we'll need to know where everything is."

"What are we looking for?"

"Shit, you tell me doc. This is your mission. I'm just a soldier following orders."

Montgomery didn't know, but he felt he had to make the exploration. Revenge had dominated his thoughts all day. During his football days, when someone got a good hit on him, he spent the whole game trying to figure out a way to get them back. And he had to clear his name to get his wife and daughter back. Not to mention the financial situation that needed repair. He wanted an all out assault on Njama, whoever they were.

If someone was home, he had no desire to try to enter the house. But he had to find out who the Aventis' were and their connection to Nia and Njama.

"So are we ready? It takes an hour to get there and we may be there awhile," said Donnie.

"Yeah, I'm starving though. We need to stop at a fast food drive thru on the way."

"You got money I hope."

"Gabrielle let me borrow some."

"So she bought the bank account story?"

"It's not a story," Montgomery frowned, and shook his head in frustration.

"I know man, just bustin' your balls."

"Let's just go. I wanted to make a quick trip to the hospital again." Donnie nodded and Montgomery printed the images.

"We need to go back to my office and get my glasses," said Montgomery.

"You leave those things everywhere. Why don't you get that laser eye surgery so you don't have to keep taking them on and off."

"I tried. They said I'm not a good candidate. I only need them for long distance."

"Yeah, I know. You've told me that every time we have to search for them."

As they stood, Donnie put his right arm around Montgomery's shoulder. "Before we head out, we have to get you into the proper gear and we need to have a long conversation on infiltrating behind enemy lines, intelligence gathering, reconnaissance and surveillance tactics."

Donnie smiled as they walked out of the lab.

41

Dusk provided a cast of gray over the Aventis estate. The office sat on the first floor with a floor-to-ceiling bay window overlooking the vast property. Maintenance workers had spent the day sprucing up the spectacular spring lilies and roses and mulching the Japanese maples and dogwood trees. The entire landscape met Paulette's tastes perfectly and she loved the view in the mornings.

The cherry wood furniture provided a rich feel to the dark executive decorations. Nothing looked out of place. Neatness was Paulette's obsession.

The wall hangings showed her appreciation of the arts.

In addition to prints of classics like Titian and Monet, several original oil paintings from local artists adorned one of the faux finished walls. Masks from her visits to Kenya and Senegal covered another. At the entrance stood a granite ornament with water cascading down the front with a single candle burning above it. Everything reflected Paulette's taste for the dramatic, yet elegant.

Nia arrived at the house around seven, after another long day of bouncing between home, work and the hospital. They had some time to kill before Sanja and Charity arrived, so they ate crème cheese pastries and sipped raspberry ice tea. Paulette listened intently, sitting on the leather chair and staring at the screen, while Nia tried to explain the program's nuances.

Sanja's lookout at ECPI had provided all of the scripts and files for the electronic fund transfer program, as well as account number accesses. She also provided a back door to access the root of the ECPI system so that they could enter surreptitiously.

Nia had been monitoring the system for some time so she knew the protocol for how the company did electronic transfers.

"So this is how it works," said Nia. "First ECPI initiates contact with computers at the various partner banking institutions. Then they wait for an alphanumeric control sequence to be sent. It looks like this."

She pointed to the screen at her script.

Mmmmmmmmmwwwwwcwwwmmmfdesfmwsdwewd
OPID = Operator ID
OBID = originating bank ID number
TT = transaction type
AT = account type
OBAN = originating bank account number
DBID = destination bank ID number
DBAN = destination bank account number
DA = dollar amount of transaction
Mmmmmmmmmwwwwwcwwwmmmfdesfmwsdwewd

"When the bank receiving a transaction gets the string and verifies it, they automatically send back an acknowledgement."

"So are we sure we can direct the flow of transactions without being detected?" asked Paulette.

"Yes, I tested it yesterday. Transferred a coupled hundred dollars to a dummy account. Got in and out, erased all evidence, and had no problems."

"So the plan is to attack some of the top accounts at some major banks," said Paulette. "We show the flaws in ECPI's security and that money has been diverted, then send a message to Frank Hill. Once we demonstrate his system is exposed, he can't report it or he'll start losing customers. That's when we attack."

"Right. He'll look like the most charitable person in the world to keep this from becoming public knowledge. We've already identified fifteen nonprofits that he will be required to support, including the homeless women's shelter we talked about."

"Good, serves his racist ass right. Now what about the second part of the strategy."

"Sanja gave me the number of the Swiss account she opened. We also have several accounts here in the U.S."

"So we use the same process?" asked Paulette.

"Except we collect the transmissions in a file I've hidden on their system. We send back the acknowledgements so ECPI thinks they went through. Once we've collected the funds, we change the destination bank identification and distribute the funds to the Swiss account."

"How do we get that ID number?"

"Pretty easy," said Nia. "Just called the Swiss Bank and they gave it to us. Once we're sure they have the funds, we request an electronic funds transfer from the New York branch of the Swiss Bank and have the money sent to where we want it in the U.S."

"Sanja says we have to withdraw the money in small amounts, less than ten thousand."

"Yeah, so we don't raise any flags."

"We're in no hurry, we'll just withdraw it slowly and then let them sit there with small balances for a few years. Then we'll close them."

"Everything will look legit internally. ECPI will have documentation that the transactions were received. The intended bank will have no records of the transaction. They'll never figure out that the Swiss bank is involved. And if they do find out, these banks rarely release this sort of information."

"What about the U.S. Banks?"

"All set up with fake IDs and social security numbers by the kizushis. They were told to disguise themselves and their handwriting so even if they were caught on tape they'll never figure it out, if they get that far."

"No traces?"

"No traces."

They gave each other a high five and raised their cups of tea.

42

Twenty miles away, Charity rode along the country highway in her green Toyota Camry. She listened to the earpiece in her ear and smiled.

The other three women had been acting suspicious, and Charity needed details. So she carefully planted a listening device in Paulette's office at the meeting on Sunday. Knowing Paulette's sensitivity for placement of everything in her home, she inserted the microphone behind an antique clock sitting on a file cabinet next to the desk in her office. She carefully placed the clock back in its exact same location, assuming Paulette would never move it again.

The powerful transmitter sent clear voices to the receiver on Charity's passenger seat. She had reluctantly agreed to the extortion plan, mainly because Frank Hill needed to be reigned in from his suspected racist activities. However, stealing money for personal wealth went beyond anything that fit within the Njama tradition. She wanted to force him to contribute to non-profit organizations once exposed, not steal money. As a member of the mzingo zima, she should have been involved in any decision like that, although she knew why they excluded her. They all knew she never would have gone along.

Grabbing another double-stuffed Oreo from the bag, she focused on the narrow road as the sun faded behind her on the horizon. The chatter in her ear made it clear that now she had to take things into her own hands.

43

From the distant road, the century old oak trees hid what the satellite images revealed. At the center of the fifty acre Aventis property sat a sprawling colonial, built with all of the splendor of an eighteenth century plantation. The white structure with red shutters had large two-story columns, and double mahogany doors that dominated the front view. Both sides of the front entrance were dominated with twenty foot pine trees and shrubs perfectly manicured to reflect elegance and beauty.

A circular drive rambled up in front of the main house.

Several other buildings were speckled about the property, including a barn, a four-car garage, a tool shed, and an abandoned old shack. Narrow gravel roads ran along two sides of the property and a turkey farm bordered the other two.

Prior to leaving the campus, Donnie made Montgomery change into black sweat pants, black t-shirt, and a pair of black army boots. The only color on either of them were the red and light gray socks Montgomery wore because Donnie forgot to include a dark pair in the duffle bag when he rushed out of the house.

About fifteen miles from the Aventis property, they stopped to finish dressing for the mission. Donnie had two Special Forces vests with several compartments designed to holster various tools and weapons. They put the vests on and began filling the pockets.

Most notable in their collection was the combat tactical SP5 bowie knife. According to Donnie, it was a fundamental tool for any tactical mission and good for hacking your way through anything. Montgomery considered it a bit overboard since he only planned to look around, but he went along with it.

The other items included a survival compass with luminous points, night vision goggles and binoculars, a night camera, and the portable GPS. Donnie also offered Montgomery a Colt .45, but he declined. Guns made him uneasy and just the thought of possibly pulling a trigger made his chest pound uncontrollably. Donnie stuck the weapon in a side holster strapped to his leg.

Throughout the car trip Donnie tried to educate Montgomery on the art of reconnaissance. This was the most serious he had seen Donnie since they'd met and it worried him. His gaze was intense and the words were bursting from his lips with military authority. A small vein bulged from his temple with every commanding inflection in his voice.

Billy Yow's brother Gene had been diving into the CD with the hacking program and had almost figured out how it worked. Earlier, he told Donnie that if they could access the computer where the program ran and install a keystroke program to capture what the programmer was typing in, that would help quicken things. Donnie looked forward to the challenge and was determined to make that happen.

Montgomery Quinn's mind drifted as he considered what they were doing and why. Still he had no answer for what exactly they were looking for, but he kept quiet and listened. And now, he wasn't sure if he got all of Donnie's instructions, or if he really needed to.

The two had studied the satellite pictures to ensure that they had a good grasp of every thing on the property before embarking on their night quest. However, the satellite images could not warn about whether any kind of security system existed. Without knowledge of cameras, armed guards, or even dogs, they had no idea what to really expect. They knew one thing for sure, they would proceed slowly and cautiously, and haul ass at the first sign of danger.

At almost eleven, Donnie turned right off Route 521, down the gravel road, and crept past the property. At the corner, he turned right and continued about a mile past the Aventis estate.

Turning off his lights, Donnie pulled behind a grove of trees along the road so that the bright yellow car didn't raise suspicion. He went into the trunk and dug into his duffle bag.

"Here Doc, put this on." He handed Montgomery a nomex hood that covered everything on their head but their eyes.

"And you may need some of this too." He held out a tube of black grease paint.

"No thanks, I think I'm dark enough. I'll let you go for the Al Jolsen look."

Montgomery's attempt at humor raised no response from Donnie.

With a look of solemnity, Donnie said, "You should probably put it on." Montgomery shrugged and obliged.

As they finished the last check of the core items, Donnie whispered, "Last chance Doc. Let's see what we can see. Any parting questions?"

Montgomery shook his head and they began their trek through the wooded area.

The trees stifled much of the light from the quarter moon and the sudden rain sent a chill through Montgomery. One thing he remembered from Donnie's constant dribble during the trip was that there would be minimal conversation. All communications would be through hand signals whenever possible. Fear tempted him to yell for them to turn around, but it was already too late. Donnie turned on a small flashlight that he had duct taped to cover all but a small beam of light and made his way ahead into the woods.

They agreed to let Donnie act as the point man. His instincts and training were better suited for this adventure and he could detect any trouble much sooner. About twenty-five yards ahead, Donnie poked around with a small stick as he walked. He used this to identify any raised trip wires that may cross their path.

Using the GPS for direction, Donnie moved slowly, about twenty feet at a time. Then he would stop, look, listen, and smell. He used all of his senses to try and identify any possible threats. Montgomery followed, keeping his distance, walking when Donnie walked, and stopping when he stopped.

Donnie had a pair of night vision goggles but refused to wear them because he believed they would desensitize his sight. Montgomery couldn't see a thing because of the complete darkness so he had on the night vision goggles, although he wasn't sure if they were helping much. The goggles produced a greenish version of everything in front of him, which confused him at first.

He noticed a raccoon standing motionless in the brush and staring directly at him. The animal waited for him to make the first move. It eventually moved on slowly, watching Montgomery suspiciously. With time he got used to them and felt like he was walking in Rock Creek Park at midday.

The trip from the car to the Aventis property was only a mile, but it would take about thirty minutes because of the deliberate pace. Everything up to that point operated just as Donnie had said. Smooth.

44

anja pulled into Paulette's circular driveway and stopped the cargo van, facing the front door. She flashed the headlights three times. The three inductees sat in the back, silent, blindfolded, hooded, hands tied, and naked. She pushed the button on the electronic voice recorder.

"Sit. Do not move. Do not talk. We are watching and listening," the electronic voice said.

Stepping out of the van and closing the door, she looked over her shoulder to make sure they wouldn't try to sneak a peek. No movements.

Paulette, Nia, and Charity were at the door, waiting. They all wore black flowing gowns with an attached hood. A velvet blue and red stripe ran down the front of the garment that matched the elbow length gloves.

Sanja walked by them all into the front door, "Looking fly as always ladies. Ready for another class?"

"Your gown is hanging in the office. Are they safe and secure?" asked Paulette.

"Ready as they'll ever be," replied Sanja.

"Cutting it close again Sanja," said Nia, looking at her watch. It read eleven forty-five.

"I hope you didn't haze them along the way," said Charity. Nia snickered at the remark.

Sanja smiled slyly, "I've done quite a few of these things, my sister. You are more than welcome to take over if you feel more adept at getting them here safely. Otherwise, you'll just have to trust that I followed procedure. You do trust me don't you Charity?"

Hell no, Charity thought. But she turned and walked toward the kitchen without acknowledging the question.

"By the way, you've got Oreo crumbs on your mouth," Sanja said with a grin. Charity huffed and kept walking.

"Just get dressed. Why does it always have to be so much drama with you?" said Paulette.

Sanja sauntered past Paulette, then turned to Nia and winked, "I trust you've been taking care of business," she whispered.

"Always. You don't trust me?"

"You've given me plenty of reasons not to lately."

"Whatever."

Within ten minutes, the four ladies were dressed and ready for the induction ceremony. They put on their multicolored beaded Mardi Gras type masks, and draped their hoods over their heads. Carrying long black candles, they exited the front door and headed toward the van.

The ceremony took place in an old shack on the property, where field hands of the previous owners once lived. It remained abandoned until Paulette discovered several years ago that it had a cellar underneath. Artifacts found there hinted that it could have been a stop on the Underground Railroad for escaped slaves.

After some clean up and added appropriate decorations, the women couldn't think of a more fitting place for the induction ceremony and it had been used for that purpose ever since. Not even Paulette's husband knew about the place, since they only performed the inductions when he traveled.

The shack stood forty yards from the house. Sanja opened the back door to the van and silently ushered the naked inductees out one-by-one. No one uttered a word.

Once they were all in line, she untied them and removed their hoods, keeping the blindfolds intact. The rain mist formed on their shivering skin. Sanja placed each woman's right hand on the shoulder of the person in front of her. She put the lead person's right hand on her own shoulder. Paulette led the parade, followed by Charity, Nia, Sanja, and the potential candidates.

With the first step, the mzingo zima began a low, rhythmic chant as the candle procession to the shack began.

"Mie ni muradi sisi ni wa muradi sisi ni mie ni. Kodi yetu salasila kaa daima imara."

I am because we are and because we are I am. Let our chain be forever strong.

45

Montgomery and Donnie's long and arduous hike through the wooded area of the Aventis property continued. The stop, look, and listen routine wore on Montgomery about thirty minutes in. He wanted to just sprint past Donnie to the end of the journey, but he stayed with it.

Donnie's energy level seemed heightened with every step as they closed in on the gravel road at the edge of the tree grove. Both of their hearts pounded like a ceremonial tom tom from the adrenaline.

Seeing the light from the main house in the distance, Donnie waved Montgomery up to join him. Dropping to their bellies, they crawled slowly until they reached a service road. The main house stood about one hundred yards directly in front of them.

Donnie put on his night vision goggles to make sure of the images he thought he saw. They looked at each other. Then they turned again to the line of naked women, slowly marching behind the four caped formless images in black. Neither of them could make out the utterances coming from the parade.

Smiling to himself, Montgomery whispered, "Some freaky shit, man."

"Yeah, I don't know what you got me into Doc, but I think I might like it."

"I wouldn't take my pants off just yet."

"I hate to miss the show, but I'm going to try to take a closer look around the house. Keep an eye on them Monty. I'll be back." Before Montgomery could object, Donnie crawled backwards into the dark woods and disappeared, looking for another alley of darkness to navigate closer.

Montgomery stayed at his post and tried to remain quiet. The group veered left and slightly faced him at a southwestern angle. The garden lights along the pathway provided a clearer view, so he abandoned the night goggles.

To get a closer look, he slowly reached into one of the pockets of his vest and pulled out the binoculars. Removing his glasses, he put the binoculars to his eyes and adjusted the focus.

Montgomery could see the leader of the clan moving slowly in the direction of the old shack. Covered in the hooded robe, he couldn't make much of the person. He assumed it was a female. Was it Nia? The person looked taller from the distance, but he couldn't be sure. The other hooded figures were just as mysterious. The mumbling of the chant was cadenced with each step as the blindfolded trio that followed tried desperately to keep up.

Adjusting the focus, he zoomed into the naked women. They were in order of height. The first was slender with a thin neck, and long hair that hung to her shoulders, which sloped like a hanger. Her curveless body looked almost boyish. Montgomery found her totally unappealing and moved to the next one.

Number two was plump and had the hardest time following the rhythm of the chant. As she stumbled the rolls on her belly jiggled. The rain drops formed a glistening on her brown body that made her look like a glazed Thanksgiving turkey.

Moving on to the last woman, as Montgomery slowly turned the wheel to focus, he felt a chill. Something about her seemed familiar, even through the limited light. He pulled down the binoculars, wiped them with the sleeve of his shirt and looked again.

The woman had ample breasts and a small waist that flowed seamlessly into a nice pear shaped ass.

"Don't I know you?" He whispered.

Slowly moving from the waistline up to the face, he zoomed in more. She had a grimace, a sense of controlled fright. As she stumbled slightly, she clenched her teeth.

The gap, he thought.

"Fuck, that's Carmen!" Montgomery covered his mouth, thinking he had spoken loud enough for them to hear. Looking again, he concluded they heard nothing as the procession continued. And he was sure it was Carmen. He'd had his hands on that body too many times to mistake it.

He quickly reached into his vest and pulled out the 220x day/night camera. He zoomed in on the line and snapped a picture. According to Donnie it automatically switched from color to black and white in low light conditions so he didn't expect high quality. But any picture might prove helpful. He zoomed in on each individual person and took a snapshot. He took three of Carmen.

Montgomery put the camera back in his vest, picked up the binoculars and stayed on lady number three until they all disappeared into the old shack.

"Holy shit," Montgomery whispered to himself. "Carmen what are you doing here?"

He noticed through the dilapidated boards of the structure that the light from the candles disappeared. Total darkness encased the building.

Montgomery stood and began to move slowly toward the shack, using what he learned from Donnie. *Stay in the shadows, move slowly, stop, look, and listen,* he thought. After a few starts and stops, his eagerness took over and he jogged to the building and pressed his back against it.

The shack looked about fifty feet square and obviously built long ago. A wood framed door that barely hung from the hinges provided the only entrance. Two small windows on the front and one on the back provided the only view from the outside. Evidently little maintenance had been done over the years as boards and planks hung loosely from the structure in every direction.

Montgomery moved around the perimeter until he found a broken window on the back. A black plastic bag covered it.

He pressed his ear against it and listened. Not a sound. After ten minutes, he noticed some muttering coming from inside the shack but he couldn't decipher the sounds.

Reaching into another vest pocket, he pulled out his knife and carefully cut a small hole in the bag. Peering through, he saw nothing but complete darkness.

Again, he put on the night vision goggles. A few busted bags of dirt and some old rusted tools littered the otherwise empty shack, along with small amounts of debris scattered across the floor.

Montgomery stood on his toes and tried to look around. Finally he noticed an aimless flicker coming from underneath a floorboard in the center of the room. Then he heard some high-pitched moans, almost like sensual pleasure coming from underneath the building. Followed by soft screams, passionate yells, and more chants. For some reason, he found it humorous, but scary at the same time.

A tap on his shoulder made him jump. "I thought I told you to stay put," Donnie whispered and smiled, realizing the jolt he sent through his partner.

Montgomery exhaled, "That shit's not funny."

"Enjoying the show I see. Sounds pretty freaky. I wonder if they'd mind if we joined them."

Montgomery tried to catch his breath and make sure his pants were dry, "Yuk, Yuk."

They quietly listened for a little longer to the chanting and moaning.

"I heard it from the other side," said Donnie. "I peeked in the door and it looks like there's a panel to a lower level."

"I saw it. What did you find out at the house?"

"I got in through the back door. Nice place. No one's home so I found a computer in the office, but I couldn't access it. Had a password. It's like a museum in there so I didn't want to risk moving anything."

"So now what."

"Going inside the shack is too dangerous. I don't know what kind of alarms or traps they may have in there. So, we either stand here like peeping toms drooling on ourselves or go to plan B."

"Which is?"

"I thought you would know."

More muffled screeching and groaning came from the floor. A female voice yelled something that sounded like a foreign language neither Montgomery nor Donnie recognized. The cold rain started to come down harder and since they weren't moving, it made Montgomery shudder a bit. He looked down at his feet and shook his head, trying to think.

"What time is it, about one o'clock?" said Montgomery.

"Almost."

"Lets get out of here and regroup before they come out. We'll come up with something. We can return here later if we have to. I got some pictures that may come in handy."

"Sounds good to me. I'll need my own personal copy of course."

Montgomery managed a smile. It had been a long day and his drained body told him it was time to punch out.

Donnie patted Montgomery on the back, "Maybe we should make an appointment next time. I want to get some of whatever is going on in the underground pleasure palace."

They crouched, back away from the shack, and headed into the darkness of the woods back towards the car.

On the ride home, they talked about the whole mission and tossed around some ideas. First, they had to talk to Gene and try to penetrate the program. Montgomery never mentioned anything about Carmen, but in between their conversations, hundreds of burning questions filled his head. He wished he could write them down. Eventually, he lost all consciousness as his heavy eyelids shut slowly. The next thing he heard was Donnie telling him to wake up, he was home.

46

The first thought that came to Montgomery Quinn's mind Thursday morning was Eliza. He stared at the ceiling from the bed and wondered what she was doing that moment.

His thoughts then shifted to the naked image of Carmen, in the mysterious ceremonial rite he witnessed the night before. A combination of humor and eroticism made him smile as he imagined what went on in the shack cellar. Carmen's involvement concerned him. The primary question was: why was she there and how did she become connected with Njama?

Montgomery didn't want to believe that Carmen had something to do with the pictures sent to Gabrielle. Yet, the coincidences were too great to ignore. But why would she set him up? The questions kept coming, but no answers followed.

Montgomery was determined, however, to find those answers at any cost. Njama, Carmen, or whoever stood in his way had better be prepared. He planned to go down fighting.

It was a little after nine. Montgomery rolled out of bed and shuffled down the hall to the office. He looked out over the wet street, as the sun tried unsuccessfully to break through the clouds. In the spot that usually kept his BMW sat an old tan Chevy Blazer. He missed his car more than he wanted to admit.

Montgomery had no classes scheduled, but he and Donnie

agreed to meet in the afternoon. Donnie had some commitments to fulfill with some other professors and Gene wouldn't get off work until four. After that they planned to play around with the hacking program.

Settling into the desk chair, Montgomery logged on to his email. A message from *Nashiha Msiri* popped up first. He quickly double clicked on it.

To his surprise, the email began a detailed instruction of the hacking plan for Njama. It told about ECPI, the banking transactions they performed and how Njama planned to intercept the transactions and move them to other accounts. This was to occur before midnight Friday. The message ended by saying,

Montgomery, I will help you get your life back. But you must use this information and your intelligence to stop this plan. I will be in touch with more so stay tuned.

Montgomery couldn't believe his eyes. His "friend and confidant" came through again. He'd tossed and turned all night trying to figure out a way to fight these women and now an angel had given him the answers he needed. This person provided more than enough information at just the right time. He believed the identity of the person would probably never be revealed. But whoever it was, he owed a debt of gratitude.

He picked up the phone and called Donnie. When he answered, Montgomery couldn't contain his excitement. "Yo man, we got a plan," he said.

"And what might that be," asked Donnie, still trying to wake up.

He told Donnie about the email, the program, and the deadline.

"Are you sure we can trust this information," asked Donnie. "Who sent it?"

"I don't know, but I have a hunch that it's someone who really wants to help me."

"I'm not big on hunches. I prefer something more tangible."

"Well, I would too. But this is all I've got so I have to believe in it."

After a brief silence, Donnie said, "I'll talk to Gene. Maybe we can figure out something. He's made pretty good progress on dissecting the program."

"Good, let me know soon. We don't have much time."

"Doc, you better be right on this one."

"I don't have many options left. I have to trust and believe in this message."

"Stay by the phone, I'll get back to you." Donnie hung up.

Montgomery perched himself by the window looking out at the space left by the Chevy Blazer. *His* space, the one for *his* BMW now sat empty. As it should be, he thought.

He had a lot of calls to make to straighten out the financial mess. He was now certain Njama was behind it all. The car, his bank account, the research grant, the pictures to Gabrielle, the IRS, all of it had to be set up by them. They were powerful and connected, but he had some help coming from the right places so he felt some relief.

Montgomery picked up the phone and dialed Gabrielle's cell phone. A moment of anxiety took over his body and his leg shook uncontrollably. Her voice mail came on. He had no idea what to say, but he needed to hear her voice.

"Hey baby. I hope we can talk today. I... uh... I plan on doing everything in my power to prove my love for you and make this right. I know I've screwed up but like I told you yesterday, what you saw is not what it appears. By tomorrow I will show you, I promise." He paused. "Anyway, kiss Eliza and call me if you want to talk. Bye love."

Montgomery had no idea how he would prove to Gabrielle this fantastic story of a secret group of women out to get him, but he hoped something would provide proof. He looked over at the pile of clothes and equipment from the night mission. Pulling out the camera, he flipped through the images on the digital display.

Since Carmen in some way contributed to his problem, she needed to contribute to the solution. She needed to help him make this right with Gabrielle. He picked up his cell phone, leaned back in the chair, and searched through the calls he'd received over the last few days. Locating her cell phone number, he pressed the send button.

After several rings the voice mail came on and he hung up. He wanted a live voice and he planned to keep calling until he got one.

47

The muffle of a familiar sound brought Carmen Underwood from a deep unconsciousness. But it wasn't enough to help her open her eyes, even though she wanted too, desperately. Her head pounded and her limbs felt stiff and tingled, resulting from a dose of the drug Rohypnol, also known as a date rape drug.

The sound eventually went away.

She felt a rush of confusing thoughts, but her memory had huge gaps. Lying on her back, eyes still closed, images of the Njama induction ceremony were fleeting. The chanting replayed vividly in her head.

"Mie ni muradi sisi ni wa muradi sisi ni mie ni. Kodi yetu salasila kaa daima imara."

What did it mean? She needed to decipher the chant. It wouldn't leave her mind, like a commercial jingle that played over and over in your mind after the first time you hear it.

She recounted the vivid image of the robed leaders standing over her in a wooden box on the floor. The dank, musty smell of the dungeon still lingered in her nostrils.

Carmen recalled the candlelight casting shadows of the distorted images on the concrete walls. Her fellow inductees were stretched out next to her, but she couldn't see them over the high walls of the boxes. She assumed they were in similar positions with the same limited perspective.

The ceremony was intense and awkward, even embarrassing at times. She remembered clearly taking an oath of allegiance to the causes of Njama. She remembered sitting in a semi circle on the cold concrete floor, listening to the history of the sect and their purpose. She even remembered being forced to lie on her back and masturbate, while telling of her most intimate sexual encounters. But she had holes in her recollection.

The ceremony lasted at least two hours, maybe more. Carmen doubted that these actions held any significant purpose, but she went along. In her research into secret societies, she came across all kinds of ceremonies intended to bring members closer. Some thought that putting candidates in embarrassing situations tended to make a person more committed to the organization.

Forcing you to let go and strip away all pretenses, to bare your soul to your sisters, makes for a stronger bond. But who wants their sex life on display, particularly if it falls a little on the outrageous side, as Carmen's did. But she had to go along so she did.

Most of the ceremony made little sense, but they were promised it would become clearer after the indoctrination. They had more tests and more ceremonies to come.

She recalled kneeling and drinking a glass of wine, while one of the women caressed her body with a feather and chanted in what she assumed was Swahili.

"Mie ni muradi sisi ni wa muradi sisi ni mie ni. Kodi yetu salasila kaa daima imara."

After that, everything else vanished from her memory bank, and she slowly became unconscious.

Several moments later, she heard that sound again. This time she recognized it as the cell phone tone in her purse. She managed to open her eyes, barely. The hazy surroundings looked like a hotel room, but she had no idea which one or how she got there.

Carmen sat straight up in her bed, but the pounding of her head forced her to lie back down. The ringing stopped again.

She realized she was still naked. Slowly reaching over, she

picked up the phone on the night stand and looked at the words. It read Red Roof Inn, Laurel, Maryland.

The other queen-sized bed had the clothes she wore the night before, folded neatly in a pile. Her purse sat next to it along with her shoes. On the clothes pile were the keys to a room in the Washington Marriott hotel where she was staying.

Moments later, the phone rang again and she pulled herself up, slowly this time, and rummaged through her purse. She flipped up the cell phone and placed it to her ear.

"Hello?" Her voice sounded hoarse and groggy.

"You're a hard person to catch up with. Had a late night huh?"

"Who is this?"

"It's Monty. You're getting too old to be hanging out all night girl."

It took a while to get her thoughts together. Slowly, the words came, "Hey Monty, I'm glad you called. I really want to talk to you about the other day."

"Yeah, I need to talk to you too. Sorry for how I acted the other day, but my life is all screwed up because of those pictures."

"I'm really sorry Monty."

"Me too. You really sound like shit. Are you okay?

"I'm fine, just a little hung over?" That's what she hoped, but she couldn't be sure. At least that's what it felt like.

"We need to talk. What are you doing for dinner?"

"Uh...I'm free, I think."

"Okay, meet me at the Cheesecake Factory on Wisconsin Avenue. Five o'clock. You know how to get there?"

"I'll find it. Be there at five."

They both hung up and Carmen threw the phone on the bed, placed her elbows on her knees, and massaged her temples. Inhaling deeply, the mix of cigarette smoke embedded in the blanket and mildew carpet turned her stomach. She just wanted to get the pounding and swirling in her head to stop and figure out where she was and how to get back to D.C.

Looking at the clothes pile, she noticed a small pin attached to her blouse. She picked it up and looked at the symbol.

Smiling, she realized that she had become an official member of Njama.

48

Montgomery needed to gather evidence to support his story. He remembered that Jovan got the GPS from a website specializing in spy paraphernalia but he didn't have time to wait for an order in the mail. Looking through the phone book before he left home, he found a spy store on Connecticut Avenue. Not sure what to expect, he thought it was worth a visit.

Phone calls all morning brought no progress on the car or the bank. So having little money Montgomery caught the subway to meet Carmen. The spy store was on the way.

Once he arrived at the small shop, he looked around at the array of gadgets on display. The proprietor, Phil, shuffled over and asked if he could help. He looked like a worn down biker, about fifty years old. He had a goatee with specks of gray and a spike pierced in his nose. Tattoos covered every inch of both arms, which drooped from his sleeveless shirt. The one of the red-eyed skull smoking a joint looked particularly menacing.

"Have anything that would allow me to secretly tape conversations?" Montgomery asked, trying to keep his nerves in check.

Initially, the tall, slender Phil ran through the company line about the legality of "unauthorized eavesdropping and/or surreptitious audio interception." He sounded like an ex-cop, which didn't match his appearance. Montgomery assured Phil that his intentions were legal. He was just curious about the technology. Phil smiled like he had heard it all before.

He obviously had to say this to all patrons, a sort of policy for spy stores or something. But they both knew he was selling whatever the customer wanted regardless of the application. He began to show Montgomery an assortment of listening devices.

The technology fascinated Montgomery and he could have spent hours playing with the crystal controlled wireless in-ear micro-mini receivers and the hand held wireless video recorder for mobile surveillance. Phil knew how best to use them all and gave vivid examples of how his customers used them in a variety of stakeouts and traps. Apparently, suspicious married couples made the spy business thrive.

Montgomery decided on the pen microphone with built-in noise filter and amplifier. Simple but effective. Phil ran down the specifications fluidly, like he'd sold hundreds of them. Up to forty-foot range, quality audio, and looks just like a ballpoint pen. The pen even worked.

With that he had to purchase the voice activated micro-bar digital voice recorder. Twenty-two hours of digital recording, sixty-four megabytes of flash memory, MP3 player, PC compatible, the list went on and on.

Total cost three hundred and fifty seven dollars. Montgomery wrote a check hoping to get his accounts straightened out before Phil decided to cash it. More importantly, he didn't want Phil coming after him to collect if it bounced. Phil's friends were probably less subtle about destroying him than Njama.

Phil wished him luck and Montgomery headed on his way. Walking back to the metro, he pulled up the collar on his sports jacket and sloshed through the puddles as the clouds smothered the city. A typical April in Washington, with rain expected to continue throughout the day. Of course, he left his only umbrella in the BMW and buying another one didn't fit the current budget.

The Marvin Gaye tune tickled his waistline. The cell phone display read "Grandma." A broad smile overtook his face and his eyes widened.

"Grandma?" he answered.

"Hey baby. I wondered if you'd forgotten about your old grandmother. I haven't talked to you since last Sunday."

"I know. I'm sorry, it's a long story Grandma."

"Everything alright down there? You don't sound too good honey."

"Well, no. My life is a wreck right now."

"Don't think I've ever heard this kind of despair in your voice. Am I gonna have to drive down there from Howard County to take care of you? You know I'm here for you Monty. You can tell me anything."

"I planned on it Grandma. Time just got away from me." Montgomery went on to tell Lila Armstrong the condensed version of his week as he walked: Jovan giving him the thumb drive and the accident, Nia's behavior, the meeting with Dr. Kelly about Njama, Gabrielle leaving him because of the pictures, the attack on his finances, car towed, research grant lost.

As much as he could recall, he quickly told Lila the whole story. He knew she would understand and not judge him in any way.

Montgomery reached the metro station and stood at the top of the escalator to finish his story. He hadn't given Lila the opportunity to say anything. She let him talk without saying a word. Montgomery felt relieved and grateful just to get it all off his chest without interruption.

Passersby stared as he expressly used his hands to display the craziness of the events. He moved under the awning of a nearby drug store to prevent getting further soaked.

A homeless man stood in front of him and stared, holding out his hands for some change. Montgomery looked at him angrily, shrugged his shoulders and turned his back to continue talking.

"God bless you sir," the man said, and he moved on.

Lila listened without saying a word until he finished. "I know this sounds very bizarre Grandma, but I'm working on fixing all of this."

"It all sounds awful Monty. You need a lot of help. You can't do this alone. I wish you had called me."

"I'm on it Grandma. I'm not down yet, you know me. I'll get revenge."

"You still plan to make it to our date don't you?"

"Miss your birthday? Nothing would keep me from that."

"I'm worried about you baby. I wish there was something I could do. Please promise to call me if you need anything."

"I promise."

"I'll be checking back to make sure you're okay."

"I love you Grandma. I'll keep you posted."

"Bye baby. And be careful."

It felt good to tell someone about this absurdity. Montgomery got on the escalator down to the subway platform to meet Carmen. He would figure out how to use his spy devices on the way there.

49

The Cheesecake Factory buzzed with chatter from the patrons. Waiters scurrying with meals on trays, and clapping of utensils and pots from the kitchen, added to the ambience of the restaurant. Carmen had arrived early and secured a booth near a window, overlooking the Mazza Gallery mall across Wisconsin Avenue.

Montgomery walked in, dripping from the sudden downpour that caught him as he walked from the metro. He noticed Carmen as he reached the top of the spiral staircase to the second floor. She sat with her hair pulled back, dark glasses, and a red spaghetti strapped tank top with a plunging neckline.

She smiled as he approached. "You're late."

"I'd say you look ravishing, but I would be lying." He managed a smile as he sat in the booth. "I don't even want to ask about your night?"

"It was a long one, you know how it is?" said Carmen.

"I used to know. Been a long time since I rolled that hard."

"God, what happened to your eye?"

"I got caught standing in front of a straight right from an angry woman."

Although not looking her best, Carmen still stood out in a room full of fashionably dressed professional women. Montgomery's eyes darted from her eyes to her cleavage. She had a spell on him, but he had business to take care of that required total focus.

With her perfectly manicured nails, she tapped him on the wrist.

"Do my shades bother you? Somehow you seem to have trouble looking me in the eye." She giggled and removed them, setting the shades on the table. A small hint of makeup covered the dark circles, but her bloodshot eyes diminished her appeal. Montgomery sensed sluggishness in her mental functions. She seemed to move in slow motion.

The waiter came over and took their drink orders, an apple martini for Carmen and a crème soda for Montgomery. As they looked at the menu, Montgomery broke an awkward moment of silence.

"So Carmen, I have to ask you honestly. Did you have anything to do with those pictures sent to my wife?"

Montgomery looked at her for any sign of dishonesty. Twitching of the eye, jittery hands, trembling lips, anything that would give her away.

The pen was in his jacket pocket and ready to record.

"Absolutely not Monty! You know I would never do that to you."

The wrinkles on her forehead, the puppy dog look, and direct eye contact made him think she could be telling the truth. He sensed sincerity. But he had more questions.

"It all seems so coincidental don't you think. We run into each other out of the blue, meet for lunch, you kiss me and someone happens to take our picture."

"I know, but I think I can explain."

"I need more than an explanation at this point Carmen. My wife is gone, with my daughter. I sincerely need you to help me make this right."

The waiter returned with the drinks and took their dinner order. Montgomery told him to come back because neither of them had an appetite at the moment. Carmen looked down and stirred her drink, avoiding Montgomery's intense glare. He waited for a response.

"Well?" Hints of impatience resonated in his voice.

"Monty, I'll confess something to you, but you can't repeat

this to anyone." She looked up waiting for some assurance. He nodded slightly, never intending to keep that promise.

"Before you do, let me show you something."

He learned from poker that keeping competitors off balance usually worked in his favor. His favorite trick was asking his friends about their wives after they had been fighting. They made more mistakes or lost their focus if he diverted their attention or annoyed them with little things.

In this case, he wanted to maintain control of the conversation to ensure that he got what he needed. Clearly, Carmen had demonstrated up to that point that she had no interest in helping.

He reached in his jacket pocket and pulled out the pictures taken from the night before and placed them in front of her. The images weren't crystal clear, but they were enough to convince Carmen that he had witnessed the event.

She looked like someone had just hit her with a taser gun. She opened her mouth but nothing came out. The photos were spread out on the table in front of her as she stared in disbelief. She examined each photo one at a time. Finally, she whispered, "Where did you get these?"

"I know all about Njama. These bitches are trying to destroy my life because I stumbled on a little software program they want back. Based on this you're connected to them, right? So if we're being honest, let's be completely honest."

Exhaling like she had been holding her breath for ten minutes, Carmen said, "You were there?"

"Yes."

"Monty, I have a lot to tell you. But let me start by saying you need to be extremely careful."

"I can handle myself, don't worry." Although he wasn't completely convinced of that, it sounded good when it left his lips.

"Okay," Carmen said. "Yes that's me in the picture. I was inducted into Njama last night. But I had nothing to do with the pictures they sent your wife."

"How can I believe you Carm?"

"Listen, I've been trying to get into this organization for a while now. There were certain tests we had to do to prove ourselves worthy. So a secured email message went out to potential candidates for volunteers to get close to you. When I saw your name I was floored. I had no idea why they wanted you followed but I volunteered for the mission. I didn't think they were trying to trap you. And I didn't know we were being followed by anyone."

"So you were not here for a conference?"

"No."

"You came here just to rekindle old times and ruin me at the same time."

"Honestly, that was not my intent. I was just as surprised as you when I found out about the pictures. But I couldn't do anything about it at that point. I came for the induction ceremony and needed to go through it."

"You needed to do it?"

"Yeah Monty, I did. There's more about me you need to know."

"Go ahead," he said. "I'm sure nothing else could blow me away at this point." Carmen drank the last of her martini and looked directly at Montgomery.

"I work for the Secret Service."

Now that did blow him away.

50

After the initial shock, Montgomery Quinn sat back in his seat and listened, and recorded.

Carmen Underwood had spent the last three years working for the Financial Crimes Division of the Secret Service, as an electronic crimes special agent. The FBI got a tip from an anonymous source that this secret society, Njama, had executed fraudulent electronic funds transfers and planned to illegally access bank records for money laundering.

They knew little about Njama, so in collaboration with the FBI, Carmen infiltrated the organization to investigate the claims. She met all of the criteria of the perfect candidate: a black woman, highly intelligent, and trained in a high tech field. She just needed an invitation and patience would make her mission a reality.

That invite had come about five months earlier and provided the opportunity the Secret Service needed. At that time Carmen went to work for a wireless company in Connecticut and Njama found her after she spoke at a high tech conference in Washington. For the past two months, she'd been doing little assignments for Njama to prove her merit.

However, the infiltration became more difficult than the government originally thought. Njama's connections in the investigative community always kept them one step ahead of the authorities. The Secret Service took great care to keep Carmen distant from any government operations. Surprisingly, they never suspected her.

As far as she knew, Carmen became the only investigator to

get close to the inside, but she still had no idea of the leader's identity. And she knew even less about their operation. They carefully kept everything secret, apparently better than the government itself.

The government had hoped to get some insight from the induction ceremony. But during the whirlwind trip to the Aventis estate the agents following Carmen lost the trail. Rumors about the naked initiation prevented Carmen from wearing any type of bugging devices. She didn't want to risk jeopardizing the operation. So they uncovered no new information other than what Carmen's fuzzy memory could provide.

By the time the food came, Montgomery's felt queasy. Just when he thought he'd heard and seen it all this week, the story just kept getting more bizarre. He doubted Gabrielle would believe this new wrinkle. She might think he had set this all up to help support his story. *But who could make this stuff up?* he thought.

The questions flooded his brain. Twirling the fork in his Thai chicken pasta, he jumped in while Carmen took a break from her story to eat.

"You know this is all very hard to believe, Carm. You, of all people, with the Secret Service."

Carmen smiled and tilted her head back, dabbing the corners of her mouth with a napkin. "I know, but I told you I'm not a nine to five type person. I needed some excitement in my work and this certainly provides it."

"So let me get this straight. You only found me because Njama sent you, right. So do your bosses know about me?"

"In other words are you being investigated?" She laughed and sipped her water. "Well, we had a feeling there was some reason they wanted me on you. Truthfully, I was recording us at lunch. But again, we had nothing to do with the pictures. We have also monitored some of your accounts and noticed some unusual transactions."

"Unusual? They've fucked my whole life up."

"We figured as much. You must have really pissed then

off." She shrugged nonchalantly and continued eating.

"So why didn't you stop it then."

"We didn't want to jeopardize the investigation. This is much larger than just you Monty."

"Oh really? Tell Gabrielle that," he said. "And while you're at it, explain to GW about my grant, the mortgage and car finance company about my payments, the bank about my pay check --"

"We'll straighten it all out."

"When?"

"I can't say just yet, but soon. We're getting closer, we just need a lucky break."

Somehow Carmen's southern charm had turned to stern government investigator and Montgomery didn't notice when the transformation occurred. Even more, he knew he didn't like what he saw or felt at that moment.

"I will tell you one thing Monty."

"What's that?"

"The kiss I gave you, that was real." She smiled and winked, trying to use her charm. This time, he found it much less appealing.

Nevertheless, the comment caught him off guard and Montgomery almost choked on a piece of chicken.

I have to remember to erase that part from the tape, he told himself.

"Carmen, I need your help here, and it doesn't look like I'm gonna get it."

She reached over and touched his hand. Her soft hands sent a chill up his wrist straight to the crown of his head. Looking around, not sure if more pictures were being taken, he recoiled.

"Monty," she said, "Trust me, I got your back."

The glistening smile left some reassurance that things would be fixed. But when and how?

She returned to her pasta Milanese.

"By the way, if you can think of anything at all that could help us, we'll listen. For instance if you were really at that ceremony last night, you could tell me where it took place. As you can see by my appearance today, I was a little incapacitated."

Montgomery felt a sense of dread. He knew how the government operated from all of his friends working in various agencies. These kinds of things could take years to resolve and his life's losses were certainly not at the top of their priority list. He now knew that if he wanted immediate results he had to make a move quickly. Considering that, he also didn't want to give up too much control of what he did know.

"I'll get back to you on that."

"Your choice Monty. The more you can help us, the faster we can get to the bottom of this."

She paused to take a sip of water. "Another thing," Carmen said, "you never did tell me why they were after you in the first place."

"I'll get back to you on that too."

Carmen shrugged and they both finished their meals in silence. Montgomery looked out the window at people scurrying on the sidewalk below trying to keep dry as the intensity of the rain picked up. The street lights flickered as the darkness set on the business corridor. It was getting late and in Montgomery's mind, there wasn't much left to talk about. He needed to get home and see what he had on tape and determine what he would do next.

"One more thing Carmen."

"Anything you need Monty."

"I know I invited you on this date, and normally I would pay. But under the circumstances, I trust the government can cover this meal, right?"

"Sure thing Monty."

"Cool, lets look at the cheesecake menu then."

51

Friday morning brought back the sunshine and Gabrielle Quinn had taken the day off hoping to relax. She'd worked some long hours on a difficult tax case for one of her clients. April brings out all kinds of tax issues, and most of the clients are so terrified of the IRS they want instant resolution.

Working long hours provided some distraction from the pictures of Montgomery kissing Carmen. The vivid imprints in her mind made it seem like she was standing there watching the two herself.

Her mother had stepped in to help with picking up and watching Eliza the last few days. To thank her, Gabrielle planned to take her out for a day at the spa. Just the two of them.

But first she had to run some errands.

She walked out to her Lexus parked on the street in front of her parents home, hit the remote control, and jumped in. On the seat, she noticed a manila envelope with her name on it. She recognized the handwriting as Montgomery's.

Gabrielle sat and stared at the envelope contemplating whether to open it. Strong memories of their life together flashed before her. She replayed the trip almost two years ago to the Poconos Mountain in Pennsylvania for their anniversary.

It was the best vacation they'd had in years. He picked her up from work and, before she knew it, he headed north on the interstate. He never told her the final destination.

"Enjoy the ride and trust me," was all he said. They eventually pulled up into the Caesar's resort property, tucked away on acres of wooded land at the foot of the mountain.

Montgomery had reserved a room with the tall champagne glass tub and the heart shaped bed. They went horseback riding, played horseshoes, and fished. He even showed her how to play golf on a small course near the resort. They spent most of the weekend alone. No interruptions.

They even participated in a version of the Newlywed Game at the resort's theater show. They won the first place prize, a gold cup and tickets to a Broadway show. The cup still sat on the fireplace mantle. They had planned to use the tickets when Gabrielle felt more comfortable leaving Eliza with her grandparents for a weekend. Their anniversary coming up in July would have been perfect.

In the room, they took bubble baths in the champagne glass, watched movies, drank wine, and made love more than she could count. She remembered it as the best, most romantic time she had ever had. Eliza was likely conceived that weekend, adding to the pleasurable memories.

Gabrielle gazed out into the vast trees of Rock Creek Park. Her emotions ran the gamut of hurt, fear, and anger, everything but joy and happiness.

Then she stared at the envelope again.

She had no doubt that Montgomery loved her. None whatsoever. But the fact still remained that he kissed another woman. And she had no clue what else happened that day. Could he be trusted to tell the truth? And if he hadn't been caught on film, would he have ever admitted it at all.

His stories had become so outlandish that she didn't know what to believe anymore. Montgomery seemed to spin more and more tails trying to cover-up his infidelity.

Her chest ached, hands tingled, and her breaths began to shorten.

She gingerly reached over and opened the envelope. It contained a letter and a CD. Unfolding the letter, she read it:

Hey baby, I miss you so much. I know I blew it and I will spend the rest of my life making it up to you, if you let me. I never meant to hurt you and I need you to believe me more than anything. Please listen to the CD. It will help support everything I told you. If you find enough love in your heart to forgive me after you hear it, please call me. I'll be waiting.

Yours in passion forever, Montgomery.

Before she could finish, tear stains had covered the letter and the ink began to smear in places. She reached into the envelope and took out the CD. Turning on the ignition, she inserted it and waited.

The background sounded noisy and somewhat muffled, but then the voices started. It was Montgomery and Carmen from the dinner the night before at the Cheesecake Factory.

Gabrielle sat and listened intently to every word. Hoping, praying for something, anything that would allow her to forgive her husband.

52

Donnie Centronelli picked up Montgomery early Friday morning. Montgomery made some progress getting his car back, in as much as the finance company finally admitted there must have been a computer error. He had taken his canceled checks to the offices to prove he had made the payments. That helped his case.

They agreed to release the car pending further investigation. But he still had to pay the tow company two hundred and fifty dollars for hookup and storage costs. He would challenge that issue later.

In the meantime, his bank still had a hold on his account, also pending investigation. He had no money and no way to get any. So the BMW sat at the lot.

Donnie did share some good news. Gene Yow had dissected the program logic and knew exactly how it worked. He also removed a tracer program hidden in the code that sent a message to Nia Givens whenever someone other than her opened it.

That's how she knew Montgomery had the program, and how the thugs found Billy and Gene.

According to the email Montgomery received earlier, this was the night. Njama had planned to hack into ECPI's system and intercept the banking transactions. Montgomery hoped they had enough information to do something about it. And he also finally had a plan.

It wasn't quite a concrete plan, but it got firmer every moment. He kept it to himself, for now.

Donnie and Montgomery would meet with Gene to discuss their options. After dropping off the envelope at Gabrielle's car, they visited Jovan together. He looked much better. The swelling in his face had subsided somewhat and the bruises were healing. He still remained unconscious and connected to the machines.

Surprisingly, Montgomery hadn't run into Nia all week at the hospital. He knew she had been there, based on discussions with Jovan's mother, but somehow they kept missing each other.

This pleased him, because he had no clue what he would say if they did meet. The day they would confront each other may come soon though, and he knew it. He also knew the temptation to slap her would be hard to resist.

They made it to the office just in time for Montgomery's ten o'clock class. It had been probably his worst performance as a professor. Even though he'd taught the class dozens of times, he forgot formulas, mixed up theories, stumbled over his words, and lost his train of thought, more than once.

After class ended, he sat in his office and just stared into the hall, trying not to beat himself up too much about the lecture. Montgomery wondered if the students noticed his lapses. Surely they did, but he hoped they allowed him one day to be off his game. *They were probably just happy I didn't assign any homework for the weekend*, he thought.

Back to the phone. More calls to make, more cases to present. Just as he reached for the receiver, the phone rang. He picked it.

"Hello, this is Dr. Quinn"

"I just listened to your CD," the voice said softly.

He stood up and closed his office door, "Gabrielle?"

"Yes."

The words didn't come. He wanted to say something, anything but he didn't know what to say. He feared hurting her more. So he sat, waiting for her to say something. He could hear birds chirping in the background, but she said nothing.

Finally, she began slowly. "Monty, I listened to the CD. If

this is all true, what are you going to do?"

"I don't know yet baby. I'm working on it. I just wanted you to know that... I mean... I don't know what to say. I'm just sorry I fell into this mess."

"How can I help?"

"Well, I hadn't thought about it," he said. "Thanks for the offer."

They spent a moment talking about Eliza, Jovan, and catching up on the last few days.

A sense of relief swarmed his body. She never said it, but he felt like she had forgiven him. Although he knew he had a lot of making up to do, this was progress. And progress was good.

"Monty?"

"Yes?

"You kissed another woman and it's going to take some time for me to get over that."

"I know baby, but –."

"Let me finish please."

Montgomery shut up immediately. He didn't want to risk the progress they had already made.

"You said that was as far as it went and I want to believe you."

"It was Gabrielle, I swear."

"Fine, but you owe me. I never want this to happen again."

"You have my word baby. I thought I'd lost you and I hated that feeling. I never want to be in this position again."

"Good, because I'd hate to have to kill this bitch."

Montgomery smiled and said, "I love you so much."

"I love you too, Monty."

Montgomery paused. "There is one more thing, Gab."

"What is it?"

"I hate to ask, but remember when you offered to help?"

"Yes?" Gabrielle said, slowly.

"Well, can I get two hundred and fifty dollars from you. You see my car –"

"I don't need to hear anymore stories Monty. I'll be right there to pick you up."

212

53

They huddled around the computer, three of the four mzingo zima, staring, and waiting. Sanja Coston's insider from ECPI had informed her that the last transaction before the cutover to the new software would occur around eleven o'clock. It was five after nine.

Paulette Aventis' office was still and dark, except for the light from the computer that reflected on all of their faces. Nia Givens tapped rhythmically at the keyboard like a classical pianist playing a complex Mozart. Paulette and Sanja sat like mannequins and watched the cryptic characters fly across the screen unaware of what any of it meant.

They waited for the precise moment to strike.

"Patience, we need to find just the right set of transactions," whispered Nia to herself.

The program intercepted wire transfers flowing from the ECPI system to any bank in the U.S. Nia figured the fewer numbers of transactions they captured, the less likely anyone would notice them inside. Which meant going for the large dollar amounts to make their effort worth anything. It would also have the largest negative impact on the ECPI when word got out about the invasion.

Nia scanned the system, looking, waiting, and tickling the keyboard. Two hours before cut over.

"We don't have much time left," said Sanja nervously.

Nia never looked up. The only indication that she knew anyone else in the room existed was when she rolled her eyes at Sanja.

"We have plenty," she said.

54

onnie had taken Montgomery to a desolate warehouse in the back of a business park in Arlington, Virginia. They had planned to meet Gene Yow to prepare for their operation.

The full moon bursting through the clouds provided the only light on the dingy parking lot. Montgomery noticed its unusual brightness, but welcomed it. It reminded him of the night light his mother placed in his bedroom as a child. Once the lights went out, it provided comfort, support, and warmth. He would stare at it until he fell asleep.

The parking lot made him uneasy. Too dark, too isolated, and too quiet. He stared at the moon as they parked the BMW.

Following Donnie, he approached a rear door and punched the buzzer. Seconds later the door released with a click. They entered and walked down a dark corridor, a light projected from a room in the distance. As they turned the corner, Gene stood there to greet them.

"What's up Don?" said Gene.

Gene Yow was short, thin and a little dorky looking. He wore oversized glasses and looked like a white Steve Orkel, without the suspenders. The only garment he wore that looked relatively recent were the brand new Nike sneakers.

Donnie turned and ushered Gene over for introductions. "Gene, this is our man. Montgomery Quinn."

Squinting and pushing up his glasses, he extended his hand.

"Nice to meet you Doc. You sure have a knack for making people angry."

"Unintentional I assure you. How's your brother?"

"He's fine. A little sore still, but he'll live. Come on in."

Montgomery noticed a set of black and white monitors by the door, scanning the parking lot. Gene looked down at them, checking to see if there was anyone else outside.

"Sure no one followed you?" he asked Donnie.

Donnie looked at him incredulously, as if to say *I can't believe you asked me that.*

Computer equipment filled the room. Servers took up one side of the room and rows of terminals lined another. They stepped over masses of wires, empty soda cans, and trash all over the floor. The smell of mildew wafted in the air. One other person sat in the room banging away on another computer.

As they walked, Gene pointed to the lone programmer. "That's Kid CodeX, he spends all his time trying to break the latest secret codes to access Pentagon data," said Gene.

Kid looked up suspiciously, gave a half-hearted wave and went back to his keyboard. He turned so fast that Montgomery never saw his face. As they passed, Kid's reflection served as a silhouette behind a colorful flash of characters bouncing across the screen in an almost musical cadence.

They had just entered the temple of hackers.

Donnie had told Montgomery all about the place as they circled the city trying to lose any potential followers. The warehouse served as a hide away for hackers to do their work in secure isolation. It had the latest in firewall security to minimize anyone tracing their whereabouts.

In case they were ever found, a number of exits provided escape routes from the warehouse, or at least a place to hide until the heat died down. The last location got busted and several guys hid in an underground tunnel for two days while the Feds swarmed the place looking for evidence. They confiscated all of the equipment and the group had to start from scratch. It took several months to get back up, but here they were.

The three men settled in front of a terminal at the far end of the room. Gene sat and rubbed his hands together like the villain in a B-movie.

"So we ready for some action boys?"

"What you got Gene?" asked Donnie.

"Based on what you and the Doc told me, I've been monitoring these transactions at ECPI. So far, nothing out of the ordinary. I rigged the program so I can sit here and not be detected while watching what's going on. It'll give me an audio alert if your girl does anything, so we'll know its them."

"I got an email today," said Montgomery. "It said that ECPI was moving to new software. Whatever they plan to do has to happen before eleven,"

"And what are they planning to do?"

"My source tells me they plan to intercept some large transactions, then they'll send back an acknowledgement so ECPI thinks they went through. They'll then move the money to a Swiss account."

"Smart, but not innovative. One of our guys did that before and got away with about two hundred thou. Right Kid?" Kid CodeX never responded, he just kept typing. Apparently, whatever he pursued demanded his total concentration.

"Damn," said Donnie, looking over at Montgomery.

"Yeah, he went out and bought a nice S class Mercedes before he got busted," said Gene.

"How did he get caught?" asked Montgomery.

"The idiot wasn't very good at covering his track. Plus he went into Nation's Bank. If you're gonna do something like that you have to get into one of the smaller banks. They're less likely to tell anyone they were hacked. They don't want that kind of negative press. Nation's Bank on the other hand wanted their money back."

"So what about ECPI?" asked Donnie.

"They're not a bank. They just move money around for the banks. It would be pretty embarrassing for them if their clients realize their security is shitty. So I doubt they would do anything but plug the hole once they found it."

They all sat and watched the monitor as numbers whizzed by.

"We know what they plan to do, but what do you want to do about it," asked Gene.

Montgomery sat up and cleared his throat. This was the first opportunity he had to share his plan. He anxiously wanted to hear what his accomplices thought.

55

We got one," announced Nia.

"About time!" said Sanja.

Paulette ran into the office with a cup of coffee. "What does it look like?"

Nia gazed at the monitor and pointed. "This transaction's going to Chesapeake Federal. Around twenty five thousand dollars."

"Let's do it," said Sanja.

"Here's another. About forty thousand to Monie Regional Bank. They must be sending all the large ones now."

Nia calmly went about the task at hand. She diverted the transactions to a temporary file that she created in the bowels of ECPI's system. The file name was "<.>", figuring something as nondescript as that wouldn't raise any suspicion.

"A couple more coming." Nia kept going. Her calm, but intense face gazed at the screen and continued to work frantically at manipulating the program. Diverting transaction files and sending ECPI back acknowledgements that read *Transaction Received,* to indicate they had been accepted.

Paulette and Sanja looked at each other and smiled. They loved the thrill of the game they played. The opponent, ECPI, had met a fierce competitor and was losing badly. The plan worked to perfection.

"You go girl," said Paulette.

56

Montgomery recalled on several occasions Gabrielle talking about some of her wealthy clients who used Swiss Bank accounts to avoid paying taxes. Anything related to law bored him. He usually just pretended to listen and appear supportive. The conversation generally consisted of Gabrielle telling detailed stories about the nuances of tax law and IRS incompetence while Montgomery nodded his head pretending to absorb every sentence. Most often, he could care less.

Somehow the stories of the Swiss Bank accounts caught his attention and he remembered them vividly. It appears that this one time his listening might have paid off.

Montgomery and Gabrielle had spent most of the day riding around as he drilled her on what it took to open offshore accounts. A consulting firm that her practice used often could do it immediately.

Montgomery never told her why he had a sudden interest in Swiss accounts, mostly because he wasn't sure himself. But, he finally convinced her to help him open one.

They called her contact and he started the preliminary application paper work. By the time they arrived at the K Street offices of Patterson, Milken, and Bosch, everything had been prepared for processing.

Lawrence Thompson, a junior partner, greeted them dressed in a tailored designer four button blue suit, Italian silk tie, and glistening black leather shoes. Lawrence was clean-shaven and wore his hair slicked back with what looked like a gallon of oil. He could easily be mistaken for a car salesman. The thick Boston accent reminded Montgomery of one of his college roommates who had a subtle dislike for Black people, but would never admit it. Montgomery disliked Lawrence from the first handshake, but he wasn't looking for a friend.

The receptionist area had cherry wood furniture and smelled like new carpet. Various artwork hung on the hall in elegant wood frames. The office looked conservative and sterile, yet typical for the D.C. law community.

Lawrence ushered Gabrielle and Montgomery back to his office and pulled out the paperwork. He guided them through the entire process, always remaining friendly and helpful. Clearly, he had done this hundreds of times before.

They completed the signatures, handed over a three hundred dollar check, and Lawrence drove them over to the Swiss Embassy on Cathedral Avenue. Montgomery and Gabrielle showed their passports to a representative for verification of signature and within fifteen minutes they headed back to the car.

After returning to Lawrence's office, he faxed the documents to Switzerland, along with instructions for two wire transfers of five thousand dollars each from Gabrielle's savings account.

An hour later, after lively discussions between Lawrence and Montgomery about whether the Washington Redskins or the New England Patriots would make the Superbowl, they received a fax with two account numbers. In less than two hours they had an account with the Bank Leu of Zurich for Gabrielle and Swiss Credit Bank for Montgomery.

Gabrielle dropped Montgomery off at the George Washington campus to meet Donnie, and the odyssey began.

In the warehouse, Montgomery shared his plan with Donnie and Gene.

"So I'm thinking we can take the transactions Nia plans to move and have them sent to my Swiss account instead."

"I could do that, for a fee of course," said Gene with a smile.

"Of course," said Montgomery. "How much?"

"How about ten percent?"

"Fine."

Montgomery knew that he gave in too easily, but he had no desire to negotiate. Nor was he in any position to at that point. Ten percent could net a substantial reward if the transactions reached the levels Montgomery expected. But it wasn't his money, so what the hell, he thought.

"I'll take care of you too Donnie."

"I ain't worried about it Doc. I trust you will. I know where you fuckin live," Donnie said, going back to his Tony Soprano impersonation. Something he hadn't performed in quite a while. Montgomery had missed it and was happy to see the silly side of Donnie again.

A series of bell tones went off from the computer and Gene jumped to his feet to look. "They're on the move."

They all closed in to watch.

"Looks like they're starting to move some of these transactions. Let's see where they're sending them." Gene began calmly typing on the keyboard.

"Ah, I got 'em." He pointed at a list of files. "They're storing them here."

His finger sat on the screen under the filename "<.>"

"So what do we do?" asked Montgomery.

"Lets just watch for a minute. Their collecting the data and sending ECPI acknowledgements back. When they stop doing that, then we'll move."

They all turned and glared at the computer screen simultaneously and waited.

57

It was ten thirty.

"That's it, I think we should stop. I have a lot of cleaning up to do," said Nia.

"Where are we?" asked Sanja.

"We've captured forty-seven transactions totaling about 1.7 million dollars."

"Holy shit," said Paulette, falling back into her leather chair.

"We're not done yet. I still have to transfer the money to the Swiss account."

"So what are you waiting for?" asked Sanja. "Lets go!"

They sipped their coffee and Nia went to the temporary file and opened the transmission string.

She went to the destination bank ID and changed the number to the Swiss Bank. Then changed the account number to Sanja's account. She did this for all forty-seven transactions and closed files.

Nia then got up from her chair.

"Where are you going?" said Sanja.

"I need to go to the bathroom. Can I get five minutes? Damn."

"Go right ahead baby," said Paulette. "You deserve it."

Nia got up and left the room, turning to roll her eyes at Sanja, who winked. Paulette and Sanja gave each other a high five and burst into a fit of laughter.

58

Gene Yow noticed a break in the action. No movement on the part of the Njama for a couple of minutes. Forty-seven transactions sat out in limbo. The lull meant it was time to make a move.

Gene copied all forty-seven of the transactions Nia had captured to another file on another sector of the server and called it <F...>.

He looked over his shoulder at Donnie and Montgomery. "I named it this because we're about to fuck 'em," he said with a chuckle.

Gene opened the first transaction, and then changed the string to the account and destination of Montgomery's Swiss Bank. He did this for all forty-seven transactions.

He then sent all of the transactions from his file to Switzerland for electronic deposit.

"Now here comes the fun part."

Gene twirled an imaginary mustache like Snidely Whiplash. He went into Nia's temporary file and changed one random character in all of the account numbers.

"The transactions won't go through without the right number," he said, staring straight ahead as his fingers nimbly navigated the keys. He changed all forty-seven transactions and closed the file.

Ten forty-five, fifteen minutes before the transfer to the new ECPI system was complete. The window was shutting quickly.

Donnie, Gene, and Montgomery sat and waited, silently.

Then, something blinked on the screen.

Transaction Received from the Bank Leu of Zurich blinked on the screen.

"Shit. If I knew it was gonna be this easy, I would have asked for a larger percentage," said Gene.

"How much?" asked Montgomery.

"Looks like about a million and half or more. I haven't calculated the totals."

Montgomery sat back and sighed. Donnie slapped Gene on the back as he began the process of removing the temporary file and directory, killing the routine that gave him access to the system, and removing all traces of his invasion.

"Oh, before I vanish, I need to do one more thing. Just for fun," said Gene.

"We don't have much time you know," said Donnie looking at his watch.

Gene moved around the system, typed in something and hit the enter key. He then erased himself from ECPI's database, as if he never existed.

"What did you do?" asked Montgomery.

"I set it up so they would automatically receive an acknowledgement when they send their files. Now they'll think their transactions went through smoothly."

59

Nia Givens had returned from the bathroom, relieved for the opportunity to stretch her legs and arms. She had been perched at the computer for more than four hours. She felt the strain in her neck, shoulders, and wrists, but still had work to finish.

Nia eased back into her chair and Paulette offered her a cup of tea. Time was running short so she hurried. She'd changed the account numbers already so it was just a matter of sending the files off, which she did.

Then she erased all evidence of her existence in the ECPI's system.

At ten fifty-five her screen blinked with a message. *Transaction Received,* from Banca Monte Paschi (Suisse) SA in Geneva.

"We're done girls." Nia hit the last key and collapsed in her chair, exhausted.

Paulette and Sanja bent over her as all three of them embraced.

The next move was to leak to the press that ECPI had been hacked and wait for the aftermath. They would destroy racist Frank Hill's life, and they scored a nice return for their work.

The three ladies retired to Paulette's dining room where she had a bottle of DuBoeuf Pinot Noir. They planned to spend the rest of the night celebrating their new wealth.

Two miles down the road from the Aventis estate, Charity Newhouse sat in her car fuming as she nibbled on some Oreo cookies. Through the earpiece, she had heard enough.

I can't let these bitches destroy the integrity of Njama, she thought.

She sat up, took out the earpiece and turned the ignition to head home. She took a sip of her Diet Coke and stared into the darkness of the wooded enclave. Putting the car in gear, she eased down the dark road past Paulette's house.

She turned on her headlights at the stop sign. Punching the gas pedal hard, the spinning tires flung the gravel as the car turned onto the main road.

Then Charity reached over and turned off the tape recorder. She had all the evidence she needed.

60

Carmen Underwood waited patiently outside the entrance to the Glenmont subway station, the last stop for the red line train in Montgomery County, Maryland.

She hadn't dressed properly for the crisp morning air. She wore Nike sneakers with no socks, short jean pants, a short-sleeved tangerine t-shirt with South Beach printed across the front and a white baseball cap. The cold made it difficult to act inconspicuous. April weather in Maryland frustrated her tremendously.

On Saturdays the station opened at seven. At seven fifteen, only a few riders had arrived to descend the escalator to the platform.

Montgomery Quinn had called at six and asked her to meet there at seven. He had an important package for her. Carmen rushed because she didn't know the exact location and feared getting lost. Now he was late.

Carmen paced near the entrance to the station, trying not to appear out of place. Her dress warranted some unwelcome gawking, but she ignored them.

Looking down the escalator, she noticed someone coming up, the first person to arrive since she'd been there. The woman wore a floppy fishing hat and a gray jogging suit. Carmen turned to walk away, assuming the woman was headed to the gym.

As the woman reached the top of the platform, she approached.

"Ms. Underwood?"

Carmen turned, startled at first. Then she tried to see if she recognized the woman.

"Do I know you?"

"No, but you know my husband."

Gabrielle Quinn stuck out an envelope and handed it to Carmen.

"You're Montgomery's wife? It's a pleasure to meet you." Carmen extended her hand, but Gabrielle stared her straight in the eye and ignored it.

"Can't say that I agree with your sentiment," said Gabrielle in a dry, unemotional response.

Carmen cleared her throat, "Well, *excuse* me then."

She opened the envelope. It contained a type written page:

Your ceremony was at the address below:
Paulette Aventis
14498 Pott Point Rd
Calvert County, Maryland

Carmen smiled, folded the page and placed it back in the envelope. "Tell Monty thank you for this."

"You're welcome. And he trusts you will honor the agreement to leave him out of this whole mess."

"No one will ever know about him in relation to this matter. I give you my word."

Gabrielle glared at Carmen intensely.

"Is there anything else Ms. Quinn?"

"As a matter of fact, yes." Gabrielle took a step closer, clenching her teeth. "If you ever contact my husband again, I will fuck you up. Do you understand me?"

Without flinching, Carmen stared back, "Are you aware of the punishment for assaulting a federal agent, Ms. Quinn."

Gabrielle took another step forward, their noses were inches apart and Carmen could feel her hot breath on her lips.

"Bitch, I don't give a shit who or what you are. All I know is this. If I hear one word about you coming anywhere near Monty, I will hunt you down and beat you like a run away slave."

A slow smile extended across Carmen's face. The intensity in Gabrielle's face frightened her, but she wouldn't let her know it. She backed up, turned around and headed to her car, never saying a word.

Gabrielle smiled as she watched Carmen walk away. Then she headed back down the escalator.

Montgomery had taken her to the spy store the night before where they had purchased a transmitter and receiver from Phil. She had a camera and microphone hidden in her hat. Montgomery felt they needed some documented assurance that Carmen wouldn't implicate him.

He couldn't trust Carmen anymore so he felt he needed a little insurance. Montgomery sat in the car near the metro station listening and recording the whole conversation.

"I hope you enjoyed that," Gabrielle said, imagining the grin on his face. Montgomery smiled and turned off the recorder.

"More than you know baby," he said.

61

Paulette Aventis hadn't gotten much sleep the night before, but she had never needed much. She enjoyed an early lunch in the sun room off the kitchen. Paulette and her husband, Harold, often shared strawberries and mimosas for brunch on Saturday mornings. He hadn't returned from his business trip yet and she didn't want to waste the beauty of the crisp spring morning, so she sat alone, taking in the ambiance of the natural environment.

She loved the view of the colorful flowers surrounded by the Patuxent River in the far distance. Spring was her favorite time of year. All of her landscape work had begun to awaken from its winter hibernation.

From her hilltop location she could see the town of Eagle Harbor across the river. Beginning in 1659, for over two hundred years African slaves cultivated tobacco crops on the land where the town originated. Even after the Civil War, the town remained predominately African American.

In 1926, an African American developer bought the parcel of land. He sold individual lots to members of the growing Washington, D.C. African American middle class who were looking for a refuge from urban living. The location proved a popular site with its beach location along the quiet Patuxent River. She loved telling the story of the town, often to the surprise of those who knew little about the history of African American inhabitants along the river.

Her grandparents were one of the first families to purchase land in Eagle Harbor. Now she sat overlooking the entire town from her estate.

A knock on the door startled her from her pleasant thoughts. No one ever visited her without calling first.

As she got close to the door she noticed several flashing police car lights in front of the house from her dining room window. They didn't look like typical county police cars and some were unmarked. She rushed to open the door, confused and concerned about what business they had with her.

A woman stood at the door with her back facing the parade of cars.

"Can I help you?" asked Paulette.

Carmen Underwood turned to face Paulette and she recognized her instantly. Paulette thought her eyes deceived her and appeared unnerved, but quickly gathered herself.

"What are you doing here?" Paulette asked cautiously.

Carmen smiled broadly and handed Paulette a piece of paper. "Mrs. Paulette Aventis, we have a warrant to search your property."

Paulette snatched the paper in disgust. She leaned forward, forcing a smile. "Ms. Underwood, right?" she said. Carmen nodded.

"It's getting harder and harder to find people you can trust these days," said Paulette.

"I agree Mrs. Aventis," said Carmen, "but I'm just doing my job."

"And who do you work for?"

"The Secret Service."

Paulette responded calmly. "So you've become a traitor to your people to prove something to your bosses. I assure you it won't get you very far."

"You may be right," said Carmen, trying to maintain her composure. "However, we have reason to believe you were involved in some illegal activities that could undermine the banking industry."

Paulette smiled. "Come on in Ms. Underwood. Feel free to search all you want. You'll find no evidence of any such thing. In the meantime, I'll call my lawyer."

Paulette walked to get the phone while Carmen waved in the

men to begin the search. The mzingo zimas had been cautious, so Paulette knew the agents would recover nothing. Her lawyer informed her not to say anything until he got there.

Carmen stood in the door supervising the action as the men began rummaging through the house. They made their way to the office and grabbed the laptop computer. Then they boxed up diskettes and CDs and other items that might help their case.

Paulette couldn't help walking over to say one final thing.

"You back stabbing bitch," Paulette whispered in Carmen's ear. "You'll eventually learn that what you have done will cause more damage to your people than you realize. We work to bring down our enemies. You're working to help them."

Carmen turned and continued smiling.

"Mie ni muradi sisi ni wa muradi sisi ni mie ni. Kodi yetu salasila kaa daima imara," Carmen said. "It took me awhile, but I figured out what it meant."

"And," said Paulette.

"Your greed contributed to this Mr. Aventis. I respect what Njama is all about and support its mission. It could have stayed underground forever and I probably would have helped ensure Njama's secrets. *You* took things one step too far and brought this to light. *Your* actions went against all this organization is about. For that, I believe the term 'back stabbing bitch' is more appropriate for *you*."

Carmen took a step closer and whispered in Paulette's ear.

"*Mie ni muradi sisi ni wa muradi sisi ni mie ni. Kodi yetu salasila kaa daima imara.* I am because we are and because we are I am. Let our chain be forever strong. *You*, Ms. Aventis, have broken Njama's chain. I hope you can live with that."

Carmen turned and walked out the door.

62

Aloud banging made Nia Givens jump to her feet from a sound sleep. She'd hoped to spend most of the day in the bed after not getting home until three o'clock am.

Nia grabbed her robe and rushed down the stairs, still a little confused and groggy. The noise came from the back of the house, but she had no clue what caused it or where it originated exactly. Half way down the stairs, the force of the pounding startled her. Someone had appeared at the back door and that scared her.

Entering the kitchen she slowly pulled the blinds back and peeked out the window, but she couldn't get a good look.

Another set of hammering beats on the door.

"Who is it?" she yelled.

"Sanja."

Sanja had never been to her house before. Nia was surprised she even knew where she lived.

She unlocked the door and Sanja pushed her way past. Adorned in dark glasses, a lime green trench coat, and a white baseball cap pulled down on her forehead, she looked nervous.

"What's wrong?"

"We have a lot of problems." Sanja walked into the kitchen and sat at the table.

"The transactions didn't go through," said Sanja.

"That's impossible."

"I checked the account this morning. There were no deposits made."

"But we got the confirmation back last night, there must be a mistake."

"Yeah, a big mistake. Something must've gone wrong."

"Shit! What do we do now?"

"It gets worse."

Nia knew Sanja had something more serious on her mind. Little things never frazzled her. Her eyes looked sad and watery and the streaks of dried tears were still visible on her cheeks. Sanja took off her coat and threw it across the back of the chair. Then she turned toward Nia and took a deep breath.

"Paulette just called me. The Secret Service showed up at her house not long ago with a warrant. They're crawling all over her place," said Sanja.

"Secret Service? What do they want?"

"They were tipped off by someone about our scheme. They're taking her computer and looking for any other evidence."

"Shit!" said Nia. She dropped her head into her hands. Everything was happening so fast, she didn't have time to process it all. "Who could have told them?"

"I sure would like to know the answer to that myself. But Paulette couldn't talk."

"Well they won't get anything from the computer."

Nia had left no trace of their activities on Paulette's computer. Not knowing this day would come, but preparing for every possibility, they were covered. Everything regarding the software program had been encrypted, so it would be virtually impossible to get anything. She'd made one critical mistake that led to Montgomery Quinn's involvement and wasn't going to make another.

But in time, she knew that federal agents trained to conduct forensic examinations of computers could gather evidence from encrypted and erased files. If her employer, the NSA got involved, it would happen even faster.

So before they started the night before, Nia had copied Paulette's system onto an identical laptop so she wouldn't lose any of her personal data. She used the second laptop for the hacking, which she had in her possession. Only she and Paulette knew about this.

She would now destroy it.

"Have you contacted Charity?" Nia asked.

"Yeah, after listening to her berate me about how she told us not to do this, she said she didn't want to meet until this blew over. But she would try to find out if the FBI was involved."

"Does she know about the money and the Swiss account?"

"Not to my knowledge, but who knows."

The two of them sat and talked about every possible way this could have happened. But it was all speculation because they had no clue who could have turned them in. They knew Paulette would never implicate them, but that didn't relieve the concern. Certainly if the government found Paulette, they weren't far off their trail.

The same questions kept coming up: Who tipped the Feds? How did they find out? What should they do? And what about Njama? Had they jeopardized something that was so important to so many people for so long?

For thirty minutes, Nia felt closer to Sanja than they had ever been. Suddenly being thrust in a situation that could destroy them both, made their differences seem less important.

63

ontgomery Quinn had a date that he had been
waiting for all week, a birthday lunch with his
grandmother Lila Armstrong.

He spent the morning cleaning up some details from Friday's
activities. Taking Gabrielle to pick up Eliza and getting them
back to the house made the horrors of the week fade, a little.
The joy of seeing Eliza rolling around on the floor and playing
with her toys comforted him. He was glad they were home.

He visited Lawrence Thompson to confirm that the money
had indeed reached Gabrielle's Swiss account. He then had
Lawrence fax the paperwork to transfer the money from her
account to the one he had at Swiss Credit Bank. He then closed
Gabrielle's account.

Knowing the Swiss regulations precluded their government
from discussing bank account transactions brought little solace.
Montgomery felt this extra step was a precaution, just in case
someone tracked the ECPI transactions to Gabrielle's account.

He had Lawrence open an international debit card for his
account so he could access the funds from any ATM machine
in the world. He didn't want to risk transferring the money to
a U.S. bank so he would just keep it there, for now.

Leaving downtown D.C., he drove the BMW towards
Virginia. For lunch, Lila Armstrong chose the Chart House
restaurant in old town Alexandria and Montgomery had no
objections.

He loved seafood and he rarely had the opportunity to visit
the Chart House. Just the thought of shrimp scampi and broiled

mahi mahi made his stomach growl. Plus, the place provided the perfect ambience for a quiet lunch with the special person in his life.

As he drove, his face radiated with a broad smile that made him look like Batman's nemesis the Joker. He knew people in nearby cars were laughing at him, but he could care less.

Ship novelties filled The Chart House and the sailing theme carried through from the lobby area to the tables. The large crowd had a surprisingly low noise level. The aroma of the fresh seafood filled the air.

Lila Armstrong sat at a restaurant table overlooking the Potomac River. Although she was turning seventy-three, she looked about fifty. Friends said she must share Lena Horne's genes, having a youthfulness that never seemed to fade.

Her reddish-brown skin glowed from the sun reflecting through the window. Lila's mother was part Cherokee and the Native American features were prominent, including the high cheekbones, round nose, and the dark colored eyes.

That morning at the salon, her hairdresser recommended a layered pixie cut and added a little brown highlight that blended well with the gray. Lila loved the youthful look it gave her.

She adjusted the pearl necklace that hung over her turquoise satin dress. Her matching pearl earrings made her look sophisticated, like she was going to the opera. A little overdressed for the Chart House, but it wasn't often that she went out.

And at seventy-three, the occasion warranted a special wardrobe since one never knows how many more birthdays there are left to celebrate. As she stared out at the water, she felt a tap on the shoulder.

"I've got to be the luckiest man in this place, having a beautiful woman like this waiting for me," said Montgomery, as he reached down and kissed her on the cheek.

Lila smiled broadly and touched Montgomery gently on the wrist. "Don't make me blush."

Montgomery walked around, pulled out his chair and sat down. "I hope you weren't waiting long, Grandma."

"No problem baby, I was just enjoying the view."

"None of the men in here were trying to pick you up were they?" said Montgomery as he laughed.

"You stop that. None of these young men in here have anything I want."

"So you say, Grandma."

"Anyway," Lila said, with a slight smile of embarrassment. "You're looking kinda classy there yourself baby."

Montgomery wore a crisp white shirt, with a colorful silk tie, and his favorite mahogany colored four-button blazer.

"I was brought up well."

"I agree."

The two of them always talked like old friends. Anyone who witnessed their interaction saw the mutual admiration they had for each other.

Since the death of Montgomery's mother, they had developed an unbreakable bond. Montgomery felt comfortable sharing anything with Lila and she loved spending time with him.

They ordered lunch. He had the mahi mahi and she ordered the shrimp platter. Montgomery ordered a bottle of French Bourgogne Blanc white burgundy wine to celebrate the occasion. And they talked about everything.

Lila talked about life in retirement and all the time she spent with her friends at the community center taking classes in sculpting and art. She was also an electrical engineer, so they couldn't resist entering into some conversation about Montgomery's research on satellite imagery. They also talked about Eliza and how Lila looked forward to taking her to the beach for a week in June. Just the two of them.

Montgomery eventually talked about Jovan and the pain of his best friend laying in a coma. They laughed about the stories of Montgomery and Jovan in their many episodes of misbehavior during their teen years.

After lunch, Montgomery ordered strawberry cheesecake for dessert and Lila had a cup of decaffeinated coffee. As they finished, Lila took advantage of a rare moment of silence to probe Montgomery.

"So Monty, how is that other situation we talked about earlier this week?"

"Much better now."

"That's it? Much better? You sounded pretty bad when we talked the other day."

Montgomery smiled and shrugged his shoulders. "Things changed drastically for the better."

She nodded, waiting for him to expound, but he kept eating cheesecake.

"Lets pay for this meal and go for a walk outside. It's such a nice spring day and I have a story to share with you that I'm sure you will find interesting," said Lila.

After paying the check, Lila and Montgomery walked down the stairs from the back of the Chart House restaurant and headed down one of the piers along the waterfront to enjoy the fresh spring air.

On the waterfront, couples sat on their yachts in the small marina sipping beer and laughing raucously. In the distance they could see people standing and waiting to board the Cherry Blossom, a replica of a Mississippi river boat that went out on the river for tours, parties and special events.

The patrons of the restaurants and shops spilled onto the pier continuously, while others enjoyed the ambience of the historic colonial town. Frisbees flung, dogs barked, children ran around in the small park area, and bicycles interspersed with the rollerbladers dominated the path along the banks.

Lila had been quiet since they got outside and Montgomery could tell she had something on her mind.

"Monty, I have something to share with you. It's important to me that you not speak of this to anyone whatsoever." Lila stopped and looked at Montgomery, waiting for his assurance.

"Sure grandmother, you know you can trust me."

Lila sighed and started to walk again. Then she began her story.

"When I graduated with my masters from MIT in electrical engineering in the 60s, I went to work for the Defense Intelligent Agency."

"I always thought you worked for the FBI."

Lila turned and looked at Monty. The lines across her forehead told him she didn't want to be interrupted. "I did, I'll get to that. Just bear with me awhile, Monty. It's a long story, but it's important that you hear all of it."

"Okay grandma. Sorry," said Montgomery.

They silently came to the end of the pier and stood under the gazebo. To the right were hundreds of cars racing back and forth across the Woodrow Wilson Bridge into Maryland and Virginia. To the left the Capital Building stood as stately as ever in the distance.

Lila looked out over the water and stared at the ducks flapping. Montgomery looked at her, and then looked out as well, wondering where this was all going.

"Monty, this is something I've been carrying for a long time and no one is to ever know. Do you understand?" Lila looked straight into Montgomery's eyes waiting for a response.

"I would never do anything to disappoint you grandma, you know that."

A young couple walked towards them. She said nothing as the couple chatted for a few minutes about the view and then wandered back down the pier. Montgomery kept quiet as well.

"Okay," she turned and began to walk back up the pier and headed down one of the walking paths away from the Chart House.

Then she said, "Monty, I'm your Nashiha msiri."

"What?" He thought he heard her correctly, but needed to hear it again.

"I'm the one whose been sending you the messages to help you."

Now it all made sense. The emails provided all the information he needed every step of the way. All along, his grandmother acted as a sort of guardian angel, directing him.

Who else could it have been? But still, he wondered how she knew so much.

Montgomery finally got the words out of his gaping mouth. "But…" he stuttered, grasping for the right words, "how do you know…"

Lila turned and smiled at Montgomery, "I'm the founder of Njama."

64

"anja, come in here quick!"

Nia and Sanja had been sitting in the family room flipping channels looking for any news story about Paulette. Nothing appeared. Secret Service agents at the house of an executive at Nanotechique, Inc. should have been a big story, so the fact that no one reported it surprised them.

Nia had wandered to her office, leaving Sanja watching the news. She noticed that her answering machine blinked. Due to her exhaustion, she had never heard the phone ringing. The call had come sometime while she slept because she had checked the machine when she got in. She pushed the button and listened to the message.

"Sanja!"

She sat and stared at the machine as Sanja turned the corner into the office, winded from the short sprint.

"What is it?"

"Listen," and she pushed the play button.

Nia, this is Monty. Long time no hear from. Anyway, we need to talk. I know all about your little group, Njama and I don't appreciate the shit you've put me through this past week. You need to fix my life back. And you know what, I'm going to give you an incentive to do just that. If you haven't already, you'll notice that your little scheme with ECPI last night didn't work. The money never went to your Swiss account. Why? Because I sent it somewhere else. We can talk about a way to redress your issue and mine so that we're all happy. I have something you want and you have something I want. Sounds like a good start to a great negotiation. Meet me at the Peirce Mill in Rock Creek Park, nine o'clock. Come alone or I'll take the information and send it to the FBI. I trust that we can work this out between the two of us. See you soon.

"That motherfucker! When did this come in?"

"It had to be sometime this morning, while I was sleeping."

"How in the hell did he find out all this information about us," said Sanja, looking curiously at Nia.

"Hell if I know. It wasn't me."

"Fuck!" Sanja pounded her fist on the desk, rattling the contents. "How did he get access to ECPI like that? And how did he intercept our transmissions?"

"Shit, I don't know, Sanja. He must have made a copy of my program before you got it back. But he must've had some help to run it though. His Ph.D. is in satellite communications, so I don't think he knows enough about computers to pull this off alone."

"That son of a bitch. He has no idea who he's fucking with." Sanja bit her lip, trying to keep from erupting into a rage.

Nia sat in her chair and Sanja paced across the office. The phone signaled another message on the machine. Nia pushed the button out of curiosity.

Oh and one more thing Nia, if you don't believe me, check your front porch. Beep.

They looked at each other, then ran to the front door. Nia unlocked it to discover a padded manila envelope sitting on her welcome mat. She ripped it open to find a CD.

They walked into the office and inserted it into her computer. The CD contained an audio recording of Paulette, Sanja, and Nia as they bantered, laughed, and celebrated their invasion of ECPI the night before.

"This is impossible. He must be connected to someone. What do we do now?" said Nia, tears streaming down her cheeks. Anxiety, fear, and every emotion of desperation had overtaken her and she felt nauseous.

"First, we have to destroy this tape. We don't want any evidence that he contacted you." Sanja calmly paced around the office, her mind racing about what they should do. She knew how to manage crisis and knew she had to take control of the situation.

"I know one thing," she said. "I want that money. You go meet him. I have to make some calls. Dr. Quinn's going to regret he ever fucked with us."

65

He finally calmed himself to ask a cogent question, just out of curiosity. "You mean you know Nia?" Montgomery asked.

He found it hard to accept his grandmother's involvement in a secret society. Even more alarming was her potential involvement in something illegal, like designing computer programs used for hacking.

"Yeah, I know her, I met her once. She has no idea that I'm your grandmother though. As I'm sure Dr. Kelly told you Njama has several layers called usawas."

"You know Dr. Kelly?"

"I sent you to her. Remember the email. We worked together back in the sixties at the FBI. We're good friends, but she is not in Njama. She helps keep the Feds off our backs by publishing enough information to make it look like she knows all about us. But she sprinkles a few falsehoods here and there to mislead folks away from us," she said with a wink.

"She was definitely helpful."

"I knew she would be. I also sent the recording last night. Did you get it?"

"Yeah, I got it. I already put it to good use. I recognized Nia's voice, but who were the others."

"Never mind that right now. You'll find out if you need to know more. Anyway, Nia just got to the highest level less than a year ago. The mzingo zima or circle of queens. While she toiled at the bottom layers and I was involved, she never knew me. I met her at an initiation ceremony once and when I realized that she had married Jovan, I kept my distance. I didn't want her to know me, or our relationship, just yet. Now I'm glad I did."

My grandmother founded Njama? Is she involved with the ECPI heist? When did she know they were out to get me? Why didn't she tell me earlier?

Too many questions. Montgomery remembered the letter Nia left on his car the night he visited Dr. Kelly. He had been carrying it around in his jacket pocket since he'd met with Erin Kelly. He pulled it out, raised it up and said, "So is your group into threatening people?"

Lila read the letter, and exhaled. "Not in that way. Listen Monty, this is not the Njama I founded. When I left last year, I thought I had left it in capable hands. Obviously, I was wrong. The women at the top now are involved in something totally illicit and I'm not happy about it. In fact, I plan to do something about it."

"So you know about the computer program?" he asked, not sure if he wanted the answer.

"I know everything. I have a protégé that has informed me of all of the events over the last few days. The original plan was to bring down ECPI, which is run by an undercover racist. That I could live with. But when they decided to try and skim money for themselves, that's unacceptable to me."

Relieved she disapproved, he looked around to make sure no one could hear, "I'm not so sure you know everything." He smiled and began telling her all about how he, Donnie, and Gene intercepted their transactions and transferred the money to his Swiss accounts.

"I guess you can take care of yourself, huh?" Lila chuckled. She then turned serious. "You know you will have to return that money though, right."

Montgomery knew she would say that, but he didn't respond.

"Do you also know the Secret Service is investigating? I sent them to Paulette's house this morning," he said.

Looking surprised, Lila said, "No. I didn't know that. And how did you know where she lived?"

"It's been a long week." Montgomery went on to explain the GPS Jovan gave him and how he and Donnie visited the Aventis estate and witnessed the induction ceremony."

"Anything else I need to know?" asked Lila.

"That's it."

"Good. You saw more than you should have. Make sure Donnie does not find out anymore. We'll take care of the Secret Service and Paulette. She may have to suffer for a while and she needs to go anyway."

"I'm trying to meet with Nia tonight. We have evidence from the computer program of their scheme. I have some other stuff too. I'm hoping to use this to force them to fix the financial mess they put me in. If they do, maybe I'll *think* about giving the money back."

"What they did to your finances will be taken care of baby. Don't worry. I can fix that for you."

"I want to meet with her anyway. I just don't like the way she treated me."

"She and the others will be taken care of too. They will be forced from their positions. I need to put Njama back in more capable hands. I don't know what these women are capable of. They're pretty ruthless."

During their wandering and talking, they found themselves back at the boardwalk outside the restaurant. Montgomery smiled and put his arm around Lila's shoulder.

"Grandma, don't worry about me. They may have attacked the wrong man this time. I don't have any skeletons in my closet that they can use against me like the cronies you went after."

They walked a little further stopping with others to admire a mime doing magic tricks along the cobble-stoned street.

Montgomery bent down to whisper in her ear. "Do I have to give the money back? I'm sure I can find something positive to do with."

Lila rolled her eyes, with a smile and never answered.

"We'll talk about it later," Montgomery said. "I certainly don't want to have you on my bad side."

They both laughed and he kissed her on the cheek.

66

Paulette Aventis sat on a nearly empty car on the subway orange line reading a Michael Crichton novel. Across from her, two African American teenage boys listened to headphones and bobbed their heads, and an elderly white man read the Washington Post. Paulette sat on the opposite end of the car, but could still hear the hip hop music blaring in the teen's ear. The old man eyed the teens frequently, nervously, and suspiciously.

Paulette found people watching intriguing, kind of a hobby for her. She realized the harmless boys were probably heading home from a movie or something. Minding their business, just trying to get to their destination. But to the elderly man, even though they ignored him completely, he saw trouble.

Paulette had been riding the train for more than an hour, changing lines and directions frequently to ensure no one followed her. As the evening progressed, fewer passengers boarded, allowing her time to relax, read, and watch.

It had been a long day. The Secret Service spent more than an hour sifting through her house. Paulette spent another two hours trying to get everything back in its place.

After the Feds left, she spoke with each member of the mzingo zima to ease their minds about the investigation. Nia Givens worried, but she knew they would find nothing. She apologized profusely for everything and promised to do her part to correct her mistakes. Nia trusted Paulette's leadership so she easily assured her that everything was fine.

Sanja Coston on the other hand was pissed, more so about the money and Montgomery Quinn spoiling their plan. She worried about the Secret Service too, because of the potential impact on her own career if they uncovered her. However, the fact that someone outsmarted her enraged her more. Paulette hoped she wouldn't do something stupid out of desperation, but also realized she had lost control of Sanja. She regretted allowing Sanja to talk her into this entire plot in the first place.

Charity Newhouse refused to talk on the phone and wanted to meet face to face. So that's where Paulette was headed. Paulette figured Charity, being the most level headed of the group, would provide a calmer response. She looked forward to a mature conversation for once.

The train finally pulled up to the New Carrolton station, the last stop on the orange line in Prince Georges County, Maryland. The two teens bounced up and raced out of the car for the platform escalator. Paulette followed, smiling at the old man who sat and watched to make sure the boys had left. Then he folded his paper and exited the train slowly.

Charity had suggested that they meet in the lobby of the MARC train station adjacent to the metro. Few people used the station, making it a good place to talk.

At the bottom of the escalator, she went through the turnstile and headed out of the gate. The lobby of the MARC station was empty. The lady at the ticket counter watched, expecting Paulette to approach. Paulette ignored her, hoping the lady would forget she ever saw her there.

Charity sat at the far end talking to someone. The other person's back was to Paulette so she couldn't identify her. She approached slowly, cautiously, unsure why Charity would engage someone in a conversation prior to their meeting.

As she got closer, she could see from the graying hair it was an elderly lady, sitting calmly. Paulette's eyes met Charity's and she nodded in her direction. Charity looked solemn, but Paulette expected that after the events of the day.

Just before she reached the two, Paulette slowed to a

stop. The elderly lady turned and smiled slightly. Paulette recognized her immediately; it was Lila Armstrong.

"Sit down dear. We need to talk," said Lila.

"Muumba Lila, what a pleasant surprise," said Paulette as she bent to kiss her on the cheek.

This caught Paulette totally off guard and she shot Charity a fierce glare after Lila turned around. She walked around and sat in the hard plastic seat next to Charity, facing Lila.

"I understand we have some issues to deal with Ms. Amiri," Lila said to Paulette.

"I assure you Muumba Lila, we will take care of it. I don't believe Njama is in any great danger."

Lila smirked. "Are you telling me that the Secret Service visiting the amiri of our organization poses no great danger? I find it hard to believe that you even let that leave your lips."

Paulette silently tried to avoid Lila's gaze. Charity sat next to her, staring as well. Her reputation for unquestionable leadership skills had been diminished now. She had no response. For the first time she had failed to make good decisions and it may have cost more than she imagined. She believed in Njama and now she was ashamed that her actions placed the organization at risk.

"Listen Paulette, let's cut to the chase." Lila leaned forward. "I am aware of your little scheme to siphon money from ECPI to a Swiss Bank."

Paulette looked surprised and wondered how she found out. Charity should have been unaware as well.

"I made it clear from the beginning that this was inappropriate. Although you tried to keep me in the dark, I knew everything Paulette," said Charity

"I'm curious as to how?" asked Paulette, looking in Charity's direction.

"That's not important now," said Lila. "I believe it is in the best interest of Njama if you are replaced as amiri. You have too much heat on you now and frankly I find your actions despicable."

Paulette lowered her head, unaware that she was slowly

sinking into her seat. Lila continued in a soft calm voice. "You took something I and others built over decades and totally destroyed it in a couple of years."

"You have every right to be upset Muumba. But give me an opportunity to--"

Lila interrupted. "*Kodi yetu salasila kaa daima imara.* You do recall the meaning don't you?"

"Let our chain be forever strong," replied Paulette.

"Your opportunity has passed. You have broken the chain under your leadership. We were created to help the disenfranchised fight the powers that held them down. Greed was never part of our mission."

"I understand."

"Effective immediately Charity is the new amiri of Njama. I'm sure you have no objections," said Lila.

Paulette looked over at Charity, feeling set up, betrayed. This angered and hurt her, but she had no defense. Her own decisions, or failure to make good ones, brought her to this point. She had no one to blame but herself.

"Sanja and Nia will also be replaced. I trust that you will take care of this federal investigation without implicating Njama. You, Sanja, and Nia will fall on the sword for this and I want nothing coming back to us. Do you understand?"

"Yes."

"Good. Charity dear, do you have anything to add?" asked Lila.

"No ma'am."

Lila stood and gathered herself. Charity stood as well, leaving Paulette slumped in the chair like a rag doll.

"My dear Paulette. I had so much hope that you would take Njama to another level. Only God knows my disappointment." Lila turned and walked way. Charity followed, looking back blankly but saying nothing.

The words pierced Paulette like an arrow. She respected Lila more than any woman she knew. The fact that she failed to meet her expectations was humiliating. Even more devastating was that she failed herself.

As the two ladies vanished from the station lobby, Paulette stood and brushed herself off. Realizing she had no place to go, she immediately sat back down. Her life had been derailed and she sat in a train station with no predetermined destination. How appropriate, she thought.

67

The Peirce Mill was an old gristmill built in the 1800s, standing in the heart of Rock Creek Park. It was once open for tours, but ceased operations in the 1990s, due to safety issues resulting from deterioration. Montgomery had ridden by the place many times on the bike trails with Gabrielle.

Night smothered the park. The trees surrounding the mill provided a darkness that made it difficult to see further than a few feet.

Nia stood by a large tree adjacent to a waterwheel attached to the mill, peering into the night. The stillness of the park made her nervous, and a bit frightened. She shifted her head from one side to the other, looking for any sign of Montgomery Quinn.

Montgomery stood near the edge of a pine tree cluster about fifty feet away. He watched her arrive and scanned the area with the night binoculars for fifteen minutes. No one else was around.

Convinced she had come alone, he stepped into a slightly lit area and whistled softly. She turned sharply and began to walk toward him.

As she approached, Nia said, "A bit dramatic don't you think." She had on a dark blue jacket and slacks. Her make-up was flawless as always.

"Maybe. But trust has become a foreign concept for me lately."

"Let's do this Monty. I don't feel comfortable out here."

He removed his glasses and snorted, "Comfort? I haven't felt that all week."

"You brought that on yourself Monty. All you had to do was give me back the thumb drive,"

"My friend, and *your husband*, told me not too. I honored his request. I thought you and I were cool Nia. Why would you allow all this to happen?"

She stood there, and stared at him blankly. He wanted her to answer, but she wouldn't. She wasn't the person he thought she was and felt sorry for Jovan's future with her, if one existed.

"Anyway, so you out-smarted us and redirected the money. Where it is?" she said finally.

"Not so fast Nia, I need some assurances first."

"Such as?"

"My bank accounts, mortgage, the IRS, my research grant, everything needs to be put back in place."

"Much of it has already been reversed. We'll take care of the rest. But first, what about our assurances? You said something about the FBI. You need to give me all the tapes and anything else you have. Original copies."

"That can be arranged."

"Now where is the money?"

He laughed, "As you may already know, I'm not stupid. You fix what you destroyed, you get your money and your tapes."

"Game over, Dr. Quinn," said a voice approaching them from the darkness of the adjacent wooded area. A shadowy figure walked up from behind Nia, with one arm stretched forward. Nia turned towards him and took several steps backwards until she was standing near Montgomery.

"I want to see both of your hands at all times."

Nia raised her hands immediately. Montgomery tried to put on his glasses.

"Raise your hands, now!"

Montgomery immediately placed his hands high, holding his glasses in the air.

"Come on man, I need these to see."

"You don't need to see shit," said the man as he took a step closer. The streetlight reflected off the silver object in his hand.

It was a gun. He stayed in the shadows.

It was Ted Jacobson. Sanja had called to have him follow Nia to the meeting. He had a baseball cap pulled down over his eyes, making it difficult for Montgomery to establish any facial features. However, Montgomery did notice his left arm was in a sling.

Nia said, "Who the hell are you?"

"A friend of a friend. Just providing you a little backup."

Montgomery knew this must have been the guy who beat up Billy Yow. The broken arm gave it away.

"What do you want?" Montgomery asked.

"I want you to stop fucking around and give the lady what she wants."

"I don't know this man, Monty," said Nia.

"Sure you don't," Montgomery said to Nia. Scared, he turned back to the stranger and said, "Listen man, please don't hurt me. I have a wife and daughter at home. All I want is to get this behind me so I can move on with my life."

"Then give the lady what she wants."

"I don't have anything to give her right now."

"Listen, I don't know who you are, but I don't need your help. Just leave us alone, *please*." Nia's voice shook.

Maybe she didn't know the guy, thought Montgomery. He now wondered who this guy really was, why was he here, and who sent him?

"Dr. Quinn, I can make life very uncomfortable for you and your family. Painful. Do you understand?"

Montgomery noticed a shadowy figure in his peripheral vision. It looked like a panther, slowly stalking its prey. The dark image approached, taking deliberate steps toward Jacobson. Montgomery knew he had to do something. He slowly attempted to put his glasses on again.

"Didn't I tell your ass to keep your hands where I could see them." Jacobson turned the gun towards Montgomery and said, "I'll say this one more time –"

The dark figure pounced on Jacobson like an NFL linebacker attacking a running back. A loud pop echoed and smoke drifted from the gun as the two men flew into the grass. Montgomery fell to the ground covering his head and Nia dropped down next to him.

He looked up to see the mysterious man drill Jacobson in the face and knock him out with one punch. With the gun still in his hand, Jacobson was motionless on the ground. The figure stood up and emerged from the dark, walking toward Montgomery. He dressed in all black and his entire head was covered, except for his eyes.

Montgomery stood and walked toward the man who slowly removed the mask. It was Donnie Centronelli, his face painted with grease and wearing a special forces vest. They both thought they needed backup, but never expected it to come to this.

Donnie and Montgomery stood over the man momentarily.

"Sorry Doc. The gun went off when I jumped him. I had to do something. He might have killed you both," said Donnie. Montgomery looked down, and then looked over at Donnie. "Is he going to be alright?" he asked.

"Probably."

"We need to get out of here."

"Yeah, we'll call the police once we're clear."

Montgomery turned around, "Nia! Come on, we've got to go." Nia remained face down and didn't move.

"Nia?"

He looked at Donnie and bent down to tap her on the shoulder.

"Nia, lets go." Still no response.

He turned her over on her back and noticed the blood covering her face. Then he saw the hole between her eyes.

"Damn!" He jumped back in shock. "I think she's dead."

"Shit. We need to get out of here before someone sees us," said Donnie.

Montgomery knelt down again next to Nia. This was never supposed to happen. No one was supposed to die. Donnie grabbed him by the arm and dragged him up. They ran by Ted Jacobson and headed for the woods.

68

A dams Morgan buzzed with the usual Saturday nightclub crowd. The cars cruised the street, bumper-to-bumper, looking for parking. The sidewalks swarmed with college-aged people on the verge of drunkenness.

Sanja Coston looked out of her closed bedroom window eyeing the jovial atmosphere. Her mood was sullen. She unsteadily poured another glass of Hennessy, spilling some on the windowsill.

The background noise of the television provided the only sound in the room. It was tuned to one of the reality shows about a bachelor selecting a potential wife from several women. She really didn't care for those shows, but could find nothing more interesting on. Not that she watched television much anyway.

Paulette had called earlier about the meeting with Lila and Charity, so she knew her days in the mzingo zima were over. During the brief conversation, Paulette's glowering voice made her even more depressed. Sanja said nothing during the conversation. She was too ashamed of the position she had put Paulette in to respond in any way.

She now wished she had apologized. But she didn't and there was no need to call back. It was over.

So once they hung up she poured a drink. Cognac straight, on the rocks. One bottle gone, half of another left.

She waited to hear from Ted Jacobson about the encounter

258

with Montgomery Quinn. She'd told him to follow Nia to the meeting place and convince Quinn to tell them about the money. The call should have come more than an hour ago. But at that point nothing surprised Sanja; things had gone wrong all week.

She had nothing left. No husband. No friends. A career she hated. A plan to make money that failed miserably. Now Njama was taken away. And for what? She searched for an answer and it kept coming back to her. She failed not only herself, but the one thing that meant the most to her. Njama.

She swallowed the drink in her glass and staggered from the window to the bed, Cognac bottle in one hand and glass full of ice in the other.

Why isn't he calling, she thought?

She sat up on the bed, as the credits from the television show rolled across the screen.

Coming up on your evening news, a bizarre murder in Rock Creek Park. We've got the story, next.

She thought nothing of the teaser and poured another drink. She grabbed the telephone and fumbled with the receiver. The numbers looked blurry. She squinted and slowly dialed Ted Jacobson's cell phone number. It went straight to his voice mail and she hung up.

Where the hell is he?

The musical jingle for the news faded and the camera focused in on the well-dressed, young, female new anchor.

"Good evening. We start tonight with breaking news of a murder in Rock Creek Park. We go now to Tonya Houser standing by. What do we have down there Tonya?"

"Well Sarah. As you can see behind me, the area here at Rock Creek Park has been completely taped off as detectives scan for clues to this heinous crime. The details are a little sketchy at this moment, but we've learned that the victim is an African American woman. The murder occurred at the Peirce Mill, shown behind me, sometime between nine and ten o'clock. Apparently, the woman, around thirty years old, was shot once in the head. The assailant, also in his thirties had a cast on one arm and was passed out near the body still holding the murder weapon. It's unclear what happened to him. Other information is still unknown tonight. We'll follow up with the police, but they aren't releasing the identification of the victim pending family notification. The investigation will probably continue into the night and we'll be right here to bring you any updates as we get them. I'm Tonya Houser for News 5. Back to you in the studio, Sarah."

"Thanks Tonya. What a bizarre turn of events. In other news..."

Sanja stared at the screen in shock. It had to be Ted and Nia. She had no doubt. A man and woman at Peirce Mill in Rock Creek Park? Who else could it be? Did Montgomery Quinn do that? But how? And where is he? Jacobson's training should have made this an easy task. Nowhere in Quinn's background was there any indication he could do anything like this. What could have gone wrong?

Regardless of what went wrong, now she had blood on her hands. Nia's blood. On top of all the other failures, this one she couldn't take. Her chest felt like it was caving in and she labored to breath.

Sanja turned her feet off the bed and onto the floor. She was now forced to do what she had been contemplating all night. Reaching into the drawer of the nightstand, she almost fell over onto the floor. The alcohol had depleted her coordination skills to that of a toddler. She gathered herself slowly, reached in and pulled out the 9mm gun.

Sanja sat back on the bed and poured the last of the Cognac into her glass and threw the bottle against the wall. She swallowed the drink in one breath.

Then she put the gun in her mouth, closed her eyes, and pulled the trigger.

69

Montgomery Quinn slept in Sunday morning. He felt like he had a week's worth of sleep to catch up on. Not even Eliza banging him on his head with her stuffed Tigger doll made him budge.

When he finally opened his eyes around noon, Gabrielle snuggled up next to him in bed. He kissed Eliza and set her down on the rug, next to the bed.

Turning on the television, he flipped the channels looking for any sign of what happened the night before. He hadn't told Gabrielle, figuring there was no need to scare her. He settled on the local twenty-four hour news channel.

The well-manicured anchorwoman began reading her stories.

"D.C. Police are still investigating the suspicious death last night of a scientist with the NSA in Rock Creek Park. The young woman has been identified as Nia Givens of Northwest Washington. Ms. Givens, a computer scientist with the NSA, was shot once in the head. The murderer has been identified as Theodore Jacobson, a Pentagon official. He was found passed out next to the body. Police have no clues as to the motive for the killing and are asking anyone with information to please contact..."

Gabrielle looked at Montgomery. "Oh my God. Did you know anything about this?"

"This is absolutely shocking." Montgomery tried to sound surprised. He hoped it worked.

"Nia." Gabrielle shook her head. "I really liked that girl. I can't believe this." She sat up and stared at the television screen.

Montgomery settled back on his pillow, looked over and kissed Gabrielle on the cheek.

"This is unreal," he said. *So far, no clues. That was good,* he thought.

"In other breaking news, a senior official with the Federal Reserve Board was found dead in her Adams Morgan townhouse. Neighbors reported hearing a gun shot late last night at the home of Sanja Coston. The Director of IT at the FED apparently committed suicide, although no note was found. Police are releasing no information until further investigation."

"What a damn shame. We're getting a fill of horrible news this morning. Was it a full moon last night or something?" asked Gabrielle.

"The scandal at ElecCheck Processing, Inc., continues this morning as officials of the company try to determine who may have accessed their computer systems. As we reported yesterday, an anonymous tip informed federal agents that someone hacked into the ECPI's system as they were converting to a new software Friday evening, stealing millions of dollars. So far, no one has come forward to claim responsibility..."

Montgomery turned up the volume on the television as they both sat up to listen intently. Images of a elderly white man standing in front of a throng of microphones filled the screen.

"CEO Frank Hill held a press conference this morning denying that the hackers were able to access any accounts and that no money was stolen. However, the online bill processor has relationships with many major banks in the country and this security breach may scare away several of its clients. The news is expected to deliver a major blow to ECPI's stock prices at the opening of the market tomorrow. Mr. Hill is the majority stock holder and will be severely impacted if investors bail out. We will keep you abreast of any further developments in this story. Coming up, sports..."

Montgomery turned off the television. "That's enough of that."

"You think we're safe?"

"So far, but we'll just wait and watch for awhile. Just to make sure."

They smiled at each other, hugged, and shared a deep kiss. Then they both got down on the floor to play with Eliza.

Montgomery looked up and said, "I guess while we wait, it wouldn't hurt to take a ride to look at some houses."

Gabrielle laughed and jumped up, "Hey, you don't have to tell me twice. Let's go."

EPILOGUE

Two months later, one early Monday morning, Lila Armstrong sat in her family room playing around on her laptop. She had just returned home from a weekend at the beach with her granddaughter, Eliza. She loved every moment of it and couldn't wait to send pictures of the two of them to all of her friends.

As she finished the email, an instant message popped up on her screen.

From: Charity
I saw you online and just wanted to say hello. I hope all is well. And again, thanks for everything. I'll be in touch.

Lila smiled. Charity was busy rebuilding Njama and was proud to have the opportunity to carry on Lila's vision. This time around, they implemented a more cautious and selective process for its new members. The women initiated in the last year would get retested, except for Carmen Underwood.

Although Carmen's cover was revealed, she took extra precautions to saved Njama from a potential Federal investigation. Her character was above reproach and under different circumstances, she may have never turned on the organization.

Carmen reminded Lila of herself. If she was sincerely interested in Njama's mission, Lila wanted to keep her engaged. She still made an ideal candidate and could become a significant contributor in the future.

Overall, Lila was happy with the direction of the group and trusted Charity to do the right thing.

The phone rang and she grabbed it.

"Hello?"

"Ms. Armstrong?"

"Yes?"

"This is Rita Flannigan from MIT Alumni Affairs. How are you?"

"I'm fine." Lila had already given to her alma mater earlier in the year and had no plans to make another contribution.

"Ms. Armstrong, I have some good news for you. An anonymous donor just gave us over one million dollars to establish a scholarship in your name. They suggested that it support African American women majoring in engineering at MIT."

"What?"

"Yes, I'm calling to talk to you about establishment of the scholarship and how you want it distributed. Isn't that exciting?"

"Yes, it is," she uttered slowly. "Do you have any idea who this person was?"

"No ma'am, we do not."

But Lila knew. She had no doubt it was her grandson, Montgomery Quinn. He said he would make good use of the money. She guessed this was as good as any.

"Can I get your name and number and call you back? This is quite a surprise and I need some time to think about it."

"Absolutely, just take your time," said Rita.

Lila took down the information and hung up the phone. She sat back in her chair and reflected. Everything worked out just right and she could go on with her retirement. Montgomery continued to make her proud. She smiled and continued sending the pictures of her beach trip on the email.

Montgomery Quinn had meditated at Hains Point, done his yoga and morning jog, and made his way to Jovan Given's hospital room at the George Washington Hospital. He was back in his routine. As he stood staring out the window, the summer activities below were in motion. The campus was less lively since classes had ended, but the government bureaucrats scurried along the sidewalks in every direction.

He stopped by to visit before heading to his office to work on his summer research grant. With the help of Njama, the NSF corrected their mistake and dropped the audit of his account, releasing the money to continue his study.

No more financial problems. Thanks to his grandmother and the new Njama, everything else returned to normal.

Jovan still remained comatose and everyone wondered if he would ever awaken. Montgomery glanced over at the bed. Many of the machines had been disconnected and he was breathing on his own now. The swelling from the accident had subsided and he looked like Jovan of old. He had lost weight because of the feeding tube and no solid food, but otherwise he appeared normal. Jovan looked like he was in a deep relaxed sleep.

The last two months had gone by quickly. Feeling safe, Montgomery had begun distributing the funds from his Swiss Account. He paid Gene Yow's commission for his help by purchasing more than one hundred thousand dollars in high tech computer equipment and software. Gene didn't want cash and that was all he requested as a reward. Plus, the hackers needed some upgrades and had no other source to get it.

Montgomery paid Donnie Centronelli's tuition for the next two years, not an insignificant amount for a school like George Washington. But well worth it in Montgomery's mind. Donnie's help during Montgomery's weakest moments was priceless. Now, he could finish his doctorate without any financial worries.

When Njama restored all of Montgomery's finances to normal, the computer programs alleviated all of his debt, so he had a fresh start. No more car payments, credit card bills, or other debt and he planned to keep it that way.

He had no reason to keep any of the money from ECPI and could never humbly face Lila if he did. What better use for the money than to give it to MIT for his grandmother's scholarship fund, he thought. So that's what he did. After the donation exhausted the remaining balance, he closed the Swiss accounts.

Montgomery sat down in the chair next to the bed and watched the Price is Right on the television.

The sound of Kool and the Gang's *Celebration* rang out from his cell phone and he reached down to look at the screen. He had changed the ring tone in honor of Jovan.

He answered. "Hi grandma."

"Hey baby, I just got a call from MIT."

"Surprise! I thought you would love it."

"I do. Where are you?"

"I'm at the hospital."

"Well, you go ahead and spend time with Jovan. We'll talk later."

"Okay Grandma, I love you."

He hung up the phone and turned off the television.

"Jo, I've got a story for you that I know you'll love."

Everyday for several weeks, Montgomery had told Jovan an account of the events that began with the thumb drive. He hoped this would help to awaken him. Every time he relayed the story, it became more elaborate as he recalled more details. He had the most difficulty when he got to the part about Nia's death. But he got better at it each time.

He always started it the same way.

"Purpose. Jo, we all are searching for purpose. Mine right now is being here with you. And I'll stay here as long as you need me." Montgomery touched Jovan on the shoulder.

"I'm going to tell you how I discovered my purpose. But before I start, I'll warn you that some parts of this story you'll love, and some you'll hate. Some will make you laugh, and some will hurt your heart. But I hope you'll wake up soon because you're recovery would make a great ending."

Montgomery leaned forward and looked directly at Jovan. "Two months ago, you came to me with a problem and this is how it was resolved..."

This and other quality books are available from

OverLookedBooks

Visit us online at:
www.overlookedbooks.com

Printed in the United States
53829LVS00004B/295-342

9 781595 940179